THE CURIOUS LIFE OF
ADA BAKER

KAREN
HAMILTON-VIALL

CRANTHORPE
MILLNER

First published by Cranthorpe Millner Publishers (2022)

ISBN 978-1-80378-043-6 (Paperback)

www.cranthorpemillner.com

Cranthorpe Millner Publishers

Prologue

Mary let her red silk dress slip over her curvaceous body and drop to the bathroom floor. She turned off the tap and swirled her hand in the warm water, feeling its soft caresses as it kissed her fingers. Dappled light filtered through the windows and sparkled on the water's surface, making it look like liquid gold. Steam filled the room and the gentle scent of roses enticed her to enter. A light breeze tickled her body and she felt her skin shiver in response. She dipped a beautifully manicured foot slowly and tentatively into the water, followed by the other, then gracefully eased herself down into the bath. The warmth radiated through her muscles, making them glow.

Mary felt a growing surge of excitement building within her as she thought about what she was about to do; her stomach turned as though she were an actor about to give the performance of her life upon the stage. Her friend, Marcus, would be here any minute to photograph her. He was going to use the images in his new photography exhibition. She was fond of him –

he'd been a wonderful lover – and working as an artist's model for him had been a fascinating experience. He valued her as an artiste, rather than viewing her as a harlot, as her sister Ellen and so many others had done. They didn't understand the art within what she did. They thought posing in the nude for artists was just another way of prostituting yourself. Well screw them – if they didn't understand it, that was their problem, not hers. It was the career path she'd chosen for herself in life. There was a creak behind her and she felt her heart race. Perhaps it was Marcus. She craned her head round to look, but nobody was there. She sighed, disappointed, and sank back into the bath. The house was old. For over a hundred years its beams and lintels had supported its Edwardian facade. It wasn't a surprise that it creaked and groaned occasionally. Sometimes she heard it creaking in the middle of the night, which had freaked her out when she was a child, but she'd grown used to its noises. It must have just been the house settling.

She'd lived here as long as she could remember. The house had belonged to her mother before she'd died and bequeathed it to Mary. She'd loved her mother dearly. She was the only person who'd ever understood her. The warm water had a meditative effect and she felt her mind drifting away to the past as though it were a cloud on a breeze. A tune her mother used to sing when she was a child entered her mind. She hadn't heard it for a long time and she started gently humming. "hmmm… hmmm… hmmm…" Mary saw a shadow suddenly loom over her then a flash of red in front of her eyes before something tightened hard around her throat. She clutched desperately at her neck, trying to loosen its grip, her legs thrashing wildly as she tried to get purchase to turn around and face her attacker. The attacker seemed to squeeze tighter still, like a constrictor squeezing its prey. She felt an intense pressure in her head. Her vision slowly faded until at last she felt a sort of serenity and slipped into unconsciousness.

Mary opened her eyes and groaned. The light was dim, as if dusk was approaching. She felt like she was sitting on a carousel after drinking ten double whiskies. She dragged herself out of the bath and dropped onto the floor. What had happened? Why did she feel like this, had she been drinking? Had she been drugged? Then, slowly, a recollection came to her mind and she put her hands up to her throat. She recalled the sensation of her neck being squeezed hard. She looked desperately around her but there was nobody to be seen. Had the attacker gone away? Had he been disturbed part-way through? She heard a bang downstairs. What should she do? It could be her attacker coming back to finish her off. The door of the bathroom cupboard was slightly ajar. She raced over to it and slipped inside. She could hear hurried footfalls coming up the stairs. Mary didn't usually panic, but she felt a tremendous sense of dread of what she might see.

"She's here, Mike," a woman's voice said. "I can't feel a pulse. She's not breathing. Call an ambulance."

Mary heard Mike talking to someone. "I think we should try CPR, Mike. Can you give me a hand lifting her?" It didn't sound like someone who was going to hurt her. Tentatively, she peeked around the door. There was the woman and man crouched on the floor. They were police. Mary burst forth from the cupboard.

"Oh thank God you're here. I was just attacked by someone. I think that they were trying to kill me. What are you both doing?" Mary looked down at the object in front of them. Staring blankly up at her from a soulless body was herself. Her mouth dropped open, gawping like a cod in the fishmonger's window.

Mike did chest compressions on her poor naked body. "I don't think there's any life left in this one. Pity, she's a stunner! I would, alive or dead!"

The woman tutted. "Mike, show some respect for the dead and keep trying."

"What! She doesn't know any different. Come on, Nikita, give a guy a break. The only pretty girls I get to meet in this job are dead or being questioned for a crime."

"You're sick!" said Nikita. Mike shrugged and carried on with the chest compressions.

Mary sank down to her knees beside her corpse. "No!" she screamed and tried slapping her face. Her hand passed clean through. She turned to look at Nikita. "I'm here! That's not me! I'm not dead!" she screamed. "You're wrong!"

Mike shivered. "Is it me or has it got really cold in

4

here?" he asked Nikita.

"Bloody freezing. The heating must be off," she responded. Mike carried on his chest compressions for a few minutes until the paramedics arrived.

"It's no good, lads, I think she's gone," said Mike. The paramedics nodded but carried on trying to revive Mary for a few more minutes.

"Looks like we've got ourselves a murder – we'd better call it in. It's going to be a late one tonight, Nikita."

Mary screamed as loud as she could and ran downstairs to shut herself in the pantry, away from the hustle of the police investigation.

Chapter 1

Ada Baker was a psychic. She was the seventh daughter of two parents who were both seventh children, and she had been gifted with some extraordinary powers. Ada had been named after her mother's best spirit guide. Personally, she disliked the name; it was so old-fashioned. Ada couldn't just hear and see the dead, she could channel the abilities they'd had in life too. It had proved extremely useful sometimes. She regularly channelled a lady called Rose Thorne when she needed to get her cleaning done. Rose had been an exceptional cleaning woman while alive, and in death she helped to keep Ada's home looking spotless. Sadly, she had died at the age of fifty-two when she'd slipped on a bar of soap. She'd hit her head, knocked herself out and ended up drowning in the toilet bowl.

When it was time for the local country fair, Ada channelled the spirit of Mrs Dorothea Entwhistle. Mrs Entwhistle had been the head cook at a large country house in Yorkshire in the early twentieth century. Ada knew that it was really a sort of cheating but her thinking was that she was helping these souls by giving them an outlet for the talents they had accrued during a lifetime of experiences. The afterlife could be very dull at times and it gave the dears something to do.

She didn't just channel women but men too. She'd never been terribly good with figures, and she regularly called upon a very suave and charming banker called Dennis. He'd died of a heart attack during the Black Monday stock market crash in 1987. His hedonistic lifestyle and the strain of it all had been too much. Dennis helped to keep her money worries in order and did her monthly accounting for her. He'd even advised her on which shares to buy and she'd done rather nicely out of him. Right this second, though, she was sitting in her garden, drinking a cup of tea, while reading the paper and enjoying the spring sunshine.

"Anything good happened recently?" asked Mrs Entwhistle, who was occupying the chair opposite her and peering closely at the back of the paper.

"There's been a juicy local murder!" said Dennis with glee. He was standing behind her and reading over her shoulder.

"Please may I have another cup of tea?" asked Rose.

Ada looked up at Rose, over the top of her paper, and smiled.

"Of course!" she said, putting her paper down. She picked up the full teacup in front of Rose, threw its contents on her petunias and poured her a fresh one. She knew the dead couldn't drink, but it made them feel more alive by being included. In a way, it was a little like having flatmates, with the strange addition that sometimes she allowed them to occupy her body. She was always still there when she allowed them in and remained in ultimate control, but she allowed them to take the driver's seat for a while. Not all spirits were as nice as the three she currently lived with; sometimes spirits were so keen to have another chance at life that they would try to take over her body completely. She'd had one particularly nasty incident with a doctor who'd thought that his uncompleted life's work was more important than Ada's own. It had been very hard to remove him and had left her with the strange taste of pineapple in her mouth ever since. She couldn't explain the pineapple. But these three she trusted. Occasionally, she would let in the spirit of Seth, who'd been the head gardener at the same house as Dorothea, but she rather enjoyed gardening herself.

"Mary Watts was found naked and dead in the bathtub of her home, with a silk scarf tied around her neck. She had been strangled. Curiously, no water was found in the tub and the house was locked. The murder remains unsolved," read Dennis. "I bet we could solve it, Ada! Or rather, you could with your powers. All you'd need to do is nip down there and ask this Mary person who did it. Easy!"

Ada looked thoughtfully up at Dennis for a second. "I don't know, Dennis, it seems a bit risky. Somewhere out there is a murderer who wouldn't be very happy about me snooping around. I don't want to end up murdered myself. Then where would you all be?"

"Oh go on, please!" begged Rose. "My life was so dull. I wish I'd spent every day of my life challenging myself and trying new things. It's too late when you're dead."

Ada sniffed. "What do you think, Mrs Entwhistle?" She trusted Mrs Entwhistle above all of them – she was sensible and level-headed. Ada could hear the gentle click-clacking of the ghostly needles Mrs Entwhistle was using to do her knitting, which she kept in the small carpet bag she carried everywhere with her. She never seemed to begin or end a piece of knitting, but it was always there. Mrs Entwhistle's bag seemed to be bottomless and all sorts of things appeared from it. All the things she'd loved and found most useful in life.

Finally, she spoke. "Well, dear, I think it'd be good for you to get out of this house and mix with some real living people. It's not healthy for someone of your age to mix with old fogeys like us all the time."

"Thank you, Mrs Entwhistle."

Ada was, in fact, twenty-eight. She didn't have many living friends. People tended to find her constant talking to herself rather freaky. She'd had quite a lonely childhood. She had been the odd child that hung around in the corners of the playground on her own, except she was never alone. When she was young, some of her ghostly friends had also been young, but as she'd grown up most of them had abandoned her to find younger

9

playmates. She had met these three in recent years.

"Talking to your ghosts again are you, Ada?" said Mr Gardener, her neighbour, peering over the fence and smiling. He noticed the four teacups on the table full of tea and chuckled to himself. Mr Gardener didn't believe in ghosts.

"Yes, Mr Gardener. They've seen a murder in the local paper and they want me to get involved in solving it. Did you know Mary Watts at all?"

His skin was weather-browned and wrinkled after spending so many years outside gardening. His name was very fitting. He had creases on the side of his eyes that, because of his tan, looked like tiger stripes. His trousers were held up by a piece of garden twine and his clothes were full of many holes. His garden was absolutely immaculate, very ordered, neat and well weeded, but his house was falling apart and one window had been repaired with a sheet of plastic over it. Paint peeled from every sill. Mr Gardener appeared to be thinking for a few seconds before he answered.

"I knew her mother at school. She was a pretty lass. Perhaps a bit too pretty, if you know what I mean. The local lads liked her and she liked them too. I often wondered if the daughter was the same. I'm not sure anyone could say for sure who Mary's father was. So, Miss Marple, will you take on the case do you think?" he enquired jokingly, with a wry smile on his face.

"Hmm, maybe, I don't know. I need to think about it. It's one thing to try to solve a murder on a TV show but quite another to solve a real one."

"Ooh, before I forget, I have some tasty forced rhubarb for you. It makes a cracking crumble." He smiled, handing it over the fence.

"Thank you, Mr Gardener, we'll enjoy that."

He smiled again, shaking his head and looking at the empty chairs. "Poor lass," he mumbled to himself as he turned back to his own garden.

Ada had a lot to think about if she was going to help with this case. What was the best way to go about it? Mrs Entwhistle was great at baking and cooking, but not, she suspected, brilliant at solving crimes. Perhaps the best thing to do would be to visit the scene of the crime and see if she could chat to the murder victim. The newly dead did tend to be very shy though. Ada cleared the tea things away.

"Time to make some dinner, Mrs Entwhistle. Rhubarb crumble is on the menu for tonight it would seem." Mrs Entwhistle followed her into the kitchen.

It was easy for Ada, letting the dead people in. She'd done it for so many years now. She just had to stay still and clear her mind to allow space for them to come in. Ada felt Mrs Entwhistle slip into her mind and take control of her body. Almost as if she was watching a movie, Ada watched Mrs Entwhistle's calm, reassured manner as she manipulated her hands with a lifetime's experience at the task.

Before long, the rhubarb was chopped and crumble-ready. It had taken Mrs Entwhistle a while to get used to using an electric oven, but she had mastered it now. When Mrs Entwhistle had been working, it was still coal or gas, and only near the end of her life did electric really take off.

Ada thought quietly to herself at the back of her mind. Perhaps they were right and this would be a good way to get out and about a bit more. Her daily life was very humdrum and consisted mainly of watching murder mysteries with the ghosts. Perhaps it was time she used her abilities to help solve a real murder and make a difference in the world. She made up her mind that she was going to do it. But how would she tell the police what she knew without incriminating herself in some way? Perhaps she'd have to tell them the truth. Trouble was, most people didn't believe in ghosts. Somehow, she'd have to find a way to make them believe.

In a short while the kitchen was smelling wonderful. Mrs Entwhistle had made a chicken casserole and an amazing rhubarb crumble with egg custard to follow. Ada laid four spaces at the table and put the casserole dish and crumble in the middle. She didn't serve it up to the ghosts, but they enjoyed the ceremony of it. Mrs Entwhistle insisted on saying grace.

"Let us be truly thankful, oh Lord, for this bounteous feast laid before us. Thank you, Lord. Amen."

"Amen," said everyone else collectively. Ada wasn't actually religious, but she liked to please Mrs Entwhistle, and she truly was thankful for the food. She ate her meal thoughtfully, listening to the ghosts chattering away to each other. She'd never solved a real murder before, only on the telly. Tomorrow was going to be an interesting day.

Chapter 2

Ada awoke the next day feeling bright and refreshed. She was excited about speaking to Mary and was keen to get going. She put on her best purple dress and fastened an amethyst pendant around her neck. She wasn't sure why but she had found that the dead were always very drawn to the colour purple. It was generally considered a very spiritual colour and associated with death so perhaps that was why. Ada gazed in the mirror as she slowly stroked a brush through her long black hair. Her dark brown eyes twinkled like pools of water on a moonlit night. She used her finger to gently apply some blusher and emphasise her high cheek bones. Her skin was golden brown and glowed with health. Ada's mother had been half black and her father had been half Thai, and she'd inherited features from both her parents. They had been very happy together but had sadly both passed on after a car accident. They had never appeared to her as ghosts, so she assumed they were happy wherever they were now. Their deaths were the reason she had been able to afford the house.

It was a lovely warm spring day, so she put on her sandals and a light cardigan.

"Do you want breakfast today?" asked Mrs Entwhistle.

"No, I want to speak to Mary and it's always easier speaking to the newly dead on an empty stomach." Ada wasn't sure why but she suspected it made her seem that little bit closer to being dead. Mrs Entwhistle looked crestfallen.

"Can we come too?" asked Rose.

"I think not today, Rose. It's the first time I've talked to a new ghost in ages and she might be a bit intimidated if we all turn up."

Rose crossed her arms and slumped in the armchair, looking decidedly fed up.

"Have fun!" shouted Dennis, who was sitting watching the business news on the telly. Dennis was a poltergeist and was getting better and better at moving things with his mind. He had recently mastered using the remote to control the TV. This had annoyed Ada at first, until they'd made an agreement that he'd watch it with subtitles on or very quietly. If Ada wanted to watch her favourite programme, she had priority. He had discovered his abilities many years before. His very sudden death at work had been a shock and he had wandered around for days trying to speak without success to those around him. Eventually, he had been so frustrated and angry with the situation he had kicked an office chair and sent it flying into one of his colleagues

15

who had run out of the office screaming. He had met Ada many years later when she had been employed in a temp job in the same office building. They had formed such a close friendship by the end of her contract that she'd invited him home and he'd been there ever since.

Ada grabbed her keys and bag and stepped out into glorious sunshine. She opened the sunray gate on her 1920s semi. Mr Gardener was in his front garden today.

"Greetings, Mr Gardener. I'm off to solve a crime!"

He waved. "Good luck, Ada. Careful you don't go around upsetting any murderers!" he joked teasingly.

Ada ignored his comment; she was used to sceptics. She smiled disarmingly at him. "The rhubarb crumble was delicious by the way. I've saved you some. I'll bring it round later. Cheerio."

The streets were lush and green and full of life at this time of year. It seemed odd to be heading off to help somebody with their death on such a beautiful day. She took her time strolling and eventually reached 31 Cherry Tree Lane. The road lived up to its name because in the early spring, the street was showered in a pink-cherry petal confetti. She stopped outside the gate. It wasn't as cheery a house as her own. It was older, perhaps Victorian or Edwardian, but somebody had rendered the bricks with horrid pebbledash sometime in the 1970s, which was now sloughing off in little pieces. It wasn't as unkempt as Mr Gardener's house, but it felt unloved in a different way, joyless. Its dark windows seemed to stare back at her and sucked in the light as if they were black holes. The garden was rather wild but showed signs that it had once been loved, as rose bushes and camellias peeked out from among the brambles. She walked through the gate. Even though a couple of weeks had passed since the murder, remnants of police tape still littered the garden. She knocked on the door loudly but nobody answered. She hadn't really expected anyone to. She opened the letterbox and looked inside. She couldn't see anyone but she thought that she could hear sobbing somewhere nearby.

"Mary?" she called out. "Mary, my love, I know you don't know me, but my name is Ada Baker and I'm a psychic. I help people that have passed on. I know this has all been a terrible shock to you being dead. It's strange, isn't it, when people ignore you. I know, I have several dead friends. I can hear the dead. I can see them too. I'd like to offer my services to you in helping to capture whoever did this to you and bring them to justice." She didn't feel like telling her yet that she could let her inhabit her body. She might want to take direct revenge on the person who murdered her and then Ada would be on a very sticky wicket. "I'll put my card through the door so you can have a look at who I am." Ada thought the crying had stopped. "I'm just going to have a look around the garden, I hope you don't mind. Sometimes I can pick up vibes or even have visions if I walk around and touch things. I'll come back again tomorrow to give you time to think."

With these words, she walked down the side return

of the house and into the back garden. It was in the same sort of condition as the front, with the exception of a small patio area near the house that had been kept quite neat. She walked closer to inspect it and found a white cast-iron table set with two chairs. An empty ashtray sat on the table, but in the bushes nearby she found traces of two different brands of cigarettes, one of which had lipstick on. She walked up to the patio doors and peered into the gloom within, seeing a red chaise longue on one side of the room. An octagonal occasional table sat beside it, and on it was a large vase of red roses, now rather dried and faded. The shelves around the room were lined with books on art and photography. Ada felt her spine tingle and she spun around to look behind her.

An older man in a grey pinstripe suit was staring at her. His eyes were so intensely blue it made Ada feel uncomfortable, as if she was standing in front of the headmaster at school. Finally, he spoke.

"Who might you be, madam, and what are you doing here at the scene of the crime?" he enquired suspiciously, while tapping a notebook in his hand with a pencil.

She decided that the honest answer was the best approach. "My name is Ada Baker. I'm a psychic and I've come to offer Mary my services." She flashed her business card at him.

"I see," he said, furiously scribbling down everything she'd just said. "And has she taken you up on the offer?"

Ada paused. She wasn't used to anyone actually

believing what she said.

"Not yet…" she said nervously. "I left a card."

"And have you seen anything else of interest?" he enquired.

"Just two different brands of cigarette – one with lipstick, one without," she said, holding out her hand to show him.

He briefly looked then carried on scribbling in his notebook. "I see… Anything else?"

"I was just looking through the window to see what else I could find and I saw the dead roses on the table. A woman doesn't usually buy roses for herself, so I guess someone bought them for her. I was also trying to make out what the books were on the shelves. Looking around someone's home can give an insight into their character. They look like art and photography books, so presumably art was a passion."

"I see, very good, Ms Baker," he said, furiously scribbling down notes. She looked at him properly for the first time. He was still handsome for a man of his age, about early fifties. He was slim with greying hair and pink cheeks. He seemed to have a very organised, competent air about him. Every time he came to the end of a page in his notebook, he licked his finger to turn the page. Every so often he would tap his pencil against his mouth thoughtfully.

"I don't think there's anything else I can do today," said Ada finally, breaking the silence. "I'm going to go, unless you need me?"

"No, no, I'm done here today," he said, snapping his book shut smartly. "I'll walk you out."

They made their way through the overgrown garden back to the front gate. They stepped through and Ada clicked the gate shut behind them.

"I'm going this way," she said.

"Oh, me too," he replied.

They walked along silently, side by side.

"What's your name, Inspector…?"

"Jolly."

"What?"

"Detective Inspector Jolly. That's my name. Thirty years' experience in the service."

They wandered up to a house near the high street.

"This is me," he said.

She looked up at the house. "What a very fitting house for a policeman to live in," she said, and smiled. It was the town's old Victorian red-brick police station. An old police gas lamp hung over the garden gate and 'Police' was carved in stone over the front door. It had been converted last year to a house, ever since a shiny new station had been built with all mod cons nearby.

He looked at her. "I shall be in touch, Ms Baker." With this, he walked down the rose-lined garden path towards the closed front door and then went straight through it.

Ada's jaw dropped. She was used to talking to the dead, but never one who'd seemed so alive before. He'd had such presence that she'd not even noticed. It could be hard to tell sometimes, but with the recently deceased it was hardest. That explained at least why he was so ready to believe she was a psychic. She smiled and carried on home. She'd have something to tell the crew anyway.

***

Mary looked tentatively down the staircase at the faded grandeur of the hall below. The little card sat on the door mat. The voices had gone and she thought it might be safe to come downstairs. She looked around nervously. It was the first time that someone had spoken directly to her since *it* had happened. At first, she was disorientated and confused, uncertain of what had happened. Then the police had arrived and the house had been full of people, so she'd gone to hide in the attic. Mary was used to taking her clothes off, but after what had happened, she felt vulnerable. She'd worked out that they couldn't see her, but she hated the way that everyone was talking about her in a past tense. She felt very much present.

She bent down to look at the little card. Luckily it had landed the right way up.

Ada Baker – Gifted Psychic. Are you missing your grandma? Was there something you always wanted to tell your husband but never had the chance? I can aid you.

It also had a phone number, address and e-mail. Mary tried to pick up the card but couldn't. Perhaps this woman could help. She'd have to wait for her to return tomorrow. She walked back upstairs to her room, her pleasantly curved naked body bouncing as it had when she was alive.

Chapter 3

Ada was right – Mrs Entwhistle, Rose and Dennis were very keen to learn everything she'd heard. They poured over the news as if asking for the latest details of a TV soap. They were particularly interested to hear about Inspector Jolly. None of them had heard of him so Ada decided to ask Mr Gardener. She put some rhubarb crumble in a dish and took it round to his house. He was in the garden as normal and was delighted to receive the crumble. He went indoors to make them a mug of tea and Ada took a seat in the garden.

"Hello, Mrs Gardener," she said. "Lovely afternoon."

Mrs Gardener never said anything. She had been profoundly deaf in life and this affliction had somehow followed her into her afterlife. She just nodded and smiled. Ada found it strange that in spirit she was still limited. She wondered if this was psychological, having spent her whole life being deaf. Mrs Gardener was able to lip-read and could understand what people said, but only Mr Gardener could use sign language and he didn't know she was there. Ada was determined that she should learn sign language so that she could have a conversation with Mrs Gardener. She thought that it must be very lonely for her being unable to speak to anyone.

A few minutes later, Mr Gardener came out with the tea. "Builder strength, just as you like it, my dear," he said.

"Ooh lovely!" Ada said, as she popped two lumps of sugar in it. It was a habit she'd never been able to drop.

"Now, what can I do for you?" he asked. "I assume you didn't come here just to give me crumble?"

"Yes, I wanted to ask you whether you knew of an Inspector Jolly? I met him earlier today when I was trying to speak to Mary, the murder victim. He was so vivid and alive, I didn't realise he was dead at first."

Ada could see Mrs Gardener jumping up and down. It was the most animated Ada had seen her. She was miming dealing out cards.

"Let me see… Yes, the name sounds familiar." Mrs Gardener seemed to grow more and more exasperated and carried on miming.

"Perhaps you met him playing cards?" Ada suggested.

"Why yes! However did you know that?"

Ada smiled and looked at Mrs Gardener standing over his left shoulder, who now looked much relieved. Mr Gardener followed her gaze.

Ada thought it wise not to tell Mr Gardener, an

unbeliever, that his wife was constantly nearby. "Lucky guess," she responded.

He looked back at her. "Well yes, Evie, my wife, and I used to belong to a bridge club. He was one of the players there. A nice man but very serious and competitive. I always had a feeling that Evie rather fancied him."

Mrs Gardener seemed to blush.

"I believe he'd been in the service a long time. I stopped going to bridge after Evie died, but I think I read in the paper that he'd died last year. Suicide, I think. Something to do with a case of a girl that was kidnapped and murdered. I'd go to the local library if you want to read more about it."

"Thanks, I might do that. I'll pop in tomorrow. I have to go for my training now or I'll be late."

She drank up her tea and said goodbye. Then she nipped home and quickly got dressed in her exercise clothes and put on her trainers.

"Are you off to see the lovely Mr Lee?" asked Rose.

"Yes, I really think I'm coming along, but I don't think I'll ever be as good as him. See you later."

Dennis and Mrs Entwhistle were watching the wrestling on TV. It might seem an unlikely hobby for an Edwardian cook, but it was a hobby that Mrs Entwhistle had got into after meeting Dennis. "Come on, Killer Kong!" shouted Mrs Entwhistle, rather overenthusiastically. Neither of them noticed Ada leaving.

It was a lovely day and it would be a good one for training. Ada made her way down to the local parade of shops, where Mr Chung Lee, master of kung fu, had once lived. The Chinese restaurant and takeaway seemed to have been there forever. Once a week her parents would take her to the restaurant for a meal. Over the years, they had become good friends with the Lees and she had often seen Mr Lee training his son Jian in the car park. He moved with such grace and agility. She had always wanted to train with him, ever since watching *The Karate Kid* on TV. Ada had always loved the movie and had secretly hoped she might convince him to be her teacher. This desire was sadly cut short when Mr Lee died after being run over by a drunk driver.

Ada had finally achieved her dream in recent years after telling the family where Mr Lee had hidden a secret stash of family valuables. She'd seen him one day at the restaurant watching his son in the kitchen. She was used to seeing ghosts everywhere and normally she ignored them. However, she could see that he was urgently trying to tell Jian something and she felt compelled to help. They had been so pleased to be able to communicate with each other again that Mr Lee had agreed to teach kung fu to Ada as well as his son Jian.

Ada entered through the door. It was quiet in here at this time of day. Behind the counter was a very handsome Chinese man of about the same age as Ada. A large and healthy money tree sat on the counter beside him.

"Hello, Jian, I've come for my training."

He beamed a snow-white smile at her. "Ada, lovely to see you. Come through, please. We've been expecting you." She followed him through a beaded curtain to a family area out the back. It had once been the car park for the restaurant, but in recent years it had been transformed into a Zen Garden. An elderly woman sat there on a two-seater swing.

"Ada has come for her weekly kung fu training with Dad," said Jian to his mum.

"*Nin hao*, Mrs Lee," Ada said, bowing to her.

"*Nin hao*," she said in response.

Then Ada turned to face a beautiful maple tree. "*Nin hao*," said Ada, seemingly to the tree.

"Is he here?" said Jian excitedly.

Mr Lee bowed back to Ada.

"Yes, he's here. Is there anything you'd like to know before we start the lessons?"

Jian shook his head. "Just tell him I love him and miss him as usual."

"He heard you. He is always here. He is very pleased with how the business is being run."

Jian beamed and old Mrs Lee smiled to herself as she swung on the swing seat. The family had agreed that Ada could have kung fu lessons with Mr Lee and his son in exchange for them being able to speak with their loved one.

"Shall we begin?" said Ada. "What shall we practise

today, Mr Lee?"

"Yoga warm-up as usual," said Mr Lee. "Then we practise the jab punches, same as last week. Have you been practising at home?"

"Yes, although only with the punchbag in my spare room," said Ada. She turned to Jian. "Your father wants us to do a yoga warm-up first, then practise jab punches again." Jian nodded.

Mr Lee walked over to his son, who was warming up. "Good muscles, strong arm," he said, admiring his son's physique. Ada passed on the comment to Jian. His face beamed with pride at pleasing his father. He had spent hours training on this very spot with him when he was alive and he was pleased to be able to carry on after his death. A small ancestral shrine stood in one corner of the garden, where Jian and his family prayed to Mr Lee and their other male ancestors. Ancestor worship was very important to the Chinese.

, After warming up, Ada practised her jabs with Jian. Mr Lee watched on, giving Ada advice on how to improve.

After they had finished, old Mrs Lee prepared oolong tea for them and went through the elaborate gongfu tea ceremony. Ada watched with awe and fascination. She never got tired of watching it. The closest she normally came to a tea ceremony was using her mother's best china and pouring it for her flatmates. Drinking the delicious tea filled her with a great serenity and was most welcome after the tiring workout. Mr Lee wasn't forgotten and a cup was placed at the shrine.

Finally, Jian spoke. "What are you up to these days, Ada? Any exciting news?"

"I'm trying to help a local woman bring her murderer to justice."

"Really? How exciting! And she has agreed to this?"

"No, not yet. I only went there today. I'm going back tomorrow, but I'm hopeful. Rose thinks it'll be good for me, but secretly I believe she thinks it'll be good for her to get involved."

"A murder though, isn't that risky?" asked Jian.

"Yes." She paused. "I suppose it might be."

"Feel free to call on us for help if you need it," said Jian.

Mr Lee nodded. "Indeed. Call Jian anytime you need me," said Mr Lee.

"Would you like a takeout to go home with? We have a special offer on beef chow mein?" said Jian.

"No thanks, Jian. I'd better head home before Mrs Entwhistle gets tetchy about cooking dinner. Thanks for the lesson. See you next week."

Chapter 4

"Come on, Ada! It's time to cook breakfast. You have to be up and out to speak to Mary today," yelled Mrs Entwhistle. Ada groaned and pulled the cover further up over her head. She wasn't a morning person. She lay there a moment listening to the fluty sound of a blackbird singing near her window, when all of a sudden her covers were rudely pulled off of her.

She opened one sleepy eye. Dennis was standing there. "Come on, lazy bones. *Carpe diem*. No good ever came from idleness." Ada resented early morning interruptions like this. It was all very well for those who had no body to get tired any more to shout about 'carpe dieming', but her muscles were complaining after yesterday's workout.

She sat up slowly. "It'd be great, Dennis, if you could learn to bring me a cup of tea in the morning, rather than a rude awakening."

"Ah, I would, but carrying things is trickier than just tugging things or pressing a button. I'll have a practise if you like, as long as you don't mind a few smashed mugs during the practise?"

Ada waved her hand half dismissively. "Whatever you like, Dennis. Why don't you practise with the paper first?"

She slipped on her pink bunny slippers, which had been a gift from Rose one year. She'd actually had to buy them with her own money, but buying gifts had become another tradition with her ghostly flatmates. The slippers squeaked with every step that Ada took. Rose thought them the height of couture. Ada wasn't so keen but like with an aged aunty buying you a present, she thought it rude to say so. At least they were nice and warm. She tramped her way downstairs. Dennis had already flicked the switch on the kettle, so the water was boiled by the time she'd made her way down to the kitchen.

"Morning!" said a sunny Mrs Entwhistle. "It's poached eggs with avocado on rye sourdough this morning." Being Edwardian, this wasn't the sort of dish she had grown up prepping, but she was ready to adapt to modern taste and modern health concerns, though she couldn't quite understand why anyone would want to forego butter.

"I need tea first," Ada said from her sleepy stupor.

Ada enjoyed the citrusy floral scent of her Lady Grey tea. It wasn't quite the oolong of yesterday, but first thing in the morning it really hit the spot. After a quarter of an hour, she was feeling much better. She looked out the window to see Seth pottering around the garden.

"What's Seth doing, Mrs Entwhistle?"

"He asked me to ask you if there is anything you wanted doing in the garden this week," she said.

Ada put her head in her hands. "Oh, I forgot, it's the first Saturday of the month, isn't it." Saturday was Seth's usual gardening day. Being religious, he refused to work on a Sunday. "Why doesn't he just come in here and ask me himself, Mrs Entwhistle? It's not the nineteenth century any more and this is hardly Frogmore Manor."

"He's old-fashioned. He doesn't like change. He doesn't think it's right for outside staff to come into the house. He's worried about messing up the floor with his boots."

Spectral mud did indeed seem to constantly fall off of Seth's boots. "It's not real mud though. I don't mind. All right, Dennis, can you ask him to have a look round and see if there's anything he thinks needs doing and I'll be back later this afternoon."

Dennis trotted out to chat with Seth.

"I'm ready now, Mrs Entwhistle. You may enter." She felt Mrs Entwhistle inhabit her body and she started cooking the breakfast. Ada felt her lips purse as Mrs Entwhistle started to whistle an old ditty that she didn't recognise. The eggs were as bright and sunny as Mrs Entwhistle's disposition this morning, and in no time at all, a delicious breakfast was ready. Ada poured the ghosts a cup of tea before she started munching. Its rosy redness filled each cup.

32

"No milk for me, please. Just lemon in Lady Grey," said Rose, trying to sound posh.

Ada was hungry and ate her breakfast in silence. "That was smashing, Mrs E!" she said with real conviction. She was now feeling much better about herself.

"Can we come along today, Ada?" asked Rose.

"Well, maybe… but not Dennis, sorry! Mary died in the bath and I think she's probably naked. She may feel shy about showing herself in front of a man."

"Okay," said Dennis, who didn't mind at all because it was 'Western weekend' on his favourite film channel.

"First, I want to go to the library to find out more about Inspector Jolly. I want to know how he died and why he feels he needs to be involved in this investigation."

Mrs Entwhistle produced a hat from her capacious carpet bag and pinned it securely to her bun with a hatpin.

"Right, I'm ready, dear. Let's go."

All three ladies left the house and Ada slammed the front door shut behind them.

It was a glorious day again. The kind of day on which it felt great to be alive, or dead in the case of her two friends. Rose prattled on all the way there about some amazing new cleaning product she'd seen on TV that she thought Ada should buy for her to use. Ada smiled, nodded and promised to give it a look next time she went shopping.

Very soon they arrived at the town library. It was an impressive building with great white columns. It had been built in the 1840s as the corn exchange and then, many years ago, it had been converted for use as the town's library, but remnants and suggestions of its previous use could still be seen in places. All three entered through its impressive arched doorway. At the reception desk was a very young woman, perhaps only nineteen years old. She gave Ada a lovely smile as she approached.

"Excuse me, please, but where might I find the section on local newspapers?" asked Ada.

The assistant looked panicked. She'd obviously been hoping for an easier question. "Oh, uhm, let me think. I know I've got a note of it somewhere. Do excuse me, Mrs Barry is off sick and it's only me in charge. I've only been here a little while."

"No problem," said Ada.

"Well really!" chipped in another stern-sounding voice from behind them. They turned to look. A woman in a depression era-length light tweed skirt suit was staring at them. She peered over the top of half-moon glasses attached to a chain resting on her nose. "She's been here a month already and she doesn't know where anything is. Standards really have slipped these days. I'm Miss Prim. Follow me and I'll show you where you can find the newspaper section." With that, she walked off.

Ada quickly turned to the girl and said, "Actually, I think I can recall where it is, thanks for your help."

"Oh okay, if you could let me know where it is before you go, I'd appreciate it." Ada nodded and quickly hurried away after the speeding Miss Prim. Miss Prim chatted as she walked.

"I was the librarian here for twenty years and this is the sort of person they have replaced me with. Who knows what a mess she'll make of my filing system. Here you go," she said, arriving at the relevant section.

"Hard copies from the last year can be found here – old newspapers are on microfiche – but in recent years they started digitising copies of the *Echo* and the *Sudfield Times*. Neville, whom you can see over there, is the one scanning the pages. He does it for fun and is a walking encyclopaedia of local knowledge. If you need anything else, just ask, but no shouting please. This is a library after all."

Mrs Entwhistle nodded respectfully and Rose curtsied for some reason. Ada just smiled and said thank you.

Rather than searching through endless papers, Ada thought she would try Neville first. He was bent down over a book. "Excuse me please, Neville, Miss Pri... the librarian advised me that you were the best person to speak to about a local story. I'm interested in finding out everything I can about an Inspector Jolly, recently deceased. Can you help me, please?"

Neville looked up, staring at her through his thick

spectacles. He was young, about her age, and his dark brown, almost black hair flopped over his eyes in a '90s boy band kind of way. His clothes were long out of fashion and matched the same decade as his hairstyle. His bright green eyes were slightly magnified by his powerful lenses. Ada thought he was exactly the sort of nerd that most people in the library would studiously ignore, especially women. Neville's mouth dropped wide open. He seemed astonished to be spoken to.

"Why, er yes, certainly." He smiled nervously, looking her over. "Let me think… I recall it." He went over to the computer and started typing into the search. "Here you go. The *Echo* had a whole page about it. It was very shocking." He pulled his chair aside and drew another one up beside him for Ada to view. He started reading aloud. "The *Echo* is sad to report the sudden death of Inspector Mark Jolly. Mr Jolly started out with the police in his early twenties and quickly made the role of detective inspector. He was found dead in his office at the local police station. Investigators stated that they believed it was suicide and they were not following any other leads at present. It was thought that a recent gruesome case Mr Jolly had been investigating, involving the kidnapping and murder of a young girl, Bethan Greene, had tipped him over the edge and he had decided to end his own life. Mr Jolly leaves behind a wife but no children. His work colleagues said the inspector was a brilliant man and a workaholic. He is to be buried in Dark Street Cemetery next Tuesday. The old police station is due for closure in two weeks as the force moves off to the new station, which has just been built using two million pounds of taxpayers' money."

"Does that help?" asked Neville.

"A little, but if you think of anything else, I'd be pleased to hear it."

She was about to go when she had a thought. "You don't know anything about a Mary Watts, who was murdered the other week, do you?"

"Not much beyond what was in the papers, but there is this." He got up and beckoned her to follow him, leading her towards the library noticeboard. He pointed out a large business card attached to the board. *'Experienced life model available for portrait sittings and photography sessions. Please contact Mary Watts at the following address.'* Contact details were also listed.

"It's been up here for some time," noted Neville. "I thought it was interesting to learn she had been murdered, given her job. I'll see what else I can find out for you if you want. I love delving into local history."

"Brilliant, thank you, Neville. My name is Ada by the way." She was just about to leave when she saw that Neville was hovering. "Is there something else?" she asked.

"Would you… erm, would you fancy having a coffee with me? Now… if you're free? I'm really thirsty and I could do with a break," he said. Neville looked slightly startled by the bravery and suddenness of his own question.

"Oh!" Ada was taken aback. It had been a long time since a living young man had asked her to have a coffee with him. "Well, that would be nice, but not right now, I'm a little busy. Maybe next week?"

"Sure, sure, I understand. Next week," said Neville, forcing a grin.

"No really, next week. I'll pop by and see if you've found anything else out and we can go for a coffee." At that, he perked up a bit.

Ada left the library after informing the librarian where to find the newspapers. Rose and Mrs Entwhistle were straight on her case. "He seems like a lovely young man," cooed Rose. "Very nice manners. Oh, I'm so excited for you!"

"Rose, it's just coffee, nothing more. I just recalled what you both said about it being good for me to go out and meet living people my age. Really, he's not my type. He seems very bookish."

The two ghosts looked at each other and then walked along in silence.

They were soon at 31 Cherry Tree Lane. Ada went to the front door and opened the letterbox as before.

"Good morning, Mary, it's Ada Baker again. I've come back for a chat. I hope you've considered my offer. I'm going to go round to the back garden so we can chat more easily."

Ada made her way round with Rose and Mrs Entwhistle following her and took a seat at the table.

Rose looked through the window at the dusty room within. "Ooh I'd love to get in there and give it a deep-down clean. It doesn't look like it's been cleaned in years."

"And she could do with Seth giving her a visit too," added Mrs Entwhistle.

"I'd love a cuppa," said Rose. "How long do you think she'll be?"

"I came prepared," said Ada, who pulled a vacuum flask out of her small backpack. She placed it on the table with four plastic beakers and filled them all up.

"Ooh lovely. Nothing better than a cup of Rosie Lee to cheer the soul."

"She's here," said Mrs Entwhistle.

Ada looked up and could see a white form in the sitting room. Tentatively, it made its way across the room and through the window. The voluptuous and naked Mary Watts stood in front of them. The silk scarf that had been used as the murder weapon was still tight around her neck. *Wow!* thought Ada. She could see why Mary might be popular as a life model.

"Please…" said Ada, indicating the chair. Mary gently lowered herself onto it.

"This is Mrs Entwhistle. She was the head cook at a great country house in Yorkshire. She's been teaching me how to cook. This is Rose Thorne. Rose was an experienced cleaner before she passed. They're both dead like you. They live with me and help me in my everyday life."

Mrs Entwhistle seemed rather embarrassed, as if she didn't know where to look. Even after a hundred years of being dead, she couldn't get used to all the modern ways.

"My name is Mary Watts. I assume you've read about what happened to me, which is why you're here?"

"Yes, just so," said Ada. "We'd love to help bring you justice. If you know who did it, we can contact the police and give them evidence to convict your killer."

"That's just the problem," said Mary. "I don't know who did it. I have my suspicions, but I never saw them. Whoever did it came up from behind me. They were strong too; I couldn't fight them. By the time I came to, as I am now, they were gone."

"Well that certainly makes things more difficult," said Ada thoughtfully. "Do you have any idea who might have done it? Did anyone have access to your house? The door was locked."

"Well a few people do. I keep a spare key here." She stood up and wandered over to a nearby yew tree. In the twisted trunk of the tree was a hand-sized hole.

Rose followed her and looked in to see the key. "Who knows the key is here?" asked Ada.

"My sister Ellen, of course. This was Mum and Dad's house and she has her own key. Then there's Gilbert Orange. He's a local art teacher and artist. I sit for him here sometimes for his portraits. He finds my house very bohemian. Then there's Marcus Strang. He's a photographer. We sometimes do photo shoots here. He loves the light in the bathroom. I was expecting him actually when I was murdered."

Marcus Strang. That was a name Ada hadn't heard in a while. She'd known a Marcus Strang when she was at art college. He was one of her teachers, although he was only a few years older than her. She wondered if it was the same man.

"It might have been Marcus, but my money is on my stalker, William Kent."

"A stalker, wow. That is big news. The police must be all over him. Why wasn't he mentioned in the paper I wonder?"

"Well, I'd not reported him yet. I only met him a month or so ago. He came along to one of the life drawing classes that Gilbert was running at the college. Right from the start I could see he was different." Mary picked up her scarf and started twirling it nervously in her hand. "He spent most of the lesson just staring at me, which I know is what they're supposed to do, but they usually draw or paint too. He just stared, mostly at my breasts. I put up with it for a few classes then I told Gilbert he was freaking me out and he refused him access after that. He would be waiting outside the college for me when I finished and follow me home. In the end, I got a cab to drive me home, but by that point he knew where I lived. He would stand out the front of the house just staring at it, writing something in a little notebook." Mary's nostrils flared. "I hate him! He's a horrible weasel-like man, with mean, sharp features and greasy hair slicked down in a comb-over."

"Where might we find his address details?"

"I'm not certain where he lives but I think it's on the new estate on the other side of town. Gilbert would probably know. You'll find him working at Newton College of Further Education. Kent's the one who did it, I'm certain of it. The man's a freak." Anger flickered through Mary's eyes.

"Okay, we'll do some investigating and then we'll suggest him to the police to investigate further." Ada was about to get up and go when she thought to say, "You know, you don't have to be naked if you don't want to be. You have no corporeal body now. People just tend to stay in the clothes they were in when they died."

Mary looked down at her body. "I took my clothes off for a living. I'm perfectly happy with my body. It's being dead that bothers me. I don't need to fit in with the old-fashioned conventions now," she said, looking at Mrs Entwhistle, who was still trying to look anywhere but at Mary.

"I could clean your house for you if you like?" said Rose helpfully. "If Ada will let me use her body to do it."

Mary eyed Rose inquisitively. "Use her body?" she repeated.

Before Ada could stop her, Rose blurted, "Yes, we can inhabit her body and use it if she lets us. Almost like having our own body."

"I'm sure someone living will be along to sort the house out, Rose. In fact, Mary, you might want to prepare yourself that it will be sold eventually and you'll have a stranger living here."

"I doubt it. My sister will probably move in. As I said, this was our parents' house before it was mine. I'm surprised she's not been over yet. Too grief-stricken maybe."

"Okay, thank you, Mary. We'll be off now but we'll be in touch if we find anything out. Thanks for your time." They wandered off but as Ada looked back, Mary had somehow found a ghostly cigarette from somewhere and was smoking it. It looked like she was going to be a quick learner.

As they walked down the street, Mrs Entwhistle started spouting off. "I can see why someone murdered her. What a sloven, and so loose in morals!" she complained.

"I rather liked her," replied Rose. "She was a free spirit, not bound by convention. I bet she was a very stylish woman."

"That's just another way of saying loose morals!" continued Mrs Entwhistle, huffing. "I hardly knew where to look."

They walked past Inspector Jolly's house again. He was there sitting in the garden under a rose arch. He saw them, waved and ran over to greet them.

"Ms Baker! Good to see you. Have you been to see Mary Watts again? Have you found out anything new?

43

Good day, ladies," he said, looking at Mrs Entwhistle and Rose. "Who might you be?"

"I'm Mrs Entwhistle. I was the head cook at Frogmore Manor in Yorkshire, and this is Rose Thorne. She was a cleaning lady in the town."

Inspector Jolly took both their hands and kissed them in turn. Both ladies cooed with pleasure.

"An honour," he said. "And how do you know Ms Baker?"

"They live with me," replied Ada.

Just then, an elderly lady walked past with her two dogs and glanced up at Ada. "Who lives with you, dear?" she asked in a friendly fashion.

"Oh! I'm just talking to myself, sorry," replied Ada. Both dogs started growling in the direction of the ghosts.

"Not to worry, dear," she said, patting Ada on the hand. "I do that all the time." She smiled and wandered off towards the park.

"Yes, we've just been to see Mary Watts, Inspector. She didn't see who committed the murder but she has a strong suspicion it was a man called William Kent, who had been stalking her. I'm off to speak to the police to convince them to find out about him. Would you like to join us?" said Ada.

Inspector Jolly looked a little hesitant but agreed. They headed off to the new police station. Its large shiny glass and concrete facade glistened in the sunlight. It looked dazzling and quite intimidating. Inspector Jolly looked a little bit like a child arriving at school on their first day.

"Are you okay, Inspector?" asked Rose. He nodded.

"I wouldn't fancy having the job of keeping all that glass clean," she said.

They arrived at the reception, and the smell of new paint and furniture wafted out towards them as the automatic doors opened. They drifted in, staring all around them like young children gazing in awe at bright, shiny Christmas lights. A kindly voice in front of them brought their attention back to focus.

"Can I help you, madam?" said a bright young woman at the counter.

"Yes, I think so. My name is Ada Baker. I have some, I think unknown, information about the murder of Mary Watts. I'd like to speak to the inspector in charge please."

"I see. The inspector is rather busy at the moment, but I can take your information down and pass it on to him," she said, smiling.

"No, I think I need to discuss it with him directly," said Ada, holding her ground.

"I see. Please take a seat."

The desk officer made a phone call, speaking in a quiet voice so they couldn't hear. She kept looking across at Ada, then nodded and put the phone down.

"He'll be with you in a short while," she said.

Inspector Jolly was clearly nervous. "Do you know her?" asked Ada, pointing at the desk officer.

"No."

"Have you been here before?"

"No."

Clearly, she wasn't going to get a lot of information from him at the moment. Nothing could be heard except for the gentle click-clack of Mrs Entwhistle's needles.

At last, a door opened and Ada was beckoned through into what looked like an interview room. A cup of tea was brought in for her.

"Well, that's rude. They might have brought us all one," said Rose in a humph.

"They can't see you, Rose."

A short while after that, a man walked into the room and sat opposite Ada. He slammed a black coffee down on the table, along with a notepad.

"Good morning, Ms..." He looked at his notes. "Ada Baker. I'm Detective Inspector Matlock. The DCI is off sick presently and I'm the lead investigator on this case. What new information do you think you can supply us that the authorities haven't been able to find?" he said, pressing his lips into a tight grimace, which only vaguely resembled a smile.

"Well, Inspector, I wondered if you knew anything about the stalker she had. His name was William Kent and she met him when she was posing as a nude life model at art classes he attended. I believe he lives on the new estate in town."

"Indeed no!" he said, sitting up straighter in his chair. "Why didn't her sister know anything about this?"

"I think it's quite a new thing. I don't know how close they were and it only started a month or two ago," Ada replied.

"And how did you come to know about this, Ms Baker? What's your connection to the victim?"

Ada paused, took a deep breath and went for her 'honesty is the best policy' approach. "You will find this hard to believe, Inspector Matlock, but I'm a gifted psychic. I've been and spoken to Miss Watts. She can't tell me who did it for definite as she was attacked from behind. Her main suspect though is William Kent. He used to follow her home after class and stand in the street and watch her house. I think it's worth investigating him at least. Does he have a record?"

Inspector Matlock stood up, closed his book and said, "Thank you for your time, Ms Baker, but it's real evidence we're after."

Just then, Inspector Jolly, who had been quiet up to this point, said, "Tell him that Inspector Jolly says he's still a wet sap and he wants the forty pounds back he owes him."

Ada sighed but repeated it to Inspector Matlock. The inspector stopped in his tracks and turned back to look at Ada. "What do you know about Inspector Jolly?"

"He's here with me. I met him while investigating. He was investigating too. He currently lives in the old police station."

Inspector Matlock's jaw dropped further. "But that's my home! I moved in there six months ago."

Inspector Jolly spoke to Ada again, and she repeated, "He also says you're out of cat food, you need to get some for Mr Whiskers, and there's a twenty-pound note in the left inside pocket of the old coat that you've put aside to go to charity." She paused as she listened. "What's that? Oh! And he said you were right. He was murdered. It wasn't suicide." Ada looked at Inspector Jolly disbelievingly.

"Hah!" said Matlock, slapping the table hard and spilling his coffee everywhere. "I knew it! I knew it!" He looked at Ada and recovered his decorum. "That's certainly very interesting. We'll consider what you've said carefully, Ms Baker." He appeared to look at her properly for the first time since she'd walked in. She stared back at him and he smiled. He was really quite pleasant-looking with a smile on his face instead of the frown he had when he walked in. He seemed to be in his early thirties. He was clean-shaven with short brown hair and azure blue eyes. His shirt was unironed and a coffee-stained tie hung crookedly from his neck. Ada had the impression that fashion wasn't really something that concerned him greatly. Strong forearms were visible below his rolled-up shirt sleeves.

"This is my card if you need me for anything else," said Ada, placing it in front of him.

"Thank you, Ms Baker," he said, taking it and showing her to the door. He even managed a wave goodbye as they departed through reception. The desk officer raised an eyebrow, as if surprised by this gesture.

They left the station and headed back to Inspector Jolly's house.

"Do you think he believed us?" said Mrs Entwhistle.

"I know him. He's a good lad really. He'll look into it," said Inspector Jolly.

"You neglected to mention to us that you thought you'd been murdered," said Ada. "That's rather a big thing not to tell somebody. Would you like to tell us about it?"

A pained expression crossed his face. "Another day maybe. Let's focus on this case first."

***

Inspector Matlock wouldn't normally have listened to the witterings of a psychic. He was a sceptic about the paranormal, and God in general, but she had said some things he thought it would be impossible to know. Sitting at his desk, he searched for information on William Kent. There was indeed a record for him. Restraining orders were in place from two other women, though nothing new had been recorded for a little while. He also had a conviction for flashing. Nothing had come through for him in the search of Mary's home though – no fingerprints or any other evidence of his being there. It was intriguing but he needed more evidence than the say-so of a psychic.

Later that afternoon, he headed to the supermarket, bought his usual cans of Tiddles cat food and returned to his house. He opened a can and fed the very hungry Mr Whiskers. He emptied the large plastic bag that he'd put his used clothes in and searched the pockets of the coat. There, as promised, exactly where she'd said, in the left inside pocket, was a crumpled twenty-pound note.

"Hmmm," mumbled Inspector Matlock. He looked around the room. "Thank you, Inspector Jolly." Then felt slightly silly and carried on with his chores.

Sitting in the Windsor chair by the window, Inspector Jolly turned to look at him and smiled. "You're welcome, David."

Chapter 5

Ada felt good about having gone to the police yesterday and telling them about William Kent. She wasn't sure if the inspector had believed her or not, but she thought she had impressed him with what she'd said. She guessed that it would be printed in the papers if he was apprehended. It had all been rather thrilling. She wasn't sure she wanted it to be over. Now, of course, there was also the mystery of who killed Inspector Jolly. Perhaps she would go and see him and have a chat. It being Sunday, he might be in a more relaxed mood.

Sunday was a special day for Rose and Mrs Entwhistle. Seth the gardener came to collect them to walk to a church service. Mrs Entwhistle thought it was still one's duty to attend church even when you were dead. Apparently, there were more ghosts attending church these days than living people. Dennis was less of a believer, especially since he hadn't found himself in heaven when he died, so stayed at home with Ada. It wasn't that Ada didn't believe in God, it was only that she'd never felt the need to go to a special place to speak to him.

Dennis was watching another Western on the telly. Ada drummed her fingers on the arm of the chair. It was the same old format: good guy gets the bad guys and probably the girl.

"Dennis, how would you like to help me catch a real bad guy instead of a fake one?"

Dennis looked at Ada, then looked longingly at the screen and sighed. It was one of his particular favourites but he had seen it before. He pressed the button and flicked the screen off. "I'd be delighted, Ada."

Ada liked Dennis. He was very easy company and was quite happy to walk along in silence without the incessant need for chitter-chatter, unlike Rose. He had been in his late forties when he'd died. His hair was greying and slicked back. Oversized glasses dominated his face. He wore a blue shirt with a pink tie and pink braces held up his trousers.

They soon arrived at Inspector Jolly's house. The inspector was in the garden sitting under the rose arbour, vaping away. Ada was always surprised at the little luxuries of life that spirits took with them into the afterlife. He spotted them and came over to chat.

"Sorry, terrible habit. I took it up just before I died. Better than smoking though, I think. I know I'm not getting the same hit but it still calms me down. I think our visit to Inspector Matlock may have worked. He certainly seems very agitated and Mr Whiskers has been fed at least. I was so fed up of his pacing, I came out here for a bit of peace. The garden was never this lovely when it was a working police station."

"Ms Baker! What are you doing here?" It was Inspector Matlock.

"Oh, well, I felt at a bit of a loose end after visiting you. I thought I'd come and talk to Inspector Jolly. My curiosity was peaked about his mention yesterday about being murdered. That was the first he'd told me about it."

"I see." He looked around him. "And is he... um... here?"

Ada nodded and pointed to where he stood. "He's been vaping under the rose arch. He couldn't stand all your pacing. He's pleased you fed Mr Whiskers though."

"I see," he said, looking at Inspector Jolly, or where he thought he might be standing. "Would you like to come in for a cup of tea and meet Mr Whiskers?"

Ada was thrilled. It was exciting to be invited in for tea by a police inspector. "Yes please!" she said. "That is, if you don't mind, Inspector Jolly?"

"Not at all, dear girl, come in. It's nice to see a different face."

Ada, Dennis and the two inspectors entered the old police house. They went in the kitchen and sat round a large pine table. Inspector Matlock put the kettle on and made a large pot of tea. "I always make a large pot. I drink a lot of tea."

"Oh, but you had coffee at work?"

"That's just to keep me awake and get me through the day. Plus, the work tea is pretty awful."

Ada laughed. "Yes, I experienced it for myself!"

Just then, a loud meowing came from behind Ada as Mr Whiskers sauntered into the room. He leapt up onto the table and started rubbing himself against Ada's hand. Then he moved across to Inspector Jolly and rolled on his back, exposing his belly. Inspector Matlock poured them both a cup of tea. Ada moved one cup in front of Dennis and another in front of Inspector Jolly. Inspector Matlock looked puzzled.

"Do you mind?" said Ada. "They really appreciate being included."

He gave her a quizzical expression but smiled and said, "Of course." He grabbed two more cups from the dresser. "Why four cups?" he said.

"And who are you, my good man?" asked Inspector Jolly, looking at Dennis.

"Oh gosh, yes, sorry. I should have introduced you," said Ada. "This is Dennis Sutherland. He was a banker in the city till the 1987 stock market crash. He lives in my house with me. He's a poltergeist and can move things with his mind."

Inspector Matlock spat out his tea.

"I'm sorry, what? Who's here? A poltergeist?"

"I'm so sorry, Inspector. I keep forgetting that you can't see them. It can be a real curse sometimes. When I first met the inspector, I thought he was real. He's so full of life still."

"Why thank you, young lady."

"You're welcome. He just thanked me."

"A real live poltergeist? Like the movie?"

"Yes, but less scary and menacing. For me it's not much different to living with normal people, except I can let them in and they can use my body. Dennis helps me with my finances, Mrs Entwhistle helps me cook, Rose helps me clean."

"Who are Mrs Entwhistle and Rose?" he said, sounding confused.

"They live with me. Until they died, Mrs Entwhistle was a cook and Rose was a cleaner. They were at the police station with me yesterday too. They're all very interested in the case."

"I'm sorry, Ada, you've told me some things I can't explain, but I think this is too much really. I'm not sure I can believe all this. It just sounds like nonsense!"

Then, before his eyes, Dennis's teacup floated up into the air and hovered there. Inspector Matlock couldn't see it, but there was a look of extreme concentration on Dennis's face.

"Oh well done, old chap!" exclaimed Inspector Jolly. "You'll have to try and teach me that trick." The cup came clattering down on the table, spilling tea everywhere.

Inspector Matlock didn't say anything. He just sat there open-mouthed.

"Sorry about that, Inspector. He's just learning to lift teacups. I'm trying to get him to bring me a cup of tea in bed, but lifting teacups with liquid in is quite tricky for some reason, although pulling off my duvet in the morning to wake me up doesn't seem to be! Would you like sugar in your tea, Inspector? How many lumps?"

"Two," he managed, still staring intently at the teacup.

"Best make it three, Dennis, I think he's had a bit of a shock." Three lumps of sugar dropped out of the sugar bowl and inched themselves across the tabletop to where Inspector Matlock was sitting.

"Apparently, pushing and pulling aren't too hard but lifting requires lots of effort and concentration. Dennis once described it as needing the same concentration as playing a chess game while running a marathon."

A strange half-giggling noise emanated from Inspector Matlock. Mr Whiskers started batting the sugar cubes with his paw then padded over to Dennis and rolled seductively in front of him. Mr Whiskers lived up to his name and did indeed have very large whiskers and long tabby fur. Dennis stroked him gently. "Oh! Mr Whiskers is a girl. Do you think the inspector knows?" said Dennis.

"I don't know, but I think he's had enough news for one day. So, Inspector Jolly, would you like to tell me more about why you think you were murdered?" she asked.

"Well, for one thing, I didn't commit suicide as the papers said. That's a pretty big clue. The other thing is that I was working on a murder case at the time. That gives someone pretty good grounds to kill me."

"What do you recall of the day you were murdered?" she asked.

"It started like any other day: I washed, I ate my breakfast, I went to work. I was working on the case of a particularly heinous murder of a young girl. I felt that I was getting close to solving it so I stayed late that night to try to complete it. I was sitting at my desk over there," he said, pointing at the window. "I made a coffee to keep myself awake. I felt sleepy, and the next thing I knew, I was as I am now. Dead. My body was slumped over my desk. There were ten empty insulin pens beside me and a printed and signed suicide note."

"So you were drugged with something to send you to sleep and then injected with insulin? Somebody staged it to look like a suicide attempt?" said Ada.

"That's what I believe. I just don't know exactly who. It was a much smaller station than it is now, as you can see. It was late, so there was a skeleton staff here. There was no reason for them to check in on me. They had their own jobs to do. They found me in the morning. I was already dead by then."

"So maybe it was someone who worked in the station?" said Ada.

"That's what I've wondered too, but I've gone over the facts of the case a thousand times in the last year and I have no idea who it might be."

They all looked at Inspector Matlock. He recovered himself enough to defend against her look. "Don't look at me! I had nothing to do with Jolly's death. I've been the one suggesting it was murder. Nobody would believe me. Jolly had been very down about the case he was working on. The insulin was his own to treat his diabetes. They found the sleeping pills in his system but they were his too. It was assumed he'd taken them to lessen the chances of his being revived and from suffering."

"Is that true?" asked Ada. "Were they yours?"

"Yes, they were mine. I kept the insulin in a fridge in my office."

"Why did you have so much of it?"

"I'd read that there might be shortage of it. I worked long hours and rarely got to the pharmacy, so the last time I ordered, I ordered enough to last me a while. Some of them were my trickle insulin. My once-a-day insulin. The rest was the regular insulin that I take with each meal." He looked at Inspector Matlock. "I think David is okay. I worked with him a long time and I've lived with him for six months now. I think you can trust him."

"David?" said Ada.

"He's really here, isn't he?" said Inspector Matlock, coming round to something like his normal self. "Yes, my name is David, but that's only for social situations like this. I'd prefer if you'd call me Inspector Matlock in front of my colleagues."

"Certainly. Now that you're with us again, Inspector Jolly has been regaling us with details of the day he died."

"Yes, I heard. At least, I heard you. Does he know who did it?"

"No, he recalls feeling sleepy, then the next thing he knew he was dead, as he is now. But he says he definitely didn't commit suicide."

"I thought it was odd that the suicide note was printed. The inspector was always a big pen user. He didn't much like technology, but all the evidence was pointing to suicide. I couldn't get permission to investigate further. His estranged wife wasn't interested, and he had no family to chase the matter except for a sister in Australia, and she just accepted the verdict of death by suicide." He looked at where he thought the inspector was sitting and said earnestly, "I'm sorry this was missed, Inspector, and I promise I'll look into this further in my own time."

"I appreciate that, but he should be careful and look after himself. Finding my killer won't change what happened to me. David's still young and has his life ahead of him."

Ada repeated what he'd said to David.

"I will, thank you, sir." He turned to look at Ada. "You might be right by the way about William Kent. He has previous for stalking and flashing. I would advise you not to look at this case any further. Sometimes flashing or stalking is the stage before they take the next step to rape or even murder someone. If he is our suspect, he's very dangerous. Your information has been useful though. I've asked the officers to find any CCTV or doorbell video footage in the area for the whole month preceding the murder. Previously, we'd only looked at that particular date. It might take some time to check through it all."

"Thank you, David. I do have my own methods of defence. I have a green belt in kung fu, you know, and I have other skills. I can channel the abilities of the dead."

"That's as maybe, but kung fu isn't going to stop someone shooting you. Please keep clear of the investigation in the future, Ms Baker." He turned to look at Inspector Jolly's seat. "I'm a little surprised, sir, that you'd even consider letting a civilian become involved."

Ada was a little riled. "I think you'll find that being dead may have had something to do with his ability to stop me, and I like to think that the inspector realised my obvious abilities."

"Yes, sorry, Ms Baker. Just take care, please, and stay away from any further investigations."

Inspector Matlock stood up, picked up the milk bottle and put it in his fridge. Ada noticed that it was full of microwave meals for one. Police work could obviously be a solitary, lonely existence, she thought.

"Well, thank you for the tea and the chat, Inspectors. Dennis and I must be getting home. Mrs E will be cooking a Sunday lunch." She paused for a moment. "Unless you'd like to join us?" she said, thinking of the contents of his fridge.

"That's very kind, but I need to think about all this."

"Another time then?" she said.

He smiled at her again with a smile so dazzling it would melt away rainclouds. "Sure."

She turned to Inspector Jolly. "You're most welcome to come too, Inspector?"

He was as enigmatic as his living counterpart. "I think I need to think on things too, dear girl, and keep an eye on David, but Dennis, I would love to meet up sometime and speak with you about your abilities."

"Certainly, anytime," said Dennis.

With this, Dennis and Ada left to get home so that Mrs Entwhistle could prepare lunch.

Chapter 6

There was a loud crash downstairs. Ada was jolted out of sleep and sat up in bed. She threw back the covers and raced downstairs to see what was going on. There was a smashed cup and a pool of liquid all over the hall floor. Dennis was there looking sheepish.

"I'm sorry," he said. "I was trying to bring you a cup of tea like you asked. As I did so well yesterday at the inspector's house, I thought I'd give it a go. I got distracted by Rose talking about the state of the dust on top of the bookshelf and I dropped it."

"Never mind, thank you for trying," said Ada. "It is appreciated."

"I boiled the kettle, put the tea in, everything. It's taken me half an hour to do it," Dennis said, sighing.

"Well, why don't I set everything up for you and tomorrow we'll use an enamel cup so it doesn't break? Keep trying, Dennis. Never give up."

Rose was itching to clean up the mess, so Ada let her in to get the job done quicker.

"Thank you, Rose," she said.

"What's the plan for today?" asked Dennis, recovering his composure.

"Oh, I don't know. I'd not really thought."

"I'd love to go and meet the inspector again and teach him my skill. As lovely as it is to live with so many ladies," he said, smiling at Rose and Mrs Entwhistle, "it'd be nice to have a male friend to chat with."

"Sure, why not. Breakfast first though."

She looked for Mrs Entwhistle, who was sitting in front of the TV absorbed in a cooking programme. "What's for breakfast today, Mrs E?" said Ada.

"Oh!" she said, looking bothered. "Would you mind just making some toast for yourself. Vincenzo Cortellini is on the telly again. He's such a lovely man. Imagine! A man cooking all that lovely food. I couldn't imagine Mr Entwhistle cooking for me like that. I wish I'd been to Florence when I was alive. It's so beautiful." Mrs Entwhistle finished with a sigh.

Ada half expected her to insert the word 'dreamy' in there. Mrs Entwhistle was in full-on 1950s teenage girl mode as she cooed and simpered over the TV celebrity.

"No problem," said Ada, who set about the task.

Following breakfast, Ada put on black and green tie-dye jeans and a T-shirt. Mrs E seemed set for a morning of TV, so Ada, Rose and Dennis left the house at about nine thirty and set off for the inspector's house to meet Jolly. It was another lovely day in Sudfield and they found the inspector in his garden, walking around examining the roses.

"Ahoy!" he said joyfully, waving at them. "Welcome! Hello, Ada, Dennis and, of course, Rose." He beckoned them into the garden and they took a seat on the bench under the rose arch.

"So pleased you've come again. I have news for you. David had a call early this morning from the station to say that they'd found evidence of William Kent, the stalker, in the area in the weeks preceding the murder. There was some good doorbell footage of him but nothing at all on the date of the murder, so they don't think he can be their guy."

"That's ridiculous!" said Ada. "It must be him. Mary didn't know of anyone that might want her dead. They must have missed him somehow. Why don't they just go and arrest him?" Ada's temper was starting to rise again.

"I guess, my dear girl, that they are following procedure. It's not an offence for him to walk down the street, and she never reported him as stalking her. Perhaps they're trying to gather more evidence. I'm sure they'll bring him in for more questioning soon. Would you like to come in for tea?" he enquired.

"Would that be all right without the inspector here? I barely know him."

"I'm sure he wouldn't mind. He likes you, I think, despite his protestations. Dennis, you'll need to let Ada in though. He left the side door key in the inside lock."

They followed Inspector Jolly round to the side of the house. The gents walked through the door and shortly after, Ada heard a loud click and the sound of bolts being drawn. She tried the door handle and entered the house with Rose, who still preferred to do things the proper way. She went over to put the kettle on and got the tea things ready.

When she finished, she noticed that Dennis was deep in a lesson showing the inspector how to move objects, so she wandered off to find the bathroom. She was astonished to find that it was behind a heavy iron door with the letters 'WC' stencilled on it. It had obviously been a police cell before the station had been shut down. Ada pushed open the door and there was a man sitting on the loo. She couldn't help herself and let out a little scream. He was wearing very old, worn, tatty clothes. His jacket was full of rips and little tears, and he had a small scarf around his neck and was wearing a flat cap. He had boots on his feet but they were so full of holes that they could barely be described as boots any more. His hair looked dirty and uncombed.

Dennis, Rose and Jolly came rushing to see what was wrong.

"Ah! I should perhaps have told you about George. George was being held in the cell in 1916, when he died. He's been here ever since."

"Murdered, miss!" said George. "I was found hanging by my bootlaces. It was the bloody bobbies that did it. No offence, Inspector," he said, looking at Jolly. "They hated me because my mother was German and because I was a conscientious objector. There was a lot of ill feeling towards Germans and conscientious objectors at that time. They made it look like suicide. It happened right here where the toilet is now. Nobody investigated it because nobody cared."

"Murder seems to be a theme at this police station," commented Ada. "I'm most dreadfully sorry, George."

"That's all right, miss. I've had a hundred years to get used to the idea. I hope they're rotting in hell now. Meanwhile, I'm stuck here at the site of my murder for eternity."

"Can't you leave the cell at least?" she asked.

"No, miss."

"I see. That must be awful for you."

"Not too bad, miss. Mr Whiskers comes to see me every day. I love cats."

"I know it sounds terribly disrespectful, George, but would you mind if I used the toilet? I'm desperate. I knew I shouldn't have had that third cup of tea."

"Sure, miss. Inspector Matlock pees here all the time."

He carried on sitting on the loo, staring at Ada. Ada looked puzzled. "Er, would you mind standing facing the corner while I use the toilet? I couldn't possibly go with you sitting there."

"Sure, miss. I forget the niceties after so long." He stood up and walked into the shower cubicle behind the shower curtain.

Ada shut the cell door and pulled her jeans down to start peeing. From the corner of the room, George started singing 'Danny Boy'.

"... And I shall hear, though soft you tread above me,
And all my grave will warmer, sweeter be.
For you will bend and tell me that you love me,
And I shall sleep in peace until you come to me!"

She paused to listen to his singing. He had a lovely voice and he sung it with real feeling.

"Thank you, George," she said, pulling up her jeans and flushing the loo. "I really am very sorry to hear your tragic tale."

She opened the door and Mr Whiskers entered the cell. George's face lit up. Mr Whiskers rolled on the floor in front of him, belly exposed.

She left George with Mr Whiskers in the cell and headed to the kitchen to pour some more tea.

The inspector was busy trying to move the sugar cube with his finger under Dennis's instruction and finally managed a tiny push, which he was thrilled by. They barely seemed to notice she was there as she sipped her tea.

"I'm bored!" said Rose. "Can't we go and find out some more about this William Kent?"

"But where would we go?" asked Ada.

"We know he lives on the new estate. It's not very big. We could ask someone there if they know him?"

"I guess so..." said Ada hesitantly. "I'm not supposed to be investigating him. I'm supposed to be leaving him well alone."

"Please!" said Rose imploringly. "We can ask a few

dead people. It'll be perfectly safe."

Ada was bored too, so she acquiesced to Rose's request.

"We're off to find out more info on Kent, do you want to come?" she asked the two men.

"No, we're fine thanks," said Dennis, only half aware of Ada and Rose, and he carried on his teaching.

"Yes, very good, Inspector! You're a quick learner." They had progressed on to moving the whole sugar bowl.

"Come on, Rose, let's go."

The two ladies left and headed off towards the new estate.

Chapter 7

Ada was worried that she was making the wrong choice to find out more info on William Kent, but she was also a very curious person and it hadn't taken much for Rose to persuade her. If she only asked the dead, she thought, there'll be no risk. It had seemed like a really good idea, but as they walked around the new estate, they found very few dead people. The estate was so new, nobody had had much of a chance to die there yet. They found a man dressed in medieval clothes who looked like he was some sort of peasant farmer. He had a wooden spade in his hand and was trying to dig the soil.

"Excuse me, sir, I was wondering if you knew which house Mr William Kent lived in?"

The peasant looked at her with a glazed expression, but from behind her she heard a voice.

"Why? Are you visiting him, miss?"

She spun round to see a postman wearing shorts. She pondered quickly in her mind why it was that postmen always wore shorts no matter the weather. "Why yes, I am," she lied. "I've been before but couldn't remember the actual address."

"It's 42 Broaks Wood Lane," he proffered helpfully. "Good day, miss."

"Good day. Thank you."

Ada whipped out her phone and entered the address in the satnav. They were at the address in no time. There was a small green near the house on which someone had placed a bench. She and Rose took a seat there and looked towards the house. It was a perfectly unremarkable house, the like of which could be seen in many towns up and down the country. They couldn't see any sign of Kent from where they were sitting, but Ada noticed a public footpath that ran past a fence at the side of the house. "Let's get closer," she said, pointing.

Rose agreed, and they walked over to the path and down beside the house. Ada stopped and listened through the fence. She couldn't hear anything.

"Go through, Rose," she whispered. "Tell me if there's anyone there."

"Really, you know I hate walking through things. Oh, all right," she said in a huff. Rose didn't like walking through things as it reminded her that she was dead.

She wandered through into the garden and looked around and then went into the house. "There's nobody here," she shouted.

Ada was curious. She paused for a moment but couldn't help herself. She tried to haul herself up over the fence and because she was very agile thanks to her kung fu and yoga, she managed it with ease. The garden was pretty ordinary-looking. She went up to the house and looked through the windows, where she could see into his living and dining room. There were many art prints on the walls, but most interesting was the fact that they were all of nude women. She looked closer and noticed that some of the photos and paintings were of Mary. There was one particularly stunning colour nude photo of her made up like a 1950s glamour model. She didn't recognise the other women, but they were all similar photos and paintings. She looked around the room to see if there was anything else that might give a clue.

"Hello?" a male voice said from nearby. "Who might you be?" The voice had a creepy resonance. She spun round to see a man in his late forties. He had a long gaunt face with vacant eyes and a sallow complexion. His eyes were red-rimmed, which made him look as if he'd been crying, and they were quite deep-set.

"I know you, don't I?" he said. "Didn't you used to work in the Bleak Street café? What's your name?" he enquired. He had a quizzical way of looking at her and cocked his head on one side like a dog as he asked each question. He stepped closer towards Ada and she felt herself backing away. He kept advancing.

"Nobody, I lost my cat. I thought I heard it in your garden so I popped in to see. I knocked first but nobody was home. I'm sorry to intrude. I'll be going now."

"No, don't go yet," he said. "I'm just trying to remember who you are. That's right. You had a badge…

'Ada'. What a lovely name, so rarely heard now." He had backed her into a corner. He touched a lock of her wavy brown hair and studied it. "What pretty hair you have. I always thought that when you served me at the café. Haven't you grown up well," he said, looking her up and down.

"I'll be going now," she said, starting to feel really scared but somehow mesmerised by his ferret-like stare.

"Not yet," he said.

"Leave her alone!" shouted Rose, who tried to punch him but failed, and her fist went straight through him.

William didn't notice but instead leant forward to kiss Ada. She squealed and instinctively kneed him in the balls and then punched him in the face. William obviously hadn't expected this attack and doubled up in pain, his nose gushing with blood. Ada ran to the fence and vaulted up over the top, down the other side and ran off as quickly as she could, with Rose struggling to keep up.

***

It took William Kent some minutes to recover from the attack but once he had, he noticed a business card that hadn't been there before lying on the ground. He picked it up. "Ada Baker, Psychic. Interesting," he said. He brought the card up to his nose and smelt it. Then he licked it and put it in his trouser pocket.

Chapter 8

Ada was crying as she ran. She kept going as long as she could, not even stopping to look behind her. She was completely freaked out by her experience with Kent. Eventually, she found herself outside the public library, which somehow felt like a safe haven. She went in and found Neville scanning copies of the local newspaper.

"Hello!" she said, panting.

"Good Lord! Have you been jogging? You look pale. Are you all right?"

"No!" she said, collapsing into a chair.

"What's wrong?" he said anxiously.

"Sssshhhh! You're talking too loudly and disturbing the other visitors." Ada recognised the voice.

"Sorry, Miss Prim. She's had a shock I think."

"You can hear her?" wheezed Ada.

"Miss Prim? Why yes, can you hear her too?"

She nodded.

"Extraordinary! Come on, Ada, I think it's time we had that coffee and a spot of lunch. My treat."

He grabbed his bag and put her arm around his

shoulder to support her as she nursed a stitch in her side with the other.

"There's a lovely new vintage tea room opened. The waitresses actually dress like Lyons Nippies and they serve the food on vintage china."

They were soon at the tea room and took a seat outside in the garden. Ada scanned the menu.

"Oh! They have afternoon tea. Do you mind if we order that?" Ada asked.

"Sounds great," Neville replied.

He ordered them afternoon tea and the waitress brought through a large teapot and a tiered wooden plate stand brimming with sandwiches and cakes.

Ada was so thirsty she drank the tea when it was still scalding hot. After a couple of cups, she felt better and then realised how famished she was.

Neville smiled at her as he ate a tuna sandwich and patiently waited for her to tell him what was wrong.

"You can hear the dead then? Can you do anything else?" she asked. "How long have you been able to hear them?"

"Since I was a child. My parents lived in a fifteenth-century timber-framed house. It had once been a local guildhall. I used to hear them particularly at night-time. There were so many there, it was like Piccadilly Circus. I got used to the noise in the end. At first, I don't think they realised I could hear them. I got annoyed with them one day and shouted at them, and they wouldn't leave me alone after that. I can't see them, all I can do is hear them. Nothing else. I tend not to tell people. They either think I'm mad or ask me to speak to their dead granny. I'm sure you can relate to that."

Ada nodded excitedly in agreement. "Yes, same. They would either try and get me to help them or be abusive. The kids at school used to call me 'Bonkers Baker' because I was always talking to the ghost children. I didn't have many friends. I use my gift now to help people, although I don't usually deal in murder." She showed him her business card.

"How long have you had the gift, Ada?"

"Ever since I can remember. I recall being in my playpen and there being a grey-haired black man standing over me. He would play peek-a-boo with me by appearing and disappearing. It used to make me giggle. I think he was my granddad, Stan, who died just a month before I was born."

"Can you see them too?"

"Yes, as if they were real people. In fact, sometimes it can be hard to tell if they're real or not. I can also let them possess my body and share it with me. I just move my presence to the back of my mind. I let Mrs Entwhistle control my limbs to cook dinner, for example. I could perhaps let a train driver use my body to drive a train. I also gain some of their strength, if they're particularly strong. I think there are probably limitations, but I've not found what they are yet. I think if an opera singer tried to use my body to sing, she might be a bit disappointed as I'm tone deaf, but I don't know.

I also have retrocognitive episodes sometimes by touching objects, which means that I can see events that happened in the past in connection with that object. Usually, it's quite traumatic events. I don't have visions when I pick up the milk bottles off the doorstep, for example, but if that milk bottle had been used to murder someone, I might have a vision of the murder taking place. I can't stand visiting antique shops."

"Oh, sorry! I didn't know that when I suggested the vintage tea rooms," said Neville.

"It's okay, I don't think anyone's ever met death by teacup. I guess they could be poisoned, but this one seems fine," she said, looking into it and swirling the tea leaves around the bottom.

"You don't read tea leaves too, do you?" said Neville as he watched her.

"No!" she said, laughing.

"Can you see the future?" he enquired curiously. "I could really do with knowing the lottery numbers this week – I've overspent!"

"No, I'm not precognitive. Not yet at least. Some psychics can. My talents seem to lie more in the past than the future."

"So, tell me about the murder and why you're investigating it."

Ada went on to explain her decision to investigate Mary's murder and everything that had happened since, including her episode in the garden with William Kent. He listened carefully, not saying anything other than 'I see' or 'Hmmm' to encourage her to carry on talking.

"You should report what happened to you to the police," he said finally.

"But I was in his garden snooping. They might prosecute me for trespassing."

"Well, how about saying you sent one of your ghostly friends to investigate? You say that the inspector seemed to believe you in the end."

"You could say I went," chipped in Rose. "Can I have a cup of tea, Ada?"

"Who are you?" asked Neville, looking towards the source of the voice.

"Rose Thorne. I live with Ada."

Ada beamed broadly at Neville. "It's so nice to have a friend who can hear them too. But you can't see her?"

Neville smiled. "No, just hear her. Of course you may have a cup, Rose." He hailed the waitress. "Please may we have a separate cup, another pot of tea and one more scone."

Rose was absolutely thrilled when a large scone with clotted cream and jam was placed in front of her. Neville poured her a cup of tea. "There you go, Rose."

Ada's jaw dropped. Neville looked at her. "They like to be included, you know. I often make a cup for Miss Prim at the library."

Ada smiled. At last, someone who understood.

"Now, I'm not sure if you're still interested after today, but I did some more research. I've not found anything on Jolly yet, but I've been speaking with the old boy network down at the care home where I work two days a week. It seems that Mary's mother had something of a reputation as a woman of loose morals, and Mary had a reputation for the same. They say that Ellen's father only married her so he could have a home for his own daughter. His daughter, Ellen, was Mary's stepsister and the complete opposite in personality. She is said to be very homely and very kind. She's a member of the local Women's Institute. More into cake competitions and flower arranging than art and nudity. They sound like polar opposites. I thought perhaps you could go to see her. Presumably she knows her sister better than anyone. She might not know about the stalker but perhaps she can give you some other detail about Mary's life that might help. She lives at 4 Mill Cottages on Mill Lane."

"Thank you, Neville. Yes, I'll go and talk to her, I think. I feel a lot better now."

"You really should report to the inspector what happened to you. At least talk to the deceased Inspector Jolly. I'm sure he could advise."

They finished their lunch and Neville offered to go with her to see Ellen, as Ada still looked shaken. It was a pleasant stroll to Mill Lane, which was in the older part of town. They walked past the old silk mill, which was now an antique centre, and along to the cottages that had been built for its workers. They were small but beautiful, with surprisingly ornate windows for workers' cottages. Number four was particularly chocolate box-like, with a yellow rambling rose growing around the door and a front garden full of cottage garden plants. It was alive with pollinating insects and birds, which flew off the feeders as they arrived. It looked like somewhere that Snow White would live. Neville used the shiny brass lion-head knocker to rap loudly on the door.

There was a noise from within and then a woman in her mid-thirties opened the door. She had floury fingers and was wearing an apron. She also had on a beautiful white 1950s-style knee-length dress. She was a little overweight, with a more matronly figure than her sister, and had blonde hair, whereas Mary's was dark brown. She was quite pudding-faced, but her hair was styled immaculately in a sort of fifties updo.

"Yes, how can I help you?" she asked.

"Good morning, Ellen," said Ada, smiling. "My name is Ada Baker and this is my friend Neville." She hesitated for a second while she thought what to say. "I'm a psychic... investigator. I can hear and see the dead, and I've been talking with your sister about her killer. Sadly, she never saw who did it. As the police seem a little stuck, we were wondering if you would mind talking to us about her, to see if we can work out who her killer might have been, please?"

Ellen stood open-mouthed for a second and went very pale. Then she seemed to recover herself. "Yes, of course, please come in. I've just been baking some chocolate chip cookies. Would you like some?"

Ada and Neville nodded, to be polite, and followed her into the tiny but perfectly formed sitting room. She gestured to the 1950s-style settee and disappeared off into the kitchen to make tea. Ellen was obviously a big 1950s fan. All her furniture and furnishings were of that era but edged rather more towards the chintz than stylish side of it. Over the mantlepiece, a black plastic cat clock gently ticked, its tail and eyes moving from left to right in a most unsettling manner, as if surveying everything they did.

Ellen popped her head through the door. "Actually, I just made some lemonade this morning. As it's so warm today, do you fancy drinking some of that in the garden?"

They nodded and followed her outside. They trooped through the kitchen, which was also very 1950s in style, with an amazing black and white chequerboard lino floor. The garden was small but pleasant, and again very 1950s in style, with a little rockery. Ada could see into next door's garden, where there was a very handsome man in old-fashioned working clothes. He doffed his cap to Rose, and she rushed over to go and talk to him.

Ellen poured them a cool glass of lemonade and proffered them a cookie each. They both took one to be polite.

"So, a psychic you say. We had a local psychic come to the WI to give a talk. Elsie Strongbottom was her name. She was very good actually. She told Mrs Parker how her deceased son was missing her. We were all in tears."

Ada smiled. She thought very little of Elsie Strongbottom. She had been to see her show, but Elsie had completely ignored what any dead people actually told her and made things up. She was convinced she was a fraud.

"Mary told us she had a stalker, William Kent. Did you know anything about him? He'd been following her for a month or so. He met her at art classes where she was a model."

Ellen gave a strained smile. "No, I hadn't, but I'm not surprised, having chosen a career like that. You must meet all sorts of strange people," she said with a sniff of disapproval. "Another biscuit?" She offered the plate and put on a saccharin-sweet smile.

"He has a previous record but the police aren't sure it's him as there's no evidence he was there. Having now met him, he seems a very likely candidate," she said as she shivered. "But I thought maybe I should throw the net wider and see what else I could find out about her acquaintances. Do you know anything about Marcus Strang, the photographer?"

Ellen's face brightened a little. "Oh yes, I used to clean for her round her house occasionally – she was never great at domestic things, unlike me. I met him there one time and he was entranced by me. He came to photograph me for an article in *Good Housekeeping* magazine about people who live in retro-style homes. He took some beautiful photos of me and my home. He said I had great bone structure. Hold on…" She nipped back into the house to retrieve a well-thumbed copy of the magazine. "Here, you can keep this copy. I have twenty other copies."

Ada flicked through the pages. They were indeed beautiful photos and he had portrayed Ellen in a very flattering light. She could see why she was so enamoured; she looked every inch the domestic goddess. There was a photo of Marcus Strang set into the article. He looked very arty, with a pale slim figure, floppy black ruffled hair and dark glasses. It definitely looked like the Marcus Strang she had known at art college, but carrying a few more years.

"Where might I find him, do you think?"

"He has an exhibition of his photos on at the Wilson Art Gallery at the moment. He's probably there, hoping to sell his photos. I've been to see it twice, it's wonderful. He even gave me a signed copy of one of the prints of me for free."

"Do you know anything about your sister's relationship with him?"

"Yes, she posed for him nude. He takes a lot of gritty images of real-life people, but he also likes taking artistic photos of nudes. There are some pictures at the gallery but I skipped over those. Who wants to see their sister posing in the nude? I don't know how she could bear to have people ogle her body like that. It's little better than porn," she said rather tartly. "They'd known each other about a year I suppose. You're best to ask him more. Anyway, Marcus would never do such a thing as murder. He's a lovely man. I'd try speaking to Gilbert Orange. He is so conceited," she said disapprovingly.

"What was her relationship with Gilbert Orange?"

"I only met him a few times. He's an art teacher and artist. She posed for his students in art classes and privately for him. She has a very lewd oil painting of herself in her home, nude and reclining on a chair in the garden, smoking a cigarette. I try not to look at it when I'm dusting, but the dust does tend to gather on the nipples as he made them stick out so. Horrid thing it is. She loved it. She's known him for some years. They used to be lovers, I think. Going to see him at the college might be your best bet of finding him. I don't know where he lives. Beyond that, I can't tell you much about him, but he's my best bet for a murderer, or perhaps this Kent fellow. We weren't very close sisters. We were very different, as you can probably tell. We didn't have long chats about what was happening in her life. I think that's all I can tell you."

"Thank you, Ellen, you've been very helpful," said Neville, beaming. Ada looked at Rose, who was still busy chatting to the handsome man next door, and gave her a nod. She seemed to say goodbye, he doffed his cap again and she walked towards them.

Ellen saw them to the door, past the gently ticking cat. "If you ever want to give a talk at the WI, please let me know. We're always looking for new speakers." She gave them another saccharin smile and closed the door. They wandered off down the lane.

"Well, that was…" began Ada.

"Saccharin sweet," finished Neville.

"Yes, but also helpful. I think perhaps I'll start by visiting Marcus Strang's exhibition tomorrow to see what he says." She paused for a few seconds, then hesitantly said, "Would you like to come with me? It'd look less suspicious if two of us visited."

"I'd love to," he said, beaming again. "Let me walk you home, you've had a nasty shock."

"Sure, that'd be lovely," she replied, smiling.

"Do you want to know what Bert, the lovely man next door, had to say about Ellen?" asked Rose.

Ada jumped. She'd forgotten for a moment that Rose was there.

"Yes, that would be great. Who was he?"

"His name's Bert and he's lived there, well died there, been dead there, since the early twentieth century. He used to work at the silk mill. He says Ellen is very much a homebody, frequently entertains her WI friends, and that Mr Strang has been to visit on more than one occasion. Mary never came to visit. He's also taking me out for a stroll next Sunday after church," she finished excitedly.

"Thanks, Rose, and good for you. I'm not the only one who needs to get out and meet new people."

They carried on the rest of the way to Ada's home in silence, each wrapped up in their own thoughts. Neville saw her to the gate, gave her a hug, and Ada and Rose went in. Neville walked off back down the road towards his home.

***

William Kent sat in an old blue Ford Anglia parked almost opposite Ada's house. He watched their arrival and Neville's departure. "Interesting," he said to himself. He opened a new notebook from its plastic wrapper and started jotting down notes.

Chapter 9

Dennis was home when she got in and Rose wasted no time in telling him and Mrs Entwhistle about what had happened.

"Foul, odious little man he was," said Rose.

"Why ever did you go in there?" asked Mrs Entwhistle.

"I don't know what compelled me to do it. I guess I just wanted to find some evidence to show his connection to Mary. He has lots of photos of her up on the wall of his living room. Rose said he wasn't there, but he must have arrived after she checked. It's no matter, he doesn't know who I am or where to find me."

"He knows your name is Ada. That might be enough for a clever man," said Dennis. "That settles it. I'm coming with you from now on."

"It's fine, Dennis. I'm going with Neville to the art gallery tomorrow."

"Ooh, that lovely young man!" said Mrs Entwhistle. "He was so helpful, Dennis. I think she'll be okay with him. It'll be good for her to spend some time with living people."

Dennis sulked off back to the sofa.

Just then, the doorbell rang. Dennis leapt up. "I'll see who it is." He ran for the door and stuck his head through. "It's Inspector Matlock." He opened the door, which swung gently open. The inspector looked across the parquet floored hall to the kitchen, where Ada was sitting.

"Thank you, Dennis. Come in, Inspector, please." Matlock looked at the door as if trying to see Dennis and stepped in. The door clicked shut behind him.

He kept looking behind him as he walked towards her. There were four cups of tea on the table. He looked down at the one nearest Ada.

"I've finished with it," said Rose. "He can have it."

Ada indicated to the chair. "Please, help yourself. What can I do for you, Inspector?"

"Well, Ms Baker…"

"Ada, please."

"I was very much surprised when I checked my home security footage to find images of you in my house earlier today."

Ada's cheeks flushed hot. "I'm sorry, Inspector. Dennis wanted to visit Inspector Jolly to teach him how to move things with his mind. He invited us in."

"How exactly did you get in?"

"Dennis unlocked the door for us."

"That's a useful trick. I must remember to take the key to work with me in future. So, am I to expect Jolly to start moving things now? Also, why were you screaming outside my bathroom?"

Ada was silent.

"Ada? What's wrong?"

She drummed her fingernails on the table and screwed up her mouth. "I'm not sure if you want to know... but you have a second ghost living in your house called George. He lives in your bathroom. It used to be a prison cell. He died over a hundred years ago during World War One. He says he was murdered by the police because his mother was German and he was a conchie. He's very nice though. If you want him to go in the shower while you're having a pee, just ask him. I was understandably a bit surprised to find a man in your loo."

The inspector raised his eyebrows. "Two ghosts? This just gets better!" he said. "I would prefer in future, if you're visiting, Ada, that you wait till I'm there."

"Yes, sorry, I get so used to hanging with dead people I forget the social niceties sometimes. Ghosts go wherever they want, whenever they want."

"That's not the only reason I'm here. I put some officers on to watch Kent's house to see if they saw any suspicious behaviour. They tell me they saw a young woman walk down the alley by his house but thought nothing of it, till a few minutes later when she came running back the other way at breakneck speed. The description of the woman matches you. Even down to the tie-die jeans. It was you, wasn't it?" He paused for her to answer. Ada just stared at him.

"Otherwise, it seems rather coincidental, don't you think, that someone of your exact description was at his house? What were you doing there, Ada?"

She sighed. "I was so annoyed that he might get away with her murder, I just thought I'd see what his house looked like, see if there were any clues. I had Rose with me so I sent her in to look around first and he wasn't in, so I shimmied over to have a look through the back window. He had lots of photos and paintings of Mary on his living room wall, and lots of other women, all naked. Then he arrived home. I don't know where he came from but he was suddenly upon me asking questions. Then... then he tried to kiss me."

The inspector raised his eyebrows again. "Did he attack you?"

"Not exactly. He just backed me into a corner and tried to kiss me."

"So what did you do?" he said.

"I kneed him in the nuts and ran off."

"Well, it sounds like you had a lucky escape. Now perhaps you can see why I asked you to stay away from him. You're lucky he hasn't spoken to us about your trespassing. Please leave it to the police to investigate him further. I don't want to speak to you again." Ada nodded. "I must be off home now. Keep safe."

The door opened for him before he reached it and closed gently behind him.

"Perhaps he's right, Ada?" said Mrs Entwhistle.

"Maybe I was wrong. You mustn't put your life at risk for the sake of Rose having an adventure. Perhaps you'd be better off joining a 'knit and natter' group. Knitting certainly helps me," she said, fondly stroking her needles.

Ada had been frightened by her experience, but she'd started this now and she wanted to finish it.

Her dreams that night were haunted by images of William Kent trying to kiss her and succeeding. She was held captive by him and unable to escape.

***

She woke up the next morning in a sweat and went straight to the shower. It was a power shower and its strong flow blasted off the sweat from her and refreshed her soul. She felt revived by the time she went downstairs. Dennis had a cup of tea waiting for her and she gulped it down.

"I'm off to see Marcus Strang now at the gallery. I'm meeting Neville at ten. See you all later." She grabbed her coat and bag and left.

***

All three ghosts looked at each other. "Well, I guess we should be pleased for her, meeting up with a living friend," said Dennis sulkily.

"Hmm, bit boring though, isn't it? Anyone fancy a

trip out? Just because she isn't going with us doesn't mean we shouldn't go out on our own. Who's up for a walk?" said Rose.

Dennis and Mrs Entwhistle smiled and nodded at her. Mrs Entwhistle put her knitting needles in her bag. "As long as we don't get Ada into any more trouble," she said.

"We're dead. Kent couldn't see me when I was there. We'll be fine, Mrs E."

"If you're sure, dear." Mrs Entwhistle pulled her hat and pin out of her bag and secured it in place. Then she wrapped a fur stole around her neck. "Ready, dear, let's go." Dennis opened the door and they strolled out into the sunshine.

***

Neville was waiting outside the front of the gallery for her, leaning casually against a pillar. He smiled in recognition as she approached, flicking his hair out of his eyes.

"Ready?" he said.

"Sure, let's go in."

The Wilson Art Gallery was in a converted Baptist chapel. Its large windows let in a tremendous amount of light, and it was used for all sorts of exhibitions and events throughout the year. A poster hung at the entrance: 'Marcus Strang – Visionary Photographer – A masterpiece in black and white'.

They wandered in. Several people were milling around looking at the photos, and at the back of the room Marcus Strang was chatting to a customer.

Ada's heart thumped hard in her chest and her palms became sweaty. It was her Marcus Strang. She'd had the biggest crush on him at college. They'd got on very well. She had dreamed at the time that he might like her too, but he had been her teacher so she'd never dared to approach him.

They took the time to look round the exhibition. There were many photos that showed the stark realities of real life: homeless people, the destitute and the poor, and a range of local characters. In one room, however, they came across the portraits of Mary. They were beautiful images, very striking. He really seemed to have captured her spirit. The images played with the light and sculptural form of the body. Mary wasn't the only model featured but she was the dominant one.

"She's beautiful, isn't she?" came a voice from behind them. "She was one of my best muses."

They turned round to face Marcus Strang. He had on his trademark sunglasses. "Mary Watts, she sadly died a few weeks back. You might have seen it in the press. There will never be another muse like her," he said, sighing.

"Actually, it was her sister Ellen that recommended you to us. She thought that you might be able to help us with our enquiries. My name is Ada Baker. We're trying to find out more about her so we can help solve her murder," she said, handing him her business card, which he took without looking at it. "I saw the photos for the article you took for *Good Housekeeping* magazine. They were amazing."

"Thank you, yes, it's all down to good lighting and a good eye for a picture. That's just bread and butter money though really. The artistic photography is what I really love." He looked at her more closely. "I feel I know you though, Miss Baker... I know where! You were one of my students at the college when I was starting out. My goodness, how are you? Did you begin a career in art?"

"Actually, no. I still draw but I never made it into a career."

"What do you do for a living then? Model maybe?"

Ada felt her cheeks glow with the flattering comment. Even now he had her in a fluster. "No, I've made some good investments and I live off the money from them. Ellen said she'd been to see your exhibition a couple of times and it was really good, so we thought we'd come to see it."

"A couple of times, try sixteen times! She's my biggest fan. She follows me on Instagram and Twitter. I can't complain though, she's bought three of my prints."

"Yes, I think you made a real impression on her." She felt really uncomfortable about asking the next question. "Do you... um... mind me asking how well you knew her sister Mary? She was your model, but were you anything more to each other?"

"Very blunt and to the point. Yes, we were lovers for a while, Ada, but we weren't in love. It was a casual relationship that suited us both. A 'friends with benefits' sort of relationship. She did have the most beautiful face and body, unlike her sister."

"I heard that you were going to see her the day she died. Did you actually turn up?"

He put his hand on his face, lifted his glasses onto his head and rubbed his eyes. Ada wondered if he might be wiping away a tear. His eyes were mesmeric. They were so dark it was hard to see where the iris stopped and pupil began. They were like black inky pools that were so deep if you fell into them you'd never climb out. Ada had never met anyone else like him. She couldn't stop staring. They suited his milky pale complexion and dark lustrous hair. He was like a cross between a goth and a smouldering Mediterranean lothario.

Ada felt rather distracted from her task. She understood why Ellen thought so highly of him as she was reminded of her youthful passion. Neville noticed and carried on the questioning.

"We understand you knew where the key was hidden. Did you enter the house?"

Marcus seemed to grow defensive at this male interlude into his thoughts. "Are you accusing me of the murder?" he said curtly.

"No, just trying to establish who had the key."

"I didn't know there was a key. Mary always let me in," he said. "I came to the door at the time we were supposed to meet. There was no answer. Mary had bad asthma, so I was worried as she'd never missed an appointment, and I called the police. Too late it seems. I told all this to the police."

"Thank you, that's very helpful. I assume the roses in the living room were from you?" asked Ada.

"Yes, we were going to do a shoot in her bath. She had a lovely old-fashioned roll-top bath. We were going to sprinkle the rose petals on the water. I suppose she'd got it ready for the shoot, which is why she was found in the bath."

Marcus looked at her thoughtfully. "You have amazing bone structure, you know, Ada? I'm guessing you've mixed-race heritage? Some of the most beautiful people are." He gently reached forward and held her chin, turning her face this way then that. "If you'd like to work with me, I'd love to take some photos of you. We can catch up about old times."

"Oh, I'm not into life modelling like these women." Fear entered her eyes.

"It needn't be nude modelling. Call me if you fancy trying something different." He handed her his card.

He looked around into the main gallery and sighed. "Oh, she's here again, my number one fan." He let go of Ada's chin. Ada turned to look and there was Ellen Watts looking around the gallery, a bunch of flowers in her hand.

"Thank you, Mr Strang, for your help. Do you know anything about Gilbert Orange, by the way? We're off to see him next," said Ada.

"Call me Marcus, please, Ada. We're old friends after all. Gilbert Orange is mediocre at best," said Marcus. "No real success as an artist so he's ended up staying as an art teacher to support himself. Mary seemed to like him though."

"Were they close do you know?" asked Ada.

"No idea. We weren't there at the same time. You'd need to ask him. Good day, Ada. It was a pleasure to meet you again after so many years." He took her hand and kissed it while looking intensely in her eyes. Then he put his sunglasses back on and walked off towards another customer.

Chapter 10

As they walked out the door, Neville turned to her and said, "It was obvious he was hiding something. You said that Mary said he knew of the whereabouts of the key."

"Yes, that's true."

"And he seemed very defensive to prove that he wasn't the murderer. It doesn't quite fit, does it? I don't like him," he said, giving Ada a sideways glance.

"You might be right, but you were a bit aggressive in there towards him. I think you offended him. Perhaps he was right about the key and Mary was wrong."

"You're just swayed by his good looks. You never told me you knew him."

"Hmmm, maybe a little." She smiled. "I wasn't sure it was him until now. He was my teacher at art college. Come on, Neville, let's go to see Gilbert Orange next."

They made their way across to the other side of town. It was lunchtime as they arrived and students were strolling out into the town, hanging out in small cliques, munching on bags of fat chips.

They strolled into reception and waited patiently at

the desk for their turn. A friendly-faced woman greeted them.

"We'd like to speak with Gilbert Orange, please?" said Ada.

"Well, it's lunchtime and he's finished for the day, so you'll probably find him down the Artichoke pub on Bleak Street having a few swift pints with the locals."

"I've not met him before. Do you have a photo to help me recognise him? I'm a private detective of sorts and I want him to help in my investigation." The woman pointed towards a photo board of teachers on the opposite wall. "You can't miss him – he'll be the loudest, most vibrant person in the pub." They nodded thanks and wandered over to look at the board, and having asked her for directions, they headed off for the Artichoke.

They found Gilbert at the bar with a few wizened men. He was hard to miss. His colourful character stood out a mile from the insipid dullness of the people around him. He was a tall and muscular black man with sleek, well-kept micro dreadlocks tied back from his handsome face. He wore a long, grey wool trench coat, but underneath his clothes were bright and vibrant colours of yellow and orange batik material. He laughed heartily at the men's jokes and had the presence of a Shakespearean actor, even down to the confident way he stood. His voice and big presence boomed across the pub.

Ada wandered up to him. "Mr Gilbert?" she said

nervously.

He turned and gave her a smile as warm as sunshine. "Yes, Miss…"

"Baker, Ada Baker."

"Miss Baker, how may I help such a lovely young lady on this glorious day?" He seemed to speak every word with joy and laughter. There was a richness and depth to his tone that was captivating. Ada yearned to hear him recite some sonnets to her.

"We were wondering if you could help us to learn some more about Mary Watts? The police haven't managed to find out who murdered her yet and… well… I have special skills. I thought I might be able to help. Her sister Ellen said you were a friend of hers. You painted her portrait."

"Yes, that's right, quite a number of portraits. She had the most magnificent bone structure and figure."

"You gave one of them to her, didn't you?" said Ada.

"Yes, it was her favourite, so I gave it to her as a gift for her birthday."

"What did you do with the other portraits?" said Neville.

"I sold a few, the rest I have in my studio at home, if you'd like to see them."

"Is that where you painted her?" Ada enquired.

"Mostly, although sometimes I did paint her at her home. I never liked painting her there though."

"Why not?" asked Ada.

"I never felt comfortable in that house. It had a very

unwelcome feeling to it. Maybe it was the poor light."

"Did you ever meet her sister Ellen?" Ada said.

"Yes, a few times, but it was always strange. Ellen would come over and clean the house, but Mary was the one living there. Perhaps that is what made me feel so uncomfortable. My own family is so full of life and joy. The house seemed empty of that. They both seemed happy enough on their own but not together. I don't think Ellen was happy for me to be there. She seemed to be Miss Prim and Proper to me."

"What happened to Mary's mum?" queried Neville.

"I don't know. It was before I knew her. They never talked about it much. I had a feeling there was something shameful there. They never knew who Mary's father was, I think. Ellen's father, John, married Mary's mother after Mary was born, but I don't think they shared the same father."

"If you don't mind me asking, what was your relationship with Mary?" said Ada softly. "Was there anything beyond your artistic partnership?"

"We were lovers for a while, if that's what you mean. She was a beautiful woman, but it was no more than that. Mary had many lovers in her life, I think. She was a free spirit," he said, gesticulating grandly with his hand as if making the impression of a bird flying off into the air. "I expect her spirit is wandering freely now, exploring this great wide world of ours."

As if reading her thoughts, Gilbert started quoting Shakespeare. "I have heard, but not believ'd, the spirits of the dead may walk again."

"*The Winter's Tale?*" asked Neville. "We read it at school."

"Yes!" said Gilbert, smiling. "Before I was an artist, I wanted to become an actor."

"I can see that," said Ada. "Something about the way you talk and carry yourself."

Gilbert seemed very pleased with this comment.

"What about William Kent? What did you know of him?" she asked.

"Oh, he was a bit of an odd fellow, but harmless I'd have thought. He made Mary feel uncomfortable though, so I removed him from the art lessons and ordered her a taxi home a few times after class."

"How long was he in the class for?" she asked.

"A couple of months maybe."

"Was he any good at painting?" Neville asked.

"Yes, actually, I think he'd had some former training. He seemed a little too fixated though on parts of Mary's body, and he focussed on them with intensity."

"Do you still have the paintings?" asked Ada.

"No, but I took photos of them, as I do of all my students' work, so I can use them in advertising and to keep a record of their progress." He pulled out his phone and started flicking through images. "You can see he started off painting full portraits, as most people choose to do."

Ada could see he was right – they were good. One of them she recognised as being one of the paintings she'd seen in his home. Gilbert kept flicking through the paintings. They seemed to become focussed on particular parts of her body and the colours more intense. The colours grew more intense and angrier as the weeks went on, as if matching the intensity of his obsession. Ada shivered. She could see why Mary was so freaked out by him. Perhaps it had all culminated in a final violent act. She felt herself lucky to have escaped him.

Gilbert looked at her as the golden afternoon sun highlighted her face. "I'm sure you've been told that you have great bone structure before," he said. "I'd really love to paint you. Would you consider posing for me or my students?"

"Funnily enough, you're the second person today to tell me that!" she replied.

"Oh really? Who else?"

"Marcus Strang. I just went to see his exhibition."

Gilbert sucked his teeth. "Well model for me before you model for him. He's very mediocre." Ada smiled but thought it wise not to tell Gilbert that Marcus had said the same thing about him.

"Thank you for your help, Gilbert. May I contact you again if I need to?" said Ada.

"Certainly, here's my card. Call me any time you like, especially if you want to model." He gave her a titanium-white smile. "Please!" he said, holding open his arms, and he proceeded to grab both of them and give them a bear hug.

Ada wasn't quite sure how to respond to such an open, friendly sort of gesture from someone she barely knew, but she went away feeling positively charged from their conversation, unlike the one with William Kent. She could see why Mary liked him.

As they stepped out of the pub, Neville and Ada looked at each other and laughed, then wandered off to the café next door to grab some lunch.

***

In his car opposite the Artichoke, William Kent licked a finger and turned the page of his notebook and wrote:

1.28 p.m. – Ada left the Artichoke with her young male friend, having spoken with Gilbert Orange. They went to have lunch in the Bluebell café. Ada ordered a cappuccino and a Caesar salad. Who is the young man?

His pencil tip snapped as he wrote the last sentence because he was pressing so hard on the page. Then he threw the pencil out the car window and drew out a brand new, completely sharpened one from his pocket. He underlined the last sentence three times.

He looked back through the pages. They contained an entry for everything that Ada had done that day outside her house, starting with what clothes she was wearing.

He took a pay-as-you-go mobile phone from his pocket, zoomed in and took a photo of them sitting in the café window. Then he took another of Ada and saved it to her contact number stored in his phone. He pressed the call button and across the street Ada answered her phone.

"Hello?" Ada said. Kent remained silent. "Hello, who's there? Hello?"

"Who is it?" he could hear Neville say in the background.

"Don't know, just a prank call or an automated call I guess." She put the phone down then rang the number back. His phone started ringing. William Kent didn't answer.

Chapter 11

"So where are we going then?" asked Dennis once the ghosts were out the door.

"I agree with Ada, I think William Kent is hiding something. I think we should investigate him further. He didn't seem to be able to see or hear me when I was there the other day. If we go and search his house for clues, it'll keep Ada safe, Kent will be none the wiser and we might find some information linking him to the murder," said Rose.

Mrs Entwhistle, ever the voice of caution and reason, said, "What do we do with any evidence we find?"

"Well let's wait and see if we find any first," said Rose. "Come on, Mrs E, if we can find something to convict him, it'll make the town a safer place for Ada and other women."

Mrs Entwhistle nodded and they followed Rose to William Kent's home. Dennis went in first to check that the coast was clear. There was nobody home, so they started searching the downstairs rooms first.

"I'll check through the drawers as I can move things.

You use your eyes to look round. Call me if you need me to open anything," said Dennis.

"We must be careful to put it back as we found it though, so he suspects nothing," said Rose.

Mrs Entwhistle looked up at the naked portraits everywhere, many of Mary, some of unknown women. She shuddered. She was born in the nineteenth century, an age where women were very well covered from head to toe. Going outside without your hat would have been considered uncouth. Of course, there had always been artists' nude models, but she felt being displayed on a living room wall like this was very lewd. A nice long dress, sensible shoes and a warm coat, that was more Mrs Entwhistle's style. Women exposed far too much of themselves these days, even nice, sensible Ada, with skin-tight trousers and dresses that looked more like undergarments than clothing. Having worked in stately homes since she was a child, she had attained very good manners. She couldn't bring herself to look around the living room so moved off to what she hoped was a safer bet in the kitchen.

Rose, however, had been born in the early twentieth century, and she found the concept of posing as a life model fascinating. Her existence had been rather humdrum. Raised in a poor family, she'd helped to raise her brothers and sisters and then cleaned for a living. She'd not had children of her own but had helped her parents in their old age. Her whole life had been spent skivvying and cleaning up after other people, until her final ignoble death. Now she craved the excitement and adventure she'd never known in life. She looked with wonder at the portraits and the art books. Even horrid, lecherous William Kent had led a more exciting life than she had.

Dennis and Rose pored over the shelves and through the drawers. They could find nothing beyond what they already knew, so eventually they all made their way upstairs.

They started with the spare bedroom. When they opened the door, it was a shock. The walls were lined with photos and paintings of different women. An entire wall was devoted to Mary. Hundreds of photos were pasted onto it, as well as a copy of Mary's advert, and various things like ticket stubs and even cigarette butts. They were almost like mini shrines to the women. Mary's wall was now encroaching on the previous women's walls.

"Bingo!" said Dennis.

"But we can't take this as evidence to the police and we don't have a camera. We need something else," said Rose. There wasn't much else in the room to help so they moved to the main bedroom.

If they found the spare room shocking, the main bedroom was worse. The walls were painted red and explicit paintings of Mary filled every wall.

"Oh my goodness, Dennis! Can you just search the drawers so we can get out of here, please!" said Mrs Entwhistle, looking pale. Dennis pulled out a drawer and lifted up something pink and plastic.

"What's this?" he said, teasing it out of the drawer. It immediately started to inflate. Rose screamed. Very soon, a pair of pink plastic breasts and a wide-mouthed doll was staring up at them.

"What's that?" asked Mrs Entwhistle.

Dennis, who was a bit more worldly-wise and had died more recently, said, "I think it's a sex doll. Gentlemen use it to obtain sexual pleasure when they don't have a real woman."

Mrs Entwhistle sat down on the bed in shock. Dennis, who enjoyed a bit of teasing, said, "I wouldn't sit there, Mrs E, considering we just found blow-up Bertha in his drawer. Where do you think he uses it!"

"Oh! Filthy beast," she said, standing up quickly. "If you want me, I'll be in the garden!" She walked off, trying to retain as much dignity as possible.

Dennis deflated the doll and put her away, then carried on looking through the drawers. In the bedside drawer he found some notebooks. The top book was labelled 'Mary Watts'. Dennis picked it up and flicked through the pages with Rose staring over his shoulder. A detailed inventory of Mary's daily life was laid out, as well as some of Kent's own thoughts about her. Clearly, he believed that she was as enamoured of him as he was of her. There was nothing for the day of Mary's murder.

"This is it. This is the evidence we need," he said.

"Maybe, but it doesn't say he killed her," said Rose.

"I think it's probably good enough. I'm taking it."

"What if he notices?" she said.

"He's not following her any more. He probably won't notice till he gets a new victim. Come on, let's find Mrs E and get out of here."

He carried the book downstairs and opened the patio door. "Mrs E, we have need of your marvellous bag. We've got it!" he said, slipping it into her bottomless bag and locking the door behind him.

"Time to head home," Dennis said, and all three ghosts left the garden.

Chapter 12

"What's the next plan of action then?" asked Neville, as he wolfed down his sticky toffee pudding.

Ada had decided to choose the healthy option – too much of Mrs Entwhistle's good cooking was starting to show. Her fruit salad looked far less exciting than the oozy stickiness of Neville's dessert.

"Go and talk to Mary again, I suppose. We've talked to everyone she mentioned. William Kent still seems like the most likely candidate, but what else can I do? I've told the police and I tried to investigate on my own – that went spectacularly wrong."

"I still think Marcus is hiding something. Let's see if she can tell us more about him."

"Okay, agreed. Let's head off there now before I'm tempted to buy a pudding!"

Ada paid for the meal and left a big tip, then they headed back to Mary's house on Cherry Tree Lane.

Ada opened the gate of number thirty-one and called through the letterbox.

"Mary, love, it's Ada. I've come back for a chat and

I've brought a friend. I hope you don't mind." Neville followed Ada round to the back garden and they took a seat at the table.

"What now?" he said.

"We wait and hope she comes down to talk to us."

They didn't have to wait long. Ada saw her approaching the French doors and suddenly they opened. Neville sat up straight in his seat and stared.

"My goodness, you are a fast learner!" said Ada. "You don't need to open doors though, you can walk through them you know?"

"I know but I thought you might fancy a cup of coffee. It looks like it's about to rain too."

Neville looked agog towards the voice.

"That'd be lovely, Mary. This is my new friend Neville. He can hear you but not see you. That's right, isn't it, Neville?" She looked at him for confirmation. He nodded but said nothing.

"He looks like he could do with something stiffer. Has he not met many ghosts?"

"Oh, I think he hears plenty, but seeing poltergeist activity is something else."

"The kitchen's through here. I'll let you make it. Top cupboard. No fresh milk, I'm afraid, but plenty of dried. I hope that's okay. I wasn't much of one for the kitchen. I usually ate out."

Ada poured them two drinks and they followed Mary into the sitting room. There, hanging in pride of place, was the nude portrait by Gilbert that Ellen had

111

described. Its nipples did indeed seem to stick out from the portrait.

"We went to see Gilbert earlier. He seems lovely. Very exuberant."

"Yes, he is, isn't he." She smiled tenderly. "It's a masterpiece, isn't it?" she said, proudly staring up at the portrait he'd painted of her.

Ada nodded to be polite. "We also went to see Marcus Strang's exhibition."

"Oh yes, I do love Marcus too. It's a shame I didn't live to see the exhibition."

"We saw the portraits of you. They're very good. He'd even put a plaque up and dedicated them to your memory."

"That's lovely. I guess they're worth more now I'm dead… limited edition," she joked. "A bit like when an artist dies."

"Yes… I guess so," said Ada. "I'd not thought about that."

"He did imply that he didn't know about the hidden key. Are you certain that he knew of it?"

"Definitely, he let himself in with it on a number of occasions."

"He said he knocked but there was no answer so he called the police."

"I can't recall everything at that time very well. I was a bit confused when I first 'woke up' to my new life. The police were already here by the time I came to and realised what had happened. I tried to talk to them but nobody would speak to me, then I saw my body and went and hid in the pantry till they'd all gone."

"Why do you think he might have lied?"

"I can't think. Fear, I guess?"

"You don't think Marcus could have been jealous of Gilbert... or the other way around?"

"No, my relationship with both of them was very casual. I don't see why they would. Maybe they were jealous professionally, but certainly nothing to do with me. Anyway, why would they kill me and not each other if that were the case?"

Ada thought carefully about how to phrase the next sentence. She stared up at the portrait. "Having seen your sister's house, I can't imagine she liked this picture very much. She didn't seem to have much in common with you."

"No, chalk and cheese, salt and pepper, that's us. She doesn't appreciate art."

"I've seen her place. It's certainly very different to yours. If you don't mind me asking, why is it that you inherited your parents' house and Ellen lives somewhere else?"

"Oh, well, Ellen is my stepsister. We had different parents. Ellen is older than me. Her mum died before I was born. Her dad was single and met my mother, who already owned this house. My mum had me after a one-night fling with somebody. Ellen's dad John died first when I was ten and my mother raised us both. She wasn't a 'mumsy' mum but she put a roof over our heads. She's where I get my love of art from. She used to model too. When Mum died, her will left the house to me. I offered for Ellen to come and live here too, but I don't think she could bear to live with her radical sister. We still saw each other but we've never been close. She tidies for me; she's a big help. She'll inherit the house now."

"I see. Mary, do you mind if I use your bathroom, please, if that's not disrespectful? I already had three cups of coffee at the tea room and I forgot to go there."

"Sure. Upstairs, first door on the left."

Ada went to find the toilet and left Neville feeling rather awkward with a poltergeist he couldn't see. "Lovely portrait," she could hear him say nervously.

She had, in fact, already peed at the restaurant, but she'd wanted an excuse to check out the bathroom. She found her way there and pushed open the door. Light flooded into the room and she caught her breath. It was a beautiful bathroom. A chequerboard of black and white tiles covered the floor, and a single roll-top bath stood in the middle of the room. Delicate chiffon curtains framed the windows and billowed gently in a light breeze that blew through a pair of doors that opened out onto a tiny balconet. There was no trace of anything left in the bath, of course, but fluffy white towels hung on the radiator to dry and a line of beautiful glass jars full of powders and exotic-looking ointments sat on a shelf. There were candles and Phalaenopsis orchids everywhere. Mary was obviously into having beautiful bath times. Another of her passions maybe. Ada could see why Marcus would want to use this room to take a photograph. It was like something out of *Ideal Home* magazine.

Among Ada's many talents, she had the ability to see events that had happened in the past by touching emotive objects that had been associated with a traumatic experience. This gift was called retrocognition. She preferred to buy new things for her home for this reason, as occasionally when touching antiques, she would get a vision of some past murder or suicide. She particularly hated objects connected to war. The object that spoke to her most in the room was, of course, the bathtub. She walked slowly up to it, knelt down and placed her hands on the edge. She felt a shudder go through her, her skin turned to goosebumps and like a movie suddenly being projected before her eyes, she could see Mary sitting in the bathtub, her back to Ada. She was luxuriating in the warm water, singing to herself. A dark shadow cut across the room and a pair of hands in brown leather gloves shot forward with the red scarf. The scarf was tied quickly around Mary's neck and pulled very tight. Mary struggled to try and loosen the scarf, her face quickly changing colour as the air was choked from her. Very soon, her body lay lifeless in the bath and the killer backed out of Mary's view. Ada sat down on the floor. Seeing someone else's death was always difficult; she avoided doing it if she could. It wasn't like watching a film, as she was always aware that it was a real murder playing out in front of her. She started humming the tune to herself. Up above her in the attic, she heard a noise. She jumped up and stepped back, falling over a stool. She picked herself up then rushed out into the hall. She hurried back downstairs to be with the others.

"Are you all right?" said Neville. "You look like you've seen a ghost? Oh... you know what I mean, sorry, Mary. What was that great bang?"

Ada paused. "I tripped up."

"Send me a postcard next time," said Neville, snorting and laughing at the most unoriginal joke ever.

"Mary... are you... the only ghost here?" Ada asked.

"Yes, of course. I'd have seen someone else if they were here."

"Okay," said Ada. "I think you might have mice in your attic. I heard a noise up there. Well, thank you for the coffee and chat. I think we'd better be off now."

Mary showed them out past the shelves of art books. "Thank you, Ada, for trying to help me," she said, smiling.

"No problem," Ada replied.

***

William Kent returned home to get some food and pick up one of his cameras. As soon as he walked in the door, he knew something was different. His precise, ordered mind could see that things were just slightly out of place. Immediately he went upstairs. He went straight to his bedroom and to his bedside cabinet drawer. He pulled it open and sat down on the bed staring into it. It was gone. His precious notebook about Mary. He treasured it. Who could have done this? Ada? But he'd just left her. A thought rolled around in his head for a while like a roulette ball on its wheel and slowly dropped into place. He picked up his laptop and started to type.

Chapter 13

When Ada got home, the ghosts weren't there. This was a peculiar thing to happen as the ghosts were always there or with Ada. The house seemed very empty without them. She made herself a sandwich, poured herself a glass of red wine and settled down in front of the telly to watch her favourite gardening programme. It wasn't too long before they returned, loudly bustling through the door.

"Ada! Are you home? We've got some news for you!" shouted Rose very loudly. "You'll never guess where we've been?" She didn't wait for Ada to guess. "We've been to William Kent's house again."

Ada looked shocked. "You mustn't, it's dangerous!"

"Oh poo! We're dead, he can't see us. If he could see me, he'd have said something last time, I'm sure. Not that many people have the gift, you know. You're lucky to have found Neville. Anyway, we all had a look around the house and Dennis found a drawer full of notebooks. There was a notebook for Mary. Look!" said Rose. Dennis thumped a small notebook on the coffee table in front of Ada. She picked it up and started reading.

Mary Watts

5.20 p.m. – Mary leaves her house. She has my favourite white dress on today that clings to her curves. She walks to the art class, stopping at the newsagent on Main Street on her way to buy a packet of cigarettes.

5.50 p.m. – She arrives at the art college. I am throbbing with excitement.

6.00 p.m. – Lesson starts. She disrobes and poses facing me. She looks at me throughout the whole two-hour lesson. At the end of the lesson, she comes to view my painting and says she is disgusted with it, but I know that really she loves it. Why else would she stare at me? She knows it's a work of art. She asks Gilbert to remove me from the lessons. The depth of her feeling must be getting too much.

8.10 p.m. – She dresses hurriedly and leaves. I follow her home across town. I don't hide myself from her as usual but follow her boldly. She hurries home and slams the door as she arrives.

9.00 p.m. – I hang my new painting in my bedroom and stare at it for hours.

Ada could feel the blood draining from her face. "But this is horrific. He was keeping a diary of her movements."

"You can take this as evidence to the police," said Dennis.

"I can't, Den, they'd want to know how I obtained it.

119

We might have persuaded Inspector Matlock of the existence of ghosts, but we won't convince the whole judicial system. I could get into trouble for this. You should know different, Den. Things weren't that different when you were alive. What are we going to do with it now? You can't put it back. If he's noticed it's gone, he might be waiting for someone to come back."

"We could post it to the inspector at his work?" said Mrs Entwhistle.

"I guess so… We'd need to wipe it clean first."

"I could nip out and post it for you?" said Dennis.

"I guess so. Come to think of it, how did you get it here anyway?"

"Mrs Entwhistle's bag."

"Really?" said Ada. Mrs Entwhistle's bag seemed to have properties beyond any other and had a capacity to hold more than its size suggested. Even tangible things it seemed. "Well, I guess we have no choice. It's too risky taking it back."

"How did you get on today?" asked Rose.

"It was good. Marcus and Gilbert were both interesting characters." She gave them a review of her day. "It turns out that I know Marcus as well. He was my teacher at art college. We used to get on well, I really liked him."

"That's lovely, dear," said Mrs Entwhistle. "Nice for you to bump into an old teacher."

Later that evening, all four of them were settling in to watch their favourite drama, an episode of *Poirot*, when Ada received a text.

"Who is it?" said Rose, not bothering to turn away from the TV screen. Rose secretly had a desire to be a famous detective like Poirot and watched every show she could find.

"It's Marcus Strang. I didn't give him my number. Ellen must have given it to him."

"What does he want?" said Dennis.

"He says he's been thinking about me all day. A friend of his has a perfect spot to take some black and white photographs for his next portfolio. It's an old RAF airfield, though it's not used by the RAF any more. A company has taken it over for use as a backdrop for films and stuff. Marcus's friend owns it and says we can shoot some photos there. What do you think? It might be a good way to get to find out more about him? I might be able to tease out of him whether or not he did let himself into the house."

"Ooh, can I come with you? I could help you think of some questions to ask him. I'd love to see somewhere different," said Rose.

"Okay, Rose, but he wants an early start tomorrow – six o'clock out the back of the gallery. The airfield is an hour's drive away and it might take most of the day. He suggests bringing food and warm clothes as it can get quite windy and cold there and there's nowhere to eat on-site. Six o'clock sounds horrendous, but I think it'll be worth it."

"Okay, but just don't let him make you do anything

you don't want to," said Mrs Entwhistle, sounding concerned.

"I won't." Ada sent the reply back: 'Yes sure, see you then.' She went off to bed early to make sure she was alert for the next morning but lay awake for a while daydreaming of Marcus sweeping her up in his arms and kissing her. Clearly, she hadn't got over her youthful obsession even now.

***

It was still dark when Dennis came in to wake her. He was more gentle than the other day when he'd dragged the cover off of her.

"There's a mug of tea waiting downstairs for you, Ada. Come on, sleepy. You don't want to miss the photo shoot. Rose is already waiting downstairs."

Ada dragged herself out of bed, brushed her hair, dressed, put on a warm jumper and headed downstairs. "My goodness, Marcus doesn't know what a sleepyhead he's asked to come along with him!" said Rose. "Drink up and let's get going."

"Hold on, you need to wipe the notebook and address the padded envelope to the police station," said Dennis. "I'll get it posted this morning."

Ada gulped her tea down, ate a quick bowl of cereal, did as Dennis asked, then put on her woolly coat. It was a cold morning. Then she grabbed the food bag as suggested by Marcus.

"See you later," said Ada, as she and Rose went out the door. The sharp morning air stung her lungs and made her nose cold as she breathed it in. Rose chattered excitedly all the way to the gallery. It was quiet at this time of day on such a chilly morning. The only person she passed was someone going to the newsagent for their morning paper.

There was a small private road that ran down the side of the gallery to where the bins were kept and a small car park for staff use. She could see a car there but no sign of Marcus sitting in it. She walked up to it and noticed that it was older than she expected a photographer's car to be. Maybe it was an artistic thing. The back windows were tinted. She walked round the back of it. 'Hmmm, a Ford Anglia,' she thought. She heard Rose scream and then there was darkness.

***

When Ada regained consciousness, her head felt like a thousand drums were being beaten inside it. It was dark where she was and musty smelling. She let out a small groan.

"Ada! Are you all right? Oh, thank goodness, I thought you might have died! I was so frightened."

She recognised the voice. "Where am I, Rose? Why does my head hurt so much?"

"It was Kent, he was waiting behind the art gallery for you. He hit you over the head when you were looking in his car. Then he bound you and bundled you in his car and drove us here."

"Where is here, Rose? Why's it so dark?"

"I think it's an airfield. I guess it wasn't Marcus Strang who texted you. How could he do that, Ada? Didn't the text come from Marcus?"

"Yes, well I thought so. It was signed Marcus Strang. I don't understand, how could it not be from him? Do they know each other? How could Kent find me? Why would he know my number? Where exactly am I right now, Rose?"

"I think it's an RAF Nissen hut. It looks old. This site is huge, Ada. It must be hundreds of acres."

"Where is Kent now?"

"I don't know. He's been gone about an hour. You've been out cold for a couple of hours or so."

Ada tried to move. "Rose, how has he bound my legs? They feel really uncomfortable."

"With large industrial cable ties. He did them up really tight. Oh, Ada! Poor you, what shall I do? Shall I go for help? Should I stay with you?"

Ada's head hurt to think, but the most logical idea that came into her brain was that Rose should go for help. "Go for help, tell Dennis. He can let the inspector know."

"But what if he comes back? You'll be all alone."

"Technically, I am alone, Rose, but if you find help, I might not be."

"Oh, I wish you'd brought Dennis with you. He could

have helped you to escape. I'm so useless. What's the point of watching all these detective shows if I'm useless when it comes to the real thing!"

"You're not useless, Rose, this is your chance to help me out of a tricky situation. The sooner you go, the sooner I'll be rescued."

"Okay, goodbye, Ada. Be strong." She felt a coldness on her forehead and she knew that Rose had kissed her.

Then there was silence. The hut was cold and dark, but she did seem to be lying on a metal-framed bed. She could hear it squeaking under her. She felt her hands and legs. They were very tightly bound and the ties were cutting into her. There was nothing for her to do but wait.

***

Outside, Rose headed off across the tarmac. The sun was up now, the site was huge and it was going to take hours for her to get home. She started heading out along the path till she passed some aircraft hangars and eventually she saw the control tower. It looked very haunting in the early morning light. Then, up in the tower, she thought maybe… Yes, a person, but who was it? She was terrified it might be Kent. She puffed her chest out in defiance. This was for Ada. If it was someone who could help, she must try and speak to them. She didn't have Dennis's skills but she could try. She ascended the concrete staircase up to the tower, her ghostly feet clacking on the steps. She could see him clearer now. Her heart seemed to thump. Thank God it wasn't Kent, but who was it? He had his back to her. She took the plunge and walked straight through the glass door.

"Excuse me, sir, can you hear me?" she asked. Immediately he spun around. Rose gasped. A dashing man of about thirty years of age in a blue RAF uniform stood in front of her. He was clean-shaven with dark hair, sparkling blue eyes and a warm, pleasant smile. His uniform was neat as a pin, without a crease in it. He wore a peaked cap.

"Good morning, how can I help you, miss?" Rose realised straight away she was talking to another ghost. It wasn't the help she needed but it was better than nobody.

"Please, you must help me. My name is Rose. My friend Ada, she's been taken captive by a man called William Kent. He's keeping her in one of the old RAF Nissen huts nearby. He's a wicked man and I'm not sure what he'll do to her. She's alive at the moment but I don't know what he's planning. He may already have killed another woman. I need to go get human help but she's all alone in the dark. Please find her so she's not alone. She's my best friend." Rose broke into a sob.

"My goodness! Certainly, Rose. Don't worry. I'm Flight Lieutenant Drake. I'll go find her. We'll work something out. I think I might know who this William Kent is that you mention. I'm sure I've seen him around the place. I agree, he seems a jolly nasty piece of work. You go find help and I'll go and find Ada. Don't worry, Rose, it'll be all right." He patted her on the shoulder and gave her a wink to reassure her. "Let's head off now."

Rose directed him to exactly where Ada was tied up and headed off at speed following his directions to the way out and onto a main road. She looked at the A road that stretched ahead of her and sighed. This was going to take some time.

***

Ada was starting to become really uncomfortable. She struggled to strain at the cable ties but Kent had done them up really tight. She was in a pickle now and it was all her own doing. If only Dennis was here, he might be able to help her break the straps. She started to cry softly to herself. Then the hut glowed with a gentle blue light that got brighter and brighter. Ghostly objects appeared around her: more beds appeared, all in apple-pie order, fire extinguishers, lockers and finally a round wooden clock mounted on the wall, which seemed to be gently ticking. A leg appeared through the wall of the Nissen hut, until finally in front of her stood the ghost of a man in an RAF uniform.

"Ah, here you are! Rose said you'd got yourself into a bit of pickle. Ada, isn't it? I'm Flight Lieutenant Drake but everyone calls me Ducky. I'm here to keep you company and find out what we can do to help you. Rose has headed off to get human help. I say, it's a bit dark in here, isn't it? Didn't the cad even leave a light on for you? What a beast."

He came nearer, and in the phosphorescence that seemed to glow off him, she could see her surroundings a little better. It was unusual for a ghost to glow so brightly; they were normally either solid-looking like a live human or semi-transparent. He appeared almost angelic. Ada was comforted by his presence.

"Yes, thank you. It's so good to see you. Do you think you could help me loosen these bonds?"

"So you can hear me? I thought you must be able to as Rose said you were her best friend. It'd be hard to be friends if you couldn't." He looked at the plastic cutting into her flesh. "I say, these are rather devilish things, aren't they? I don't think I can, you know. Poltergeisting is not really my thing. I might be able to manage a light switch if I really try."

"Thank you but no, best not to, I guess, or Kent will wonder how it's turned on when he comes back. What are you doing here?"

"Oh, I was based here during the war. My plane crashed with some other planes in a mid-air collision while on a training exercise. It was all my fault. I've been here ever since."

"It must get rather lonely here?" she asked.

"Oh, not really, not these days. Anyway, enough about me. I've seen this Kent fellow around the grounds.

I think he's some sort of security or caretaker."

"Oh no, that makes it more difficult. I was hoping there might be some security doing the rounds who would find me."

"Sadly no, I think he's the main security for this part of the site, apart from the security cameras, but if he's meant to be here, nobody is going to question him and he'll probably be the one watching them. Do you know if he can see ghosts?"

"I don't think so. He didn't seem to notice Rose and she's been near him twice."

"Well, that's something at least. I'm going to have to put my head together with the boys and see what we can work out. Do you have any ideas?"

"Well, there is one thing…" She hesitated as she said it but Ada had a good feeling about Drake. He seemed to ooze calm reassurance. "I'm a gifted psychic. I can hear and see you but I can also let you in to take control of my body and see things through my eyes. Perhaps you could break my bonds for me that way with your extra strength."

"Goodness, never tried to possess a living person. I didn't even know it was possible. How do I do it?"

"I relax and let you slip in. You just slip into my body as if it were your own, like putting on a suit of clothes. I know I'm not in the best position, but do you want to try it now?"

"I'll give it a go, dear lady, with your permission. If that's what you want."

Ada relaxed her mind as best she could in this strange situation. She felt Drake slip into her mind.

"I can feel… pain. Ow! He's done those restraints really tightly. I can feel your breathing. This is amazing." Ada could hear him as he moved her lips. It didn't sound particularly like either of them but somewhere between the two.

"Try breaking the bonds," she said from the back of her mind. She could feel him straining on the ties. She cried with pain in her mind. Drake stopped.

"I'm hurting you, I'm sorry."

"No, carry on, please."

Drake tried again but it was no use. Even with his extra spirit energy the bonds were fiendishly strong. He leapt out of her body.

"It's no use." She could see him pacing up and down the room thinking.

"Don't worry. You tried. I'm sure Rose will come with help before too long."

He turned to look at her. "I'm going to put my head together with the lads and see what we can work out. Will you be all right on your own?"

"Sure, I'll be fine," she said, lying through her teeth. She was absolutely terrified. Drake left through the side of the building again. He obviously didn't have Rose's inhibition of walking through solid objects. In the darkness and on her own again, she didn't know what to do. She was cold, hungry and tired from her earlier concussion. She felt herself slipping back into unconsciousness.

***

Ada was awakened by the sound of the door opening. Light streamed in. It took half a minute for her eyes to adjust but there, standing silhouetted against the light, was the figure of William Kent. He walked over and flicked on the light then shut the door behind him. He had a holdall with him from which he withdrew a chain. He walked over towards Ada and she recoiled on the bed as far as she could. She couldn't help but let out a little scream.

"Don't worry, Ada," he said, picking up a lock of her hair and twisting it round his fingers. Then he gently brushed her head with his hand as if soothing a child. "I'm just going to make you more comfortable." He swung her round into a sitting-up position, attached one end of the chain to the bedstead and the other to her legs, until both legs were manacled. He put a galvanised bucket near the bed and then cut off her leg and arm restraints. She rubbed her arms where the ties had dug in.

"I'm sorry about that. It was necessary to get you here safely. I couldn't risk you kneeing me again and running off."

She tried to rub her ankles but the rough metal chain made it difficult. She put her hand up to the back of her head and could feel a lump rising. Dried blood crumbled off in her hand. "Sorry, that was necessary too. You'll come to understand eventually once we've spent some time together. We're meant to be together. I like art. You obviously like art. I felt in the garden that we were kindred spirits. You must have sensed it? It was fate us meeting like that again after so many years."

She shook her head but remained silent. "Come on, Ada, we're going to be spending a lot of time together." He reached into his bag and brought out some of the food that Ada had taken with her and placed it on the bed in front of her. She was famished and dived forward, opening a packet of crisps and a can of orangeade.

"That's better, isn't it?"

She looked him up and down as she scoffed her crisps. "How did you know who I was?" she enquired.

He fished in his pocket and pulled out her business card. "I knew you wanted us to be together when you dropped this in my garden. I knew it was fate."

Ada groaned and cursed herself for leading him to her. She thought again, then asked, "Is Marcus in on this with you?"

"No, I sent you a message from my phone," he said, waving it in the air. "He knows nothing about this. I guessed you hadn't swapped numbers yet. Quite ingenious, I thought, and you fell for it." He looked very smug. "Women, so easily led by the promise of a handsome face. Mary fell for him too, foolish woman."

Ada suddenly felt brave. "You killed Mary, didn't you?"

He smiled and looked bemusedly at her. "Never mind Mary, she's old news. It's you we're concerned about now." He drew out a notebook from his holdall and started sketching Ada as she sat on the bed. Kent frowned as he framed the scene with his hands. He came forward and took her hair out of its tie till it hung all around her. "That's better," he said. "More like how I remember you in the café." His mouth screwed up as he stared at her. He walked forward again and ripped her top till it hung off one shoulder, revealing her smooth golden-brown skin. She angrily pushed him back and tried to pull it up again, but it was no use. It stubbornly refused to stay there. "Beautiful," he said.

"I need to pee," she said. "Can you leave?"

"Oh, I'm not going anywhere for a while, Ada. You'll just have to pee in the bucket, or on your bed through your clothes if you wish." He carried on sketching.

Ada decided to try a new tack and screamed at the top of her lungs.

"Scream as much as you like, there's nobody for miles. There are no film companies booked for months and the flying club are only here on weekends. Their hangar is a long way off. I'm the security here. There's nobody to help you."

Ada felt deflated. She really needed to pee too. She could feel the pressure on her bladder increasing. She tried to think of other things but as the minutes ticked by, she couldn't hold it any longer. She walked over to the bucket, pulled her trousers down gingerly and squatted as best she could. The pee made a loud tinny noise as it hit the bucket. Kent sat and watched her. She tried to hide herself as much as possible with her hands but she felt the full indignity of her position. She was completely reliant on Kent and she felt like this is what he wanted. She stood and pulled up her trousers.

"Why have you captured me? What did I do to deserve this?"

"Well, I was happy just observing you. I was keeping notes, see." He showed her his journal of her movements. "Then you upped the ante and stole my notebook about Mary from my room. I don't know how you managed it but I know it was you. Who else could it be? I couldn't have you showing my journal to the police. What did you do with it by the way? Is it in your home? No matter, I can find it. I see you live alone, so there's nobody to find it. That young man from the library you've been hanging with, who is he? I've been reading about you online. No parents, no family. Few friends. You claim to be psychic. Is there anybody here?" he asked, chuckling.

"Will you kill me like you did Mary?" she queried.

"I do have footage of Mary. Would you like to see it? You seem very interested in her. She was a very interesting person to watch. She pretended she liked Marcus and Gilbert, but I know it was really me she was interested in. I have a complete record of her movements on video." He brought his phone closer to Ada to show her. She loathed his presence but was keen to see what he was showing her. He flicked though various images on his phone. There was also video footage that appeared to be shot on a wildlife camera in her garden.

Ada was horrified. "These shots are in her garden?"

"Yes, I set up some trip cameras while she was out so I could keep a proper watch on her."

"So you could plan the best time to murder her you mean?"

"What is this obsession with murder? I didn't kill Mary. I was rather devastated in fact when I found out she'd been killed. I felt we had a real connection."

"Who else could it be but you?" she said.

"Why would I want to kill my darling Mary?" He smiled in a creepy way. "We were going to be married eventually."

Ada sat quietly as she thought on his words. He was obviously insane, but she had a feeling he really meant what he said. How could she have been wrong about him? If William Kent hadn't killed Mary, who had?

"If it truly wasn't you that killed her, what about Gilbert Orange? You knew him. Is he dangerous?"

"Oh yes! Watch out for that one, he's a real ladies' man!" he said, snorting. "Mary doesn't matter now though, because I have you, Ada." He looked at her with a fierce intensity and moved and sat beside her on the bed. He had a bowl with water and a sponge and he gently wiped the blood off the back of her head. When he'd finished, he squeezed the sponge and the drops fell down her front, wetting her T-shirt. He brought the sponge down to her legs and gently bathed her ankles, then his hand moved slowly up her leg to her thigh. Ada was frozen with fear and he took this as an invitation to go further. He moved the soaking sponge up higher, then forcefully pushed her back on the bed. He clambered on the bed below her, but at this point Ada had had enough. She kicked him with her legs so hard that he fell backwards off the bed and hit his head on the chair. Then she jumped on the bed in a crouching position as if ready to strike again and defend herself. Kent sprang up quickly, as if he was going to strike her for what she'd done. She'd struck him in the nose with the chain and a trickle of glistening blood oozed down his face. He stepped forward and she raised her fists in readiness. He thought better of it and moved to sit back down in his chair.

"You'd better be nice to me, Ada. Nobody is coming here for months, maybe years. I'm going to be your only source of food and company."

"And what happens at the end of those months?" she asked.

"By then, you'll realise that you're in love with me."

Ada felt a dread creep over her. Rose was her only hope. The thought of years spent with Kent was unbearable.

Kent stayed with her for most of the day, writing or sketching her. She tried to think of a way out of her chain, but the bed was very heavy and strong and the chain was even stronger. She was just going to have to hope that Rose was successful and would bring help soon. Eventually, when the light had gone, Kent went away, she assumed to undertake his security duties on-site.

"I'll be back in the morning. Sleep well."

As if it were an afterthought, he pulled an extra blanket from his holdall and put some more food on the bed. Then she heard him get in his car and drive off. He'd turned the light off and she was alone in the dark once more. After a short while she heard footsteps.

'Is he back already?' she thought. Then the room lit up with a familiar blue light and Drake reappeared through the side of the Nissen hut, but this time he wasn't alone. Beside him was a man who appeared to be a doctor. He carried a medical bag with him.

"Are you okay?" asked Drake.

"Apart from having some of my dignity stripped from me, I'm fine."

"Dr D'eath is here to give you a check over."

"Death?" she enquired.

"Yes, not a great name for someone who's supposed to heal people, but it was the name I was born with. Now let's have a look at you." He examined her head and shone a ghostly torchlight into her eyes. Then he looked down at her leg chains.

"I think the head wound is relatively minor, though you might have some mild concussion. I'm more worried by these chains he has you in. That metal doesn't look too clean. Do you have anything here to bind the wounds or clean them? It'll be hard to do, but with your small fingers we might just manage it."

"I have some honey in one portion of the split yoghurt he left. I also have some herbal tea."

"Herbs are great at killing germs, so is honey. Let's wash them with the tea and apply a little honey on the bandage. We'll rip some material off these bed sheets, they seem clean enough. Drake says you don't mind if I use your body to apply the bandages?"

Ada tensed. The last time she'd let a doctor in, it had all gone horribly wrong. Should she let this one in? She looked at Drake. He gave her a nod. She didn't have much choice but to trust him. She nodded okay.

She felt Dr D'eath slip into her body and she could feel him looking out through her eyes. He picked up the bed sheet and ripped off a strip, carefully poured the still warm herbal tea over her cuts and spread a little honey along part of the bandage with the teaspoon Kent had left her. Then, with difficulty, he wound the bandages around her leg in the small space between the chain and her leg.

"There we go, all done. If only I'd had hands like this in life. They're so small and nimble," he said, holding them up and looking at them. Ada felt worried for a second, but then she felt Dr D'eath leaving her and he was once again standing in front of her.

"Thank you," she said sweetly.

"Now, the boys and I have a plan to get you out of

here. It's a bit madcap, but we think it'll work. Our main problem is how to get you out of those leg restraints, but we think we've got that solved too. We just need to find someone. Do you know how long we've got until he comes back?"

"He said in the morning. I think he might be working a night shift," she said.

"Right, so ideally by dawn. Don't worry, Ada, we've got this in hand. Make sure you get as good a night's rest as you can and we'll see you at first light."

Drake and the doctor left her in the dark once more and she turned over to go to sleep as best she could.

Chapter 14

Rose walked along the road using the signs to try and find her way home. She'd never had great directional sense, even when she was alive. The traffic whizzed past her at such speeds. She found it slightly terrifying. There hadn't been so many cars back when she had died in the 1960s. They seemed to get faster year on year. The good thing about being a ghost was that you didn't get tired, but it was going to take her a long time to get back at this rate. She plodded on for most of the day, following signs and the direction of the sun, but by evening she felt that she was getting no nearer. She wondered if she was, in fact, lost. She so wanted to help rescue Ada. She sat down by a yew tree on the edge of a churchyard and started to cry.

"Dear lady, what's bothering you?"

She turned around to see who was there. Standing behind her was a vicar. He clearly wasn't a living vicar as his clothes were very antiquated and he sported the most amazing walrus moustache.

"Oh, hello," Rose said, sniffing. "I'm lost and my

friend has been kidnapped. She needs me to find human help. I'm trying to get back to Sudfield but I have no idea where I am. Can you direct me, please? If I don't bring help soon, I don't know what might happen to her."

"You're in Little Piddling. This is St Nicolas's church and I was the vicar here for many years. I'm Reverend Bumble. You're not too far off. I see the great green horseless omnibuses going past here every day. There's a stop just there," he said, pointing further down the street. "It's the number eighty-nine. I think the next one is due in ten minutes." He looked up at the church clock. "I know because it always arrives when the clock strikes the hour. Just hop on board, my dear, and you should be home in half an hour."

"I'm a little scared of using transport. What if someone sits down on me? I hate it when that happens."

"I quite understand. It's an unpleasant experience, but Mrs Wicklow over there gets the bus every week to go and see how her family are getting on without her. Why don't you go with her? The bus is rarely full up.

"I say, Mrs Wicklow, would you mind showing this young lady how to use the omnibus? She needs to get to Sudfield." Mrs Wicklow looked up. She was dressed like someone from the 1950s. She had a good-humoured face with rosy cheeks and she carried a wicker basket on her arm.

"Why certainly, Mr Bumble, it'd be a pleasure. Come on, dear."

"Thank you, Mr Bumble, I'm indebted to you."

"Not a problem, dear lady. Good luck." Then he wandered off through the gravestones and walked through a disused blocked-up door.

"Don't worry, my dear, it's easy. It's only nerve-racking the first time you do it. You'll wonder what you ever worried about afterwards."

Mrs Wicklow chatted away and Rose felt easy in her company. When she saw the bus approach, her stomach started to knot. It pulled up at the empty stop and an elderly woman got off with a stick.

"That's Rosemary. I can recall her as a young child. Such a naughty thing she was. You'd never know to look at her now. Come on, dear," she said, indicating for Rose to get on the bus.

"Let's sit here." She beckoned for Rose to sit next to her. "Don't worry, I'm very good at suggesting to people that they shouldn't sit where I am. They don't know why, but they'll usually go and sit somewhere else."

Mrs Wicklow talked during the whole journey to Sudfield and Rose felt her tension ease slightly.

"Do your family know that you're there?" asked Rose.

"I don't know that they exactly do, but I like to think that they sense me around."

"If you have a short message you'd like to pass on, I know someone who can help."

"Oh really? Well just tell them I'm so pleased that

they named their daughter Edith after me. They live at 12 Clear View Terrace. Thank you."

Finally, the bus trundled into Sudfield. Rose was very relieved to get off, although the journey had been better than she imagined it would be. She thanked Mrs Wicklow profusely before rushing off.

Eventually, she reached home. She shut her eyes and ran straight through the door.

"Hello, Rose," said Mrs Entwhistle, who was watching her favourite baking show on TV. "She's had that cake in far too long. It'll be dry as toast if she doesn't take it out soon."

"Where's Ada?" asked Dennis, who only suffered the show for Mrs Entwhistle's sake. Rose's first reaction was to burst out crying. Both ghosts rushed forward to comfort her.

"Whatever's happened? Has there been an accident?" asked Dennis.

"Ada has been kidnapped by that horrible man William Kent! It was him all along. He hit her over the head this morning, bound her and now he has her chained up at an old RAF base in Suffolk. I had to leave her on her own with him. Who knows what he's done by now. What do we do, Den? I found a nice RAF man at the base to stay with her, but we need to find human help for her somehow."

"Why's it taken you so long to get back?"

"I was walking, then I got lost, and a nice vicar and a woman called Mrs Wicklow told me where I was and how to catch the bus," she said between hysterical sobs.

"Now, Dennis, there's no use in berating poor Rose. What we need to do is find that nice young policeman, Mr Matlock. He can help her out. Let's head off there now." Mrs Entwhistle reached into her voluminous bag, pulled out her hat and hatpin, put on her ghostly coat, and all three headed off at speed towards Inspector Matlock's house.

***

Matlock was enjoying his first beer of the evening. It had been chilling in the fridge all day and its icy coldness was very refreshing. Suddenly, there was a loud rapping at the door. He leapt up to answer it. He opened the door but there was nobody there. He looked around outside but could see nothing.

"Kids," he mumbled, and went back in and sat down on his favourite armchair. It was a chilly night, so he'd lit a fire in the wood burner and he was enjoying watching the flames. All of a sudden, the door sprang open and he almost dropped his beer. Then, on the red-tiled hearth in front of the fire, the ashes appeared to be moving and a letter started to form slowly into the letter A.

"Inspector Jolly, is that you? George?" He watched as a word formed. Next was a D, then another A.

"Ada? What about Ada?" The invisible hand began writing again.

"Hold on!" said David. He ran off and fifteen seconds later he returned with a shopping list chalkboard and a piece of chalk. "My aunt gave it to me," he said, feeling as if he needed to explain his ownership of this object. He placed it flat on the floor with the chalk beside it. The chalk was lifted up and started to write.

'ADA KIDNAPPED KENT.'

"William Kent has kidnapped Ada Baker?" clarified David.

The words were rubbed out and 'YES' appeared.

"When? How? Where is she now?" David asked.

'6.00 A.M. GALLERY. KNOCKED OUT. CAR.'

"Blast!" shouted David.

The ghostly writer paused to make sure this had been read before rubbing it out and writing, 'AT DISUSED WW2 RAF BASE, SUFFOLK.' It paused again, rubbed out the words, then wrote, 'NISSEN HUT, CHAINED UP IN DARK.'

"Oh Jeez!" said David. "Can you be more precise? Which base? There are loads of them. This part of the world is littered with them."

The words were rubbed out again. New words appeared. 'NO. BLAME ROSE!' The piece of chalk seemed to be batted out of the hand and went flying across the room.

"Dennis, is that you?"

The chalk was retrieved, then wrote, 'DEN, ROSE, MRS E, JOLLY.'

"Okay, don't worry. Thanks for letting me know. I'll get this sorted. Hold on."

He ran back into his bedroom and appeared a minute later fully dressed, if a little dishevelled.

"There won't be many people working this time of night. First, we'll have to find out which RAF base he's at. Then I'll need to gather a team before we go there. Do we know if he was armed?"

'NO.'

"We'd best bring that board and chalk with us," he said, grabbing it. "Come on, we'll take my car." He grabbed his keys and ran out the door, slamming it behind him.

A ghostly face appeared around the bathroom door. "Blimey!" said George. "What a furore."

Chapter 15

It was still dark when Ada next woke, but she could hear the sound of a robin singing nearby, so she assumed the world was waking up outside. She was cold and her body ached. She missed her cosy house and even Rose's bunny slippers. She was lying there a few minutes when she heard footsteps again. She sat up straight. Was it going to be Kent or Drake? Drake emerged through the side of the building with a different man. This one didn't look like a member of the RAF, more like a caretaker. He was much older, with white hair and a long brown work coat.

"Right, we've got it sorted, Ada. Alfred here was the site odd-job man. He was a bit of a jack of all trades."

"And a member of the Home Guard too in the war, ma'am," added Alfred. "I'll soon have that lock unpicked with your help." He had a set of picks in his hand. "It took me half the night to find them. I've not had to use them in a long time. They're a little rusty, but I reckon they might still work." Alfred was obviously a poltergeist like Dennis. "Do you mind, miss? I can try doing it on my own but it might be quicker with your hands. Dr D'eath said you have very nimble fingers."

Ada nodded. "That's fine, thank you, Alfred."

She tried to relax and clear her mind. She felt him slip in and she could feel what made him uniquely him. Two souls in one body was a strange experience. He got straight to work.

"Ah yes, quite easy, he's used an old padlock. Give me a minute." He fiddled with the lock until she heard a click and the padlock dropped off. She regained control, pushing Alfred out, and immediately removed the wicked chains and rubbed her sore legs.

"Sorry, thank you, Alfred. You don't know how good that feels. It was so uncomfortable. Why do people do this for pleasure?"

"Sorry?" asked Alfred.

"Oh nothing," she said, smiling.

"Now let's get you out of here," said Drake.

Ada made for the door and pushed it, but it wouldn't budge.

"Hold on," said Alfred, slipping through the door and out the other side. "It's another padlock. This might take a bit longer without your help."

Ada could hear his lock-pick set jangling again.

"So, what's the plan?" she asked.

"Well, you're not able to walk very well, I imagine, having had those heavy chains on, so we need to find a quick way out of here for you before he comes back. It might be easier to show you rather than tell you."

Outside, a blackbird started to sing. They heard the other lock drop on the concrete.

Ada pushed the door and this time it opened. "Not too hard actually, a bit like riding a bike," said Alfred proudly.

"Thanks again, Alfred."

"Quick, this way," said Drake. "I'm sorry I can't help you by giving you a shoulder to lean on."

"No problem. Just show me the way out of here." She followed Drake as quickly as her sore, cold legs would allow. They made their way along a path through a copse of trees and emerged on an area of grass near a runway. It was getting light now and a strand of shining gold highlighted the trees. Gradually, the dawn chorus was growing to a crescendo. A roe deer dashed out in front of them, paused and looked at her, then carried on across the tarmac, quickly followed by several more. Ada paused for a moment to watch them go by.

"This way, we're heading to those buildings there."

She looked and saw some large buildings in the distance. She kept pushing herself, willing herself to keep going and fight through the pain that coursed through her legs. A noise came in on the edge of her hearing and got louder and louder. She recognised that it was a car. She looked behind her and saw a car heading at speed towards her. As it got nearer, she could see that it was Kent driving it. He'd spotted her and was heading straight for her.

"Shit!" exclaimed Ada.

Drake turned to look at her. "Ruddy hell! Quick, take cover in the trees."

Ada dived into a nearby copse and started running through the undergrowth, but it was much slower with all the tree roots. Kent slammed on his brakes and jumped out of the car.

"Ada, Ada love, what are you doing? There's nowhere to go. Come here."

Ada didn't stop but kept going, the bracken and branches stinging her legs as she pushed through. Kent wasn't injured so could move much quicker. She tripped over a root and hit her knee. She screamed in pain and turned to see that Kent was almost upon her. She made a desperate attempt to get back out on the runway, thinking she might stand a better chance against him there. She broke through the greenery and emerged back in the open. She realised she couldn't outrun him in her current state. She was going to have to fight.

Kent emerged next to her. She took up a protective stance but was hobbling. Kent could see she was in pain. "Come on, Ada, we can have a look at your leg and make it better. Come back home with me."

"Home? You psycho! You had me chained up in a Nissen hut. Keep away from me," she screamed, as panic took hold and hot tears ran down her cheeks.

Kent rushed forward to grab her, but Ada jabbed him hard in the nose and it sent him reeling back. His nose started to gush again and he held it for a second, then rushed forward to grab her once more. This time she used a step kick and whacked him hard in the side, which seemed to wind him but shot pain right up her leg as she landed the blow. He shot forward and knocked her flat on the floor. Then he pinned her arms down by her sides and sat on top of her. He looked down on her as if triumphant, and Ada could tell that he was getting aroused by this. He lowered his head as if he was going to kiss her.

"No! No! No!" she screamed. Ada was strong though. She had trained with Mr Lee, learning kung fu for some years. She managed to roll onto her side and kick Kent off, before rolling and hobbling painfully back onto her feet. She went for the soft spot again and kicked him in the groin with the heel of her foot. He winced with pain on the floor, so she took her opportunity and ran off towards the buildings that Drake had pointed out.

"Quickly, Ada!" Drake said, and they both ran off as fast as they could.

***

Kent writhed on the floor for a few minutes, then recovered himself enough to stand up and head towards his car. He opened the driver's door to get in but then felt a tap on the shoulder. Kent turned around and Alfred's fist met him square on the chin. Kent dropped like a sack across the car seat, out cold.

"I don't think so, sunshine, do you? Treating a lady

like that. It's not gentlemanly. They didn't call me Alfred 'Knuckles' Johnson in the trenches for no reason. Still got it!" He smiled and wandered off back into the woods.

***

"We're nearly there, Ada. Come on, you can do it."

Ada was working on pure adrenalin now. Her blood was pumping and she was determined to get away from Kent. They arrived at the buildings, which turned out to be an aircraft hangar with 'Stockwood Flying Club' written over the doors. They ran inside and found a light aircraft and about twelve other RAF crewmen standing around.

"Ducky! You made it, well done, old sport," said a suave-looking Brylcreemed man with a neat and natty moustache. "You must be Ada. We're ready for you. Bill's opened the doors, removed all the control locks from the plane, the hangar doors are open and you just need to get it started."

Ada stood open-mouthed. It was like a scene from a TV drama.

"What? What are you planning, Drake?" she said, feeling slightly alarmed.

"We're going to fly you out of here. It's another two and a half miles to the exit. This site is huge. I don't think you're going to be able to walk out of here and get away from Kent before he's on his feet again, do you?

More correctly, you are going to fly us out of here."

"Me? How?"

"Well, if you don't mind letting me in, I'm certain I could fly this crate. I've been watching the modern crew and it's much like a training aircraft. Things haven't changed that much in all these decades." He tried to take her hand between his and she felt his cold touch. "We can do this, Ada. Please give me this chance to help you."

Her adrenalin was pumping and a thrill went through Ada's body. A real World War Two RAF pilot flying a plane with her body. It would be an experience like no other, and Kent might be here any minute.

"Okay," she replied, breathing excitedly. Ada sat down on a stool and cleared her mind. "Ready," she said.

Drake stepped forward and slipped into her body. She could feel him getting used to the sensation of touching and moving a body again. He stood up and headed for the plane. Bill wolf-whistled. "Looking good, Ducky," he said, winking.

"Thanks, Bill." Ada and Drake headed into the aircraft. He took her to sit at the controls and then seemed to be getting his bearings for a minute. The controls were gobbledygook to Ada, but she sat back and let him move her body. She could feel his confidence and excitement growing. He kept repeating in his mind, 'We can do this, we can do this.' He put on his headset, checked various gauges, flicked switches, and eventually the plane hummed into life. He looked out the windows to make sure everything was clear.

"Clear prop!" he shouted. The plane gradually taxied forward out onto the runway and moved into position.

"We're in the green," said Drake. "Ready for take-off." The plane began to taxi forward.

***

William Kent wasn't out for long, but it had been a good punch. He had no idea who it was that hit him. He just knew he had to find Ada before she escaped and told anyone what he'd done. He was a little hazy, but he started up the car and headed up the runway in the direction he'd seen her running. He didn't want to drive too fast in case he missed seeing her hiding in the trees, but she couldn't get very far with an injury like that.

***

As the plane taxied forward, Ada could hear its prop engines turning, but she was aware of another much louder, throatier noise. She wanted to turn and look but Drake was in charge of her body so she couldn't take control and risk messing up the take-off. She felt her stomach turn over as she felt the plane lift up into the air.

***

Matlock and the two police cars that were with him pulled into the old RAF base. He flashed his ID at the security on the gate as he went through and confirmed which direction he had to drive. He looked at the site map he'd printed off the internet and tried to follow the directions to the Nissen huts. The car sirens weren't on as they didn't want to give a warning of their arrival to Kent. He looked at the empty seats of his car. He knew that the ghosts were there but, unlike Ada, he couldn't see or hear them. Was he nutty to follow the scribbled directions of a poltergeist? He'd never live this down in the force if he was wrong. He might even need to change his career. He was starting to rue the day he'd met Ada Baker. He could see the aircraft hangars ahead of him. What was that? A plane was starting to taxi out of the hangar and along the runway. A blue shimmering mist appeared alongside the plane, and before his eyes, the mist started to form into shapes. As he got nearer, the shapes became more obvious.

***

Kent was driving along the grass beside the runway searching for Ada when he was suddenly aware of a strange noise ahead of him. He turned to look and couldn't believe what he saw in front of him. The flying club's Cessna aeroplane was heading straight down the runway towards him. But that wasn't the strangest thing.

Taxiing along beside and behind it were twelve Spitfires. He was so astonished by what he saw speeding towards him that he didn't think at first about taking evasive action. It was only as the Spitfire in front of him was almost on top of him that he swerved his car and drove straight into a tree. He had no seat belt on and went crashing through the windscreen. As his lifeblood slowly ebbed out of him, he could hear the drone of Spitfires disappearing off into the distance.

***

"Bloody Nora! What's that? It can't be!" exclaimed Matlock. The mist had formed into the shape of twelve Spitfires. As the light aircraft sped up and headed down the runway, the Spitfires followed it into the air. As they did, Matlock heard the most almighty crashing noise. At first, he couldn't see what it was, but at the side of the runway a car had crashed into a tree. He pulled up beside it and leapt out of his car. His attention should have perhaps been on the crashed car, but he couldn't stop himself from watching the Spitfires as they sped off into the early morning sky. The other cars had pulled up beside him.

"Did you see that?" he asked, looking at the other officers, but the pallor of their skin and open-mouthed expressions answered his question.

"Twelve Spitfires forming out of a blue mist and taking off into the sky, you mean? Yes, I saw it, but I don't believe it," said Sergeant Thomas. He looked across at the man lying crumpled on the floor. "How am I going to call this one in, sir?"

"Damned if I know, Sergeant," said Matlock, finally walking across to look at the man and see if he needed assistance. He stared down into the lifeless face of William Kent, saw the odd angle of his neck and was certain he was dead, but he felt for a pulse anyway. He was more concerned whether Ada was still here, injured somewhere, but he looked up at the now disappearing Spitfires and somehow he was certain that she wasn't.

***

William Kent picked himself up off the floor. "Bloody hell, that hurt," he said, rubbing his neck. "Bloody girl, she's for it now."

"Oh, I don't think so, sunshine, do you?"

Kent turned to look at the source of the voice. Alfred 'Knuckles' Johnson stood in front of him.

"I think you and me are going to be spending a lot of time together from now on." Knuckles took Kent's arm and twisted it behind his back. "You've got a lot of explaining to do, sunshine. Picking on young ladies. We don't take kindly to that here."

Kent yelped with pain as Knuckles led his spirit off through the trees.

Chapter 16

"Well done, Ducky!" Ada could hear over the earpiece.
She could still hear the strange droning noise. She felt
that Drake had got the plane up in the air, so she felt it
was safe to quietly ask, "What's that noise, Drake?"

She could feel him making her mouth muscles smile,
and he looked around out of the window to their right.
There, flying in formation with them, were six ghostly
Spitfires. She could see Bill in the cockpit of the nearest
plane, wearing a flying helmet, and he gave them a
salute through the window. Drake turned her head to
look out the other window. There on the other side were
six more Spitfires. Ada worked very hard not to push
herself forward in her mind but instead to quietly take
in the astonishing sight. They didn't look spectral, but
so real that she could touch them. The sunlight seemed
to glint off their paintwork and canopies.

"Keep in formation, boys."

"I knew you could do it, Ducky," said Bill.

"I've got to land this crate yet," said Drake. He could
feel Ada's panic at the back of his mind. "But so far it's

been really easy, it shouldn't be a problem."

"How long before we land, sir?" Drake heard over the headphones.

"Hadfield airfield isn't very far as the crow flies. I've heard the flying club talking about it. They use it all the time. We should be there in twelve minutes. Are you all right, Ada?"

"Uh huh, thank you, Drake," was all she could manage to say. In truth, she was absolutely blown away by the fact that a ghost was flying a plane by using her body and that a squadron of ghostly Spitfires and their World War Two pilots were flying along beside her. This sort of thing just didn't normally happen, not even in her unusual life. It was an amazing feeling, as if she was part of a real squadron in World War Two.

The pilots were laughing and joking over the radio when Ada heard Bill say, "By Jove, there's a Jerry, two o'clock!" Drake looked where Bill had said and sure enough there was a Messerschmitt 109 fighter plane heading straight towards them. It let out ghostly tracer bullets straight at Drake's plane.

"Spinks, Jones, Howard, acquire the target and get him off our tail, will you? This mission is too important to be upset by a Jerry."

Three of the Spitfires on the right wing broke off and headed straight towards the Messerschmitt. When they were in firing range, Ada could hear gunfire and see the bullets streak across the sky. The Messerschmitt made evasive manoeuvres, and for a minute Ada could see them circling each other, trying to get a clear shot, until one of them was successful and the Messerschmitt seemed to take a hit. Smoke plumed from its tail and it went plummeting downwards, where it crashed into the ground, sending up an explosion of mud and smoke.

"Well done, lads!" said Drake. "Re-form. We're nearly at base."

They circled around the airfield to ensure that no other planes were arriving or departing, then Drake lined them up on the runway and slowly brought the plane down to land. He seemed to be concentrating extremely hard. Ada could feel he was a little anxious, but he brought it down nice and smoothly and it landed with the smallest of bumps, then he taxied it along the runway. The other Spitfires were still up in the sky. Eventually it came to a halt. Drake switched off the plane and moved out of her body.

Ada felt tearful. She stood up painfully and turned to look at him. "I owe you my life, I think, Drake. How can I ever thank you enough?"

He smiled and said, "Actually, I must thank you. Ever since I crashed my plane back in 1940, I've been afraid to fly. The crash was my fault, you see. A mid-air collision on a training exercise. Bill was one of the other pilots. Three of us died that day. The boys have been waiting for me to find the courage to leave with them. At first, they weren't all here, but as the years passed by, more and more of them appeared. I feel like I have redeemed myself at last and it's safe to fly on now. I hope you'll be safe from Kent now, Ada. Live a good, full life for me. Live the life that I never had the chance to."

They exited the aircraft and there waiting on the runway was another ghost Spitfire. Drake scrambled up the plane, turned back to Ada, smiled, waved and climbed in. The Spitfire engine started, its famous streak of fire shooting out the fuselage. He taxied forward down the runway and flew off into the sky. By this time, a group of men had run over and were standing next to her watching the Spitfire as it joined the others. They flew up towards the sun until they disappeared from view.

Ada turned to the nearest man, who turned to look at her open-mouthed. "I think perhaps you'd better call the police. Please ask for an Inspector Matlock." He nodded at her, too dumbstruck to say anything.

***

When Inspector Matlock arrived at Hadfield airfield, he found Ada sitting on a sofa in their staffroom, a mug of sweet tea in her hand and a blanket around her shoulders. She looked tired and unkempt. The men on-site had looked after her but were staring at her as if she was some sort of alien being.

Matlock's first concern was whether she was okay. He looked her over and could see the cuts and chafe marks, and her ankle was looking swollen. "What did he do? Did he hurt you? Did he… assault you?"

"Generally, I'm okay. Nothing that a hot bath and a good night's rest wouldn't fix," she said, smiling, although he could see in her eyes that she was terrified.

"It's okay, Ada. Kent is dead. He crashed into a tree on the runway, went head first through the windscreen and broke his neck. He can't hurt you now," he said, trying to be reassuring. "I think, all things considered, he must have been our killer. You were right."

Ada shook her head. "No, I don't think so. I confronted him about it. He sounded surprised and he showed me his phone. He had video footage of Mary's house. It was taken from a wildlife camera he set up in the garden. I didn't see it all, but I think you might want to flick through them. His phone code was one, two, three, four. I don't think he was our man."

Matlock looked round the room, and in a lower tone of voice said, "Ada, did I really see what I thought I saw? A squadron of Spitfires taking off with your aircraft? How did you fly the plane? Do you have a pilot's licence?"

She shook her head. "No. I met a truly great man. He helped me fly the plane."

"Where is he now?"

Ada pointed upward.

"I see. You know there's going to be a big furore about this? Lots of people saw you. Saw the dogfight. At first, they thought it was part of an air show, until the ME-109 crashed. That freaked quite a few people out. I don't think you're going to be leading quite such a quiet life after this. We'll have a discussion about that later, but first of all I think we need to get you checked out at the hospital. Oh, and there's a few people waiting outside to see you. I asked them to wait there so I could get my job done."

She nodded.

"Come on then." He helped her up and put his arm around her for support. "Thank you, gentlemen," he said, nodding at the airfield staff who were being questioned by the officers. "We'll be in touch."

***

Outside, Ada could see Mrs Entwhistle, Rose, Dennis and Inspector Jolly.

"Ada! I'm so sorry it took so long to get help," said Rose.

"Dear girl, it's so good to see you." Mrs Entwhistle was choking back a tear.

"We'll chat in the car, if you don't mind," said Ada. She was acutely aware that everyone was staring at her. She climbed in the passenger seat behind Matlock and the ghosts squeezed in the back.

Ada explained everything she'd been through while Matlock drove her to the hospital.

"Well, I wouldn't believe it if I hadn't seen it with my own eyes," said Matlock. "The fallout of this is going to be huge. Half a dozen police saw it, several airfield workers, as well as civilians on the ground."

"How did Rose let you know what was going on?"

"Rose got Dennis to write me a message on my chalkboard shopping list. She was a bit hazy on exactly which airfield you were at, but luckily you mentioned that it had been used for filming recently. We managed to piece it together from Rose's description of her journey home."

"If Rose had just come straight back, instead of trying to walk half the way home, we might have been there sooner," said Dennis beratingly.

"Den, you're being too hard. Rose saved my life. She stayed with me and followed Kent to the airfield. If she hadn't found Drake, I don't know where I'd be now. Thank you, Rose."

Rose blushed.

Ada was checked over at the hospital but all was fine. Afterwards, Matlock drove them home. He saw Ada inside and onto the sofa.

"As the doctor advised, you should rest up for a few days to let yourself heal. Try not to have any adventures for a few days at least. I've already got the team onto checking out the phone footage of Mary's house and searching through Kent's home, so you can sit back, relax, watch some TV and let the professionals take over."

Ada felt that Matlock was warming to her, and he finally seemed to have embraced the ghosts.

"Thank you, Inspector."

"I think you can call me David now after that experience. At least in private," he said.

Ada smiled. "Thank you, David."

"I'm off back to work now. I'll be in touch." He nodded and left the house.

Dennis flicked on the TV. "It's Agatha Christie crime day on this channel if you fancy it?" he said enthusiastically.

"Okay," she agreed. The ghosts settled around her to watch. She sighed inwardly. Somehow watching it wasn't as satisfying as solving it herself. She pondered on who had really committed the murder. If Kent really hadn't done it, then who had? She thought some more on what Neville had said. Perhaps Marcus Strang really had been involved. He certainly did seem to be hiding something. Ada felt sure that Miss Marple or Hercule Poirot would have had this case wrapped up already. Perhaps she could channel Agatha Christie to help her solve it. Now there was an idea!

***

The night passed quietly if rather uncomfortably for Ada. She had slept downstairs to make life easier and she was awoken by the sound of the kettle flicking off. Dennis was pouring a cup of tea for her.

"Morning," she said, yawning. He brought the cup over, managing to spill only a tiny bit.

"Ada…" he said, then paused.

"Yes, Dennis?" she replied expectantly.

"There seem to be a few people outside the front of the house."

"People?"

"Yes… and cameras."

"Oh my God!" She jumped up, winced and grabbed her crutches. She went to look through the peephole of the door. There were indeed two film crews outside her house.

"Oh, what should I do?" she said.

"Just ignore them. They'll go away."

"I never knew they were going to conjure up all those Spitfires, let alone that they'd be visible to everyone."

She hobbled back into the living room. Her ankle seemed to have swollen up overnight. Dennis got her some ice blocks out of the freezer to put on it.

The doorbell rang but she didn't answer it. She heard a voice coming through the letterbox. "Miss Baker, it's *East Anglian News*. We wondered whether you wanted to speak to us about your experience yesterday?"

Dennis put his finger to his lips.

"Miss Baker?" she heard again. She heard the letterbox swing shut.

"Well, this is an unexpected turn of events," said Rose. "Shall I go out there and have a look?"

"Okay, thanks, Rose." Rose braved the front door and pushed her way through with her eyes shut.

Ten minutes later she came back. "They've moved on to talking to Mr Gardener next door. Mrs Gardener

166

is very excited. I think they're producing a news article on you. I think I heard them say it's going out on the lunchtime news."

Ada groaned and held a cushion over her face. There was nothing to do but sit it out. She couldn't go anywhere for a few days anyway.

"More Miss Marple?" asked Dennis.

Ada nodded. "Why not."

Apart from texting Jian to apologise and cancel this week's kung fu lesson, not much happened till lunchtime, when Ada switched on the telly with dread. It appeared under the 'story of interest' section.

"Suffolk residents were treated to a rather special air display yesterday when a squadron of twelve ghostly Spitfires were seen flying over the skies of Suffolk alongside a Cessna aeroplane." The presenter gave a porcelain white smile. "It's not known where the fighters appeared from, and at first people thought that the planes were practising for an air show, until a German Messerschmitt ME-109 appeared and several of the Spitfires broke off to intercept the aircraft. It wasn't till the Messerschmitt appeared to crash into the ground that people realised that this was something more than your average show." There were several ropey, shaky phone videos showing footage of the dogfight. "Some people claim that the footage is just footage from an air show. It has been leaked to us, however, that the Cessna pictured landed at Hadfield airfield. Crew on the ground there said that the pilot of the plane was a Miss Ada Baker and that they had indeed seen several ghost Spitfires in the area. We tried talking to Miss Baker but there was no answer." They showed a photo of her front door. "We did, however, manage to speak to her neighbour, Mr Gardener." A smiling Mr Gardener appeared, standing outside the front of his house.

"Mr Gardener, what can you tell us about Ada Baker? Has she said anything to you about her experience?"

"Ada is a lovely young lady. She claims to be a psychic and that she lives with three ghosts. She treats them like living people, even pours them cups of tea. I regularly hear her talking to herself, although she says she's talking to them. I've not seen her for a few days so she hasn't told me anything about the Spitfires."

Ada let out a low groan. He made her sound like a crazy person.

"Well, viewers, what do you think? Are ghostly Spitfires and Messerschmitts really haunting our skies, or is it all just a big hoax? I expect a lot of you will be scanning the skies tonight. This is Kimberly Warrior reporting for *East Anglian News*."

"There was nothing about Kent and the kidnapping at least. Matlock must have made sure it stayed out of the news. I bet he came down on those police officers like a ton of bricks to ensure nothing leaked out," said Dennis.

Ada was mortified at making the local news and

hoped it didn't appear on the national news.

Later that afternoon, there was a knock at the door. Rose looked through the spyhole. "It's Neville."

"Let him in will you, please, Dennis."

Dennis opened the door into the empty hallway. Neville looked surprised for a moment until he heard Rose welcome him in. He stepped inside and Dennis slammed the door shut.

"Oh hi, Neville. Are they still out there?" said Ada.

"I think the TV cameras have gone, but there's someone out there who looks like a newspaper reporter. I bought you some supplies," he said, dumping a bag of shopping in front of her. "I thought you might have trouble getting out with reporters at your door. I bought some microwave meals and, more importantly, chocolate ice cream."

"Oh, you star!"

"I'll pop it in the freezer for you. What happened to the leg?"

"It's a long story."

"I have time."

Ada relayed everything that had happened to her since she'd seen him last.

Neville sat with his mouth open the whole time. "Oh crikey, you poor thing. But also, what a mind-blowing experience. It's like something out of the movies. You've blown the whole 'Is there life after death?' thing out of the water."

"Well maybe, but people have short memories. They

prefer to doubt than believe. People are already saying it's a sham."

"So, what's next with Mary's case?"

"I guess we leave it up to the police. I've already got in deeper than I meant to."

"I found out some more about the family on the town grapevine. Apparently, Mary and Ellen have always been at loggerheads. Ellen actually contested the will. Mary didn't mention that now, did she?"

"Nor did Ellen," said Ada, intrigued.

"I also heard that the dad was a bit of a brute. The girls would appear at school regularly with bruises, poor things," he added. "I bet they were glad when he died.

"I'm still most suspicious of Marcus Strang though. What was he hiding? There was something he wasn't telling us. I didn't like him, Ada."

"Hmmm, I don't know how to get him to tell us though." She thought for a few seconds. "He did seem to like me. Maybe I could really go and do a photo shoot for him."

"I think not!" said Dennis. "You might end up dead this time!" Dennis was like an overprotective father sometimes, but Ada loved him for it.

"No, maybe not," she replied, but secretly Ada itched to know what had truly happened to Mary.

Neville stayed with Ada most of the day, which took her mind off the problem. He was good fun to spend time with. Mrs Entwhistle was appalled at the idea of microwave meals but accepting of the fact that Ada was incapacitated for a day or two. Meals, she felt, should take time and soul to prepare. She had learnt from the great French chef Georges Auguste Escoffier in her time. He had been famous for creating the peach melba for Dame Nellie Melba. She knew how to make the most exquisite dishes. She had even cooked for royalty on one occasion. Now she watched as the little plastic tray whizzed soullessly round and round in the microwave before it ended with a little 'bing'. All her years of training had led her to this. She sighed and walked out into the garden.

Neville left about eight p.m. and Ada was so dog-tired that she went to bed upstairs, preferring the comfort of her own bed. She was exhausted. It had been a long, strange and trying couple of days.

***

Ada awoke to some sort of kerfuffle going on downstairs. She could hear lots of loud voices. Voices she didn't recognise. She dressed as quickly as possible and made her way downstairs. Dennis was standing at the door looking angry, and Ada found Rose and Mrs Entwhistle in the kitchen. Mrs Entwhistle was clearly upset.

"What's going on? What's all that noise I heard?"

"You've attracted a bit of attention with your recent activities," said Rose. "I think you'd better have a look out on the street."

Ada hobbled to the door and Dennis opened it for her. There, out on the street, were hundreds of people staring at her. They clearly weren't living people though. Georgian gents jostled alongside ladies wearing crinolines, teddy boys and punks. They all started pushing forward as a throng.

"Whoah! Whoah! Whoah! What did I say: no pushing in. This is Ada's home and is sacred. No ghost may enter without her permission," said Dennis authoritatively.

"What about you!" the punk roared.

"I happen to live here, under her invitation."

"What do they all want?" said Ada bewildered.

"My dear young lady, I would be most obliged if you could tell the family who live in my house to vacate the premises. I have tried no end of haunting but they still won't leave," said a particularly rakish fop with a beauty spot by the corner of his left eye.

"Please tell my Bet that I love her. I never got the chance. Oh, and that the pools ticket is under the microwave. She's won fifty thousand pounds on it! I went to see that psychic down the town hall the other week, but she wouldn't bloody listen to me, despite Bet being there. Bet had to pay to see her too," said a man with a balding head.

"Not all at once!" shouted Dennis. "They have all sorts of requests it seems. They're frustrated they can't communicate with people. They've seen what a powerful psychic you are. What happened with the

Spitfires could never be generated around an ordinary person, or even an ordinary psychic. Those planes must have been generated off of your psychic energy."

"I can't help them all! It'd take me forever!"

"I don't think they're going to go away any time soon. They do literally have forever," said Dennis.

"Oh, all right! I guess I'm not going anywhere today. Order them to queue up. I'll get some paper and a pen. I'll hear their cases one by one. If I think I can help, I'll endeavour to pass the info on."

"Right, you horrible rabble, line up if you want to be heard. No promises, mind, and a one in, one out policy." They took a minute to do so but eventually there was a long queue stretching down the middle of the road. A large white van drove down the road and through all the ghosts. Ada could hear lots of cursing and 'Do you minds' as it drove through the unseen horde.

Ada sighed. It was going to be another long day.

***

By teatime, she'd managed to get through all the ghosts, and their list of grievances or messages of love were all written down. Approaching people with loving messages from beyond the grave was not her usual remit, but she felt it had helped all these souls to finally be heard by a living person. She'd been extremely patient with them, even the fop, who was called Valentine Amos. She found out what it was that was really aggravating him about the family and promised to pass on his grievances.

She was exhausted and, much to Mrs Entwhistle's chagrin, she opted for another microwave meal. Shortly after, her phone rang. It was Marcus Strang.

"Hello, Ada. I've been thinking about you. You're kind of hard to miss these days. I wondered if perhaps you might like to consider that offer of being photographed?"

Ada paused for a second while she considered. Her last experience of agreeing to be photographed had not gone well.

"Fully clothed of course. I'd like to photograph the essence of what is you. I have some great ideas."

The young, youthful part of Ada was seeing her dream come true. She'd have given everything she had when she was twenty to be photographed by him. It might also be a subtle way to find out more about Marcus's relationship with Mary without having to force the conversation.

"Okay, where would you like to photograph me? When do you want to do it?"

"My studio, day after tomorrow? The gallery is shut so I have the day free." Marcus gave Ada the address, wished her the best and hung up.

Chapter 17

The next day, Ada's foot was starting to feel a lot better. She'd been using Seth's herbal ointment recipe for easing torn and sore muscles. It had been one that he'd used in his days as a gardener. It had helped his tired muscles after a day's work in the kitchen garden. Consequently, she'd slept quite well. She made her way carefully down the stairs. The ghosts were sitting watching breakfast TV.

"Oh, Ada!" said Dennis. "I was going to try to bring you a cup of tea in bed. I didn't think you'd be up yet. I was going to let you sleep."

"No problem, Den. I can make it."

"Let me fix you a nice breakfast at least," said Mrs Entwhistle.

"I'm fine. You watch your TV. I'll just grab a croissant." The diet was not going well. She slouched on the couch next to them. Flaky crumbs dropped onto her lap and down the cracks of the sofa. Luckily Rose was too absorbed in the TV to notice.

"Anything on the news today about my adventure?"

"Strangely, no," said Rose, sounding disappointed. "I thought there might be. What are you planning to do today, Ada? Are you going to answer more ghost queries?"

Ada rolled her eyes. "No, I need to get out of the house. My foot's feeling a lot better, so I might phone Neville and try and get out and exercise it a bit. Are there any reporters out there today?"

"Not that I've seen," said Dennis.

Ada took her phone out of her pocket. Firstly, she texted Gilbert Orange. She hid what she was typing from Dennis and the other ghosts. **OK for us 2 come and view your art studio 2day? Ada.**

It took a few minutes, but a reply came back full of lots of smiley faces. **O wonderful, wonderful, and most wonderful, wonderful! 11.00 a.m.?**

Ada didn't know but she suspected it was another Shakespeare quote. **Great. C U then. Address?** His address came straight back.

Next, she texted Neville. **Fancy doing sum investigating?** She sent the message.

Bing! Almost instantaneously, the reply came back. **Sure, Marcus?**

She replied. **No, Gilbert. He invited us 2 his studio.** *Bing!* **Sure, C U in 1 hour.**

Neville arrived in one hour on the dot from when he'd sent his message. Ada took this as a good omen of their friendship. She was waiting by the door for him, ready and dressed to go. When she heard the knock at the door, she shouted out to the ghosts, who were still absorbed in breakfast TV.

"Neville's here, I'm going out for a walk with him. I might have lunch out too. See you later." Then she opened the door to a smiling Neville.

"My lady," he said, proffering his arm for support, his floppy nineties boy band hair falling over his eyes.

"Why thank you, Jeeves," she said, linking her arm through his. Her ankle only hurt a little, but it was nice for once to have a friend to lean on. She pulled the door shut behind them.

"To Gilbert's then," said Neville. "Where does he live?"

"I think it's one of the old warehouses near the river that's been converted into flats. It's on Barge Lane."

They made their way there, chatting amiably. Finally, they came to the address, and it was as she'd predicted – a converted warehouse. It had been cleaned up smartly but there were still a few hints left in place to show what it had once been. She pressed the doorbell excitedly.

Thirty seconds later, Gilbert answered the door. "Have I thought long to see this morning's face, and doth it give me such a sight as this?" he said, as an electrifying smile lit up his face. He took Ada's hand and kissed it.

"*Romeo and Juliet?*" asked Neville.

"Indeed," he replied, grinning.

"Wasn't that from the scene where they thought

Juliet was dead?"

"Maybe, but I like the words. Welcome to my home," he said, bowing to Ada. "I'm pleased to have such a famous honoured guest in my humble studio." He chuckled then turned and walked off up the stairs to the top-floor apartment. Even before she'd made it up the stairs, Ada could smell oil paint and turpentine. They walked into a well-lit loft-style room with bare brick walls. An easel stood near a window with a half-finished painting on it. All around the room on shelves and tables were tin cans of paintbrushes, tubes of paint and palette knives. A well-used artist's palette sat on the table near the easel, and paint splodges covered the floor and every work surface. Clearly, Gilbert wasn't a tidy worker. Paintings were hung all around the walls. There was a kitchenette on one side of the room and a small sofa and armchair. Gilbert gestured for them to sit.

"Please, have a seat. I'll fix us a drink. Coffee okay?" he said, shaking some beans in his hand like the well-known Nescafé advert.

"Yes, please," they both said. Very soon, the coffee aroma was mixing with turpentine. Ada spied another room off of the main room.

"Do you live here too, Gilbert?"

"Yes," he replied, smiling.

"Isn't the smell of turps quite overwhelming?"

"I love the smell," he said, opening his arms wide like an evangelical preacher.

They took their cups and wandered around the small

studio, while Gilbert showed them some of his favourite paintings.

"When did you start painting?"

"When I was very young. I used to paint on the back of cereal boxes. My mother used to buy me those cheap powdered pigments that you'd mix with water. I loved the bright colours and the scent of the paint. She was a great gardener and I would paint the flowers in her garden. She worked very hard so that I could have my paints and brushes." His mind seemed to vanish from the room for a moment as he thought of her.

"Is that Mary?" asked Neville, pointing at a painting.

"Indeed. One of the first paintings I did of her. She was so beautiful." He paused before changing the tone of his voice to a sorrowful one. "Beauty is but a vain and doubtful good; a shining gloss that vadeth suddenly; a flower that dies when first it gins to bud; a brittle glass that's broken presently: a doubtful good, a gloss, a glass, a flower, lost, vaded, broken, dead within an hour." A cloud of thought darkened his features.

"You seem like you were closer to her than you suggested in the pub?" said Ada, seeing a change in his usual cheery countenance.

A sad smile crossed his face. "Indeed so, she was a good friend to me."

"Then why pretend like she was more of a casual relationship in the pub?" asked Neville.

"Does anyone tell their true feelings in front of pub friends? Pub friends are not true friends."

179

"Were you jealous of her new friendship with Marcus?" asked Ada.

"Maybe a little. She was my muse first and he stole her. Marcus's work has no life, no vitality. His soul is dead," he said, beating his chest with his fist, imitating a heartbeat. "There is nothing within him."

"You don't seem to like him very much. Were you angry with Mary for taking up with him?" asked Neville.

He turned and gave him a condescending look. "No, young man. It was her life, her passion, she could do as she wished. I just think she was wasted following such a man."

There was an awkward silence. Ada filled it by asking where the bathroom was.

"It's just through my bedroom over there. It's an en suite," he said, pointing, but clearly still riled by Neville's comment.

Ada made her way into the bedroom and shut the door behind her. As she crossed the floor to the loo, she didn't lift her weakened ankle enough and tripped over the rug. She put her hand out in haste to try to catch hold of something and stop herself falling. As she did this, she touched a pile of canvases hidden beneath a cloth. A very clear vision shot through her mind of a man beating a black woman, with a small boy watching on. FLASH! Then she saw another image of a small boy in his mum's high heels and a dress. FLASH! Another image of perhaps the same boy as a teenager in women's clothes. FLASH! A man dressed in women's clothes being hugged by Mary. She gasped as she steadied herself and pulled backwards, grasping the cloth. As she did, the cloth slipped off and fell to the floor. She gasped again. In front of her was a very powerful portrait of Gilbert dressed like a nurse, leaning forward and kissing Mary on the lips, who was dressed very becomingly in a sailor's outfit. It was reminiscent of the famous World War Two VJ Day Times Square photo that appeared in *Life* magazine. She sat down on the bed and stared open-mouthed. As she did this, the door crashed open and Gilbert and Neville came rushing in.

"Ada, are you okay? We heard a– oh!" said Neville.

They both just stared at Gilbert, who sighed and looked at the ground.

Ada spoke first. "I'm so sorry, Gilbert. I didn't mean to look. I tripped on the rug and the cover came off in my hand. I... I... had a vision of a boy and a young man in ladies' clothes. Was that you?"

"Come, help me carry them out to the studio," he said.

They did as he asked and he set the paintings out against the wall. They depicted a male at various ages in his life dressed in women's clothes. They were very powerful pieces and Ada thought they were the best work he'd shown her. There was a depth of feeling to them not found in some of his other work.

"They're amazing!" she said. "Are they all you?"

He nodded. "Yes, they are part of my latest project.

It is going to be part of my new exhibition entitled 'Gilbert Orange – My Secret Life in Women's Clothing'. My father died when I was young and my stepfather wasn't a nice man. A violent man. He would beat my mother. It's why I abhor violence. I had no grandfather to follow, but my mother was very strong. She stood up to him in the end and left him. It must have been hard for her to leave the security of extra money. I had three sisters, too, who idolised me. They used to love loaning me their clothes and shoes and make-up. I'm not sure they saw at first how much I liked it. I don't think I understood. It wasn't till I was thirteen that I realised how much I loved wearing women's clothes. I was confused and ashamed for many years, although my family were always supportive and understanding. Then I met Mary and she understood too. She made me feel comfortable with myself and told me it was nothing to feel ashamed of. It was her idea that I should have an exhibition to tell the world. She was always so encouraging. I feel lost without her. She was my rock."

"I'm so sorry, Gilbert," she said, getting up and giving him a hug. "I don't know if you believe in such things, but I'm a psychic and I've been speaking to Mary. She's very fond of your painting of her. She didn't mention these paintings. I imagine you were keeping it under wraps until the exhibition took place. If you have anything you'd like to ask her, I can put questions to her. It's not quite the same, I know."

He looked curiously at her. "My mother always

believed in spirits. She said they were around us all the time, guiding us." He smiled and wiped a small tear that was forming. "Tell her... she was my best friend and the greatest lover I ever had. Tell her I'm going to carry on with the exhibition and dedicate it to her memory."

"So, you really were lovers?" said Neville curiously.

"Yes. I'm straight. I'm still attracted to women. I like doing manly things like Ironman races and tinkering with my motorbike. It's just that I also like wearing women's clothes. Would you like to see?" he asked excitedly.

"I'd love to," said Ada sincerely. He disappeared off into his room for ten minutes. Then he opened the door suddenly and there he stood, resplendent in a 1960s zebra-print mini dress, knee-high white boots and a bouffant wig.

"Normally I'd have painted my face and nails too, but this was the best I could do in the time."

He was still very obviously a man, with his muscular physique, but Ada felt that this was the effect he was going for. He wasn't pretending to be a woman.

"You look stunning," she said.

"Why thank you," he replied, holding her hand and fluttering his false eyelashes at her.

"Definitely go ahead with the exhibition. It's some of your best work. It speaks of your soul. Thank you for speaking so sincerely to us about it."

"Thank you! It feels like a weight off my chest to tell someone else. I've been lost without Mary to confide in.

I've hidden my true self for too long."

They stayed a little longer while Ada and Gilbert chatted about which make-up brands they liked. Ada spotted that Neville clearly felt out of place, so finally she said that they had to go. They left Gilbert, still in his mini dress as he waved goodbye to them at the door.

As they walked along the road, Ada spoke first.

"So that's clearly Gilbert out of the running as the murderer then. I felt he really loved Mary and all women. In my vision I felt his absolute love for them. Without Mary, he has lost his support and his muse. I don't think he killed her."

"Uh huh," was all Neville said. Clearly, he was still processing the morning's events.

"Do you fancy lunch at the tea room?" said Ada.

"What? Er, no. How about lunch at mine instead?" he asked.

"Okay, thank you."

Neville's flat was above a shop on the other side of town and it was approached from behind the shop. They made their way down a long, unwelcoming muddy alleyway, past concrete backyards and bins, and they were greeted by a mangy, geriatric cat, who was crawling with fleas. A strange unearthly meow came from its skinny body.

"Don't mind him. That's Mickey Bins, the shop cat. He's half feral."

Ada felt a slight revulsion as it tried to rub itself against her. Never had she seen something alive that looked so dead.

They made their way up uncarpeted wooden stairs, their feet clunking with every step. Clearly, the flat hadn't seen a lick of paint or a new carpet since sometime in the 1970s.

"Sorry about the look of the place. It's rented from a friend. I can't afford to decorate it. Seems kind of pointless too, as it's not mine." He led her into the kitchen. "It won't be anything exciting. Just cheese and beans on toast, if that's okay? I'm not much of a chef."

"Fine by me. It's nice to have something basic. Mrs E used to try to force all sorts of strange things on me when I first met her. She tried to give me brawn and pigs' trotters. She was very disappointed when I refused it."

The grill was on and lunch was made in no time. They sat at the little table in the kitchen looking out over the view, though it wasn't much of one. Just industrial buildings and tarmac, but large picture windows ran down the whole side of the kitchen. Ada wondered why the windows were so big. Perhaps it had looked over fields and not concrete when it was built.

From behind her, Ada heard a voice. "Who's this then?"

"Oh, hi, Aunt Beth. This is Ada. Do you remember I told you about her? Ada, this is my great aunt."

Ada turned towards the voice. In front of her was a woman, perhaps in her sixties, wearing a brown and white zigzag cardigan and a knee-length skirt. A polyester scarf was tied securely under her chin and her eyes were framed by NHS glasses. Her feet were shoved into tight-fitting sensible shoes and her ankles looked swollen and puffy. Behind her, she dragged a rectangular box trolley so beloved by grannies in the 1980s.

"Good afternoon," smiled Ada.

"I'm sure it is for some!" said Aunt Beth. "My varicose veins are giving me hell again. You wouldn't believe the price of meat in the shop these days. I didn't buy anything, Neville."

"That's okay, Aunt. I'll go later."

"A cup of tea would be nice, love." She wheeled her trolley over to a spare chair and sat down, putting her leg up on another.

Neville put down his cheese toastie and ran off to fetch a drink.

"Some Garibaldi biscuits would be nice too, Neville, if you don't mind. I do love a Garibaldi, don't you? The little currants look like squashed flies."

Ada smiled in response, and Aunt Beth eyed her up and down. "So, what are you two doing today? I hear you're leading my Neville into a life of crime?" she said, chuckling, clearly enjoying her own joke. Neville popped tea and biscuits down in front of them. "Did you find out any juicy gossip?"

"Yes, Aunt, we went to Gilbert Orange's art studio to chat with him and find out more about his connection to Mary."

"Oh yes, and what did you find?" she said, as she picked up a ghostly Garibaldi and dunked it in her tea. Even though it hadn't actually been dunked, it seemed to come out soggy.

"Gilbert is a cross-dresser..." Neville started to say.

"A what, dear?" she said, appearing to turn up a hearing aid.

"A cross-dresser, Aunt."

"No, I still don't understand, Neville. Speak clearly."

"A transvestite, Aunt. Cross-dresser is the name used now."

"Oh! Why didn't you say so first time, dear? There was always a rumour at the WI that Mrs Middle's husband was a transvestite." She carried on, ignoring Neville's comment. Neville rolled his eyes at Ada. "What does that have to do with the case?"

Ada answered. "I had a vision when I touched one of his paintings. He clearly loved Mary. She was helping him to prepare for a new art exhibition about his life as a cross-dresser. He lost his emotional support when she died. He clearly wasn't her murderer; he relied on her too much."

"Oh, I see. What a strange world it is now."

"Yes, Aunt."

Neville looked across at Ada. "I think we'll go out for a walk now, Aunt. I take it you don't want to come as your veins are hurting?"

"Oh, no, thank you, dear. Don't forget to stop at the supermarket on the way back and pick up some more

Garibaldi biscuits."

"Yes, Aunt Beth."

"And do the dishes first before you go. Don't be a slob like your Great Uncle Bill."

"Yes, Aunt Beth." Neville did as she said, then they headed towards the door.

"Hold on, dear," said Aunt Beth. Neville stopped and turned. She licked a ghostly hanky and rubbed at a tiny area of Neville's face. "There you are, dear, spick and span. You always were a grubby boy."

"Thank you, Aunt." Neville forced a smile and they walked down the stairs and along the alley. Neville said nothing for a while as they made their way towards the park. When they reached it, he felt free to talk. "She's not here, is she?" Neville enquired nervously. Ada shook her head.

"I'm sorry you had to see that," he said, plonking himself down on a bench and putting his head in his hands. Ada sat next to him and put her arm on his shoulders. He turned to look at her.

"I love my aunt, as I should and all. It's just... it's just that..."

"You thought all that finished when she died and she doesn't seem to realise that you're a fully grown man now who needs to lead his own life."

"Exactly!" he said loudly, getting excited and waving his hands in the air. "She never gives me any space to make my own decisions. She even insists on coming clothes shopping with me. Most of my clothes aren't even my own choice."

"The spit on the face thing used to freak me out. I had an aunt who did that too," she said.

"I'm just glad that nobody can see it." He gave her a sideways glance. "Well, nobody but you that is. I'm so embarrassed. I wanted to make a better impression on you. I thought she'd be out for hours yet."

"Don't worry about it. If anyone understands, I do. I love my ghost friends, but sometimes I just want a little space to do my own thing and be myself. They're not as bad as your aunt though."

"She insists I make my bed and fold up my pyjamas each day."

"Well, that's a nice tidy thing to do," said Ada.

"Maybe, if she didn't make me put them in Mr Zippy, my pyjama case that I've had since I was ten years old. What sort of grown man uses a pyjama case?" He sighed and put his head in his hands again. "I don't know what to do about it, Ada. I'm going a bit stir crazy, but I don't want to offend her. I don't know why she's still here."

"Have you ever asked her?" Ada queried.

"Yes, but she keeps saying it's because I need her. I can assure you it's not."

"Why is she there in the flat? Did she follow you there?"

"It was her flat originally. She used to run the shop downstairs. She left it to my cousin, who I rent it off. He also rents the shop out downstairs."

"Have you spoken to him about it?" she said.

"No. He'd think me crazy."

"Maybe it's something to do with him rather than you?"

"Maybe. Fancy a stroll around the lake?"

They walked around the lake, as Neville called it, though it was more of a boating pond. "I'd better go and buy the Garibaldis and do some more work at the library. It's been a lovely day. See you soon, Ada. Do you know, I wouldn't mind the Garibaldis if it wasn't me that had to eat them. She insists I give her new ones every time. I can't bear to waste them, but I don't even like the bloody things."

With these parting words, he headed off towards the shops and Ada headed home.

When Ada got home, she told the ghosts about Gilbert Orange but not about Neville's aunt. She thought they might be insulted by the suggestion of her interfering in his life.

There was a loud rap on the door.

"Oh, Neville must have forgotten something!"

"I'll get it," said Dennis.

Dennis opened the door. An unknown voice was heard saying, "Hello, anyone there, can you help me?"

"Oh, not another ghost needing help!" said Ada. She got up and walked over to the hall entrance. She stopped in her tracks. It wasn't a ghost. It was a newspaper reporter.

"Ah good day! It's Miss Baker, isn't it? My name is Dustin Nevery, of the *Sudfield Times*. You might have seen my column on the strange and unusual occurrences that happen in the area? I was rather blown away to find your name connected to the twelve ghostly Spitfires the other day. I didn't know we had such a talent in our local area. I wondered if you'd mind speaking to me about it? Your experience, I mean, or anything else that you might like to share."

The Spitfire flight felt like it had happened months ago to Ada.

"Well, really, I don't know if I should. I'm not sure I want my life spread across the pages of the paper."

"Oh, please, Miss Baker. The editor has threatened to cull my slot if I don't report something more interesting soon. Another story on a piece of toast that looks like Elvis will get me fired."

She thought carefully for a minute, eyeing him up and down. He was a small late-middle-aged man of slight build and dark hair with a comb-over. He had big cow eyes and Ada reckoned that he might once have been quite handsome as a young man, but he obviously wasn't vain beyond covering his baldness, and he seemed a little unkempt. His clothes were like something out of the early 1980s. He had a long, brown leather jacket on and *Kojak*-style sunglasses rested on his head, though he wasn't obviously as comfortable with baldness.

"I do believe in ghosts, you know. I don't make anything up. Not intentionally anyway. Not everyone is honest in what they tell me. I believe in UFOs,

191

poltergeists, guardian angels, large black cats, black dogs, Herne the Hunter, psychics, telekinesis and much more. There's a lot of unexplained things in the world; it doesn't mean they're not real. We just don't know what they are."

"How did you get into this job?" asked Ada curiously.

Dustin was pleased that someone was taking an interest and he bristled with pride. "I had an experience as a young man. There was a ghost living in my house. It was a Victorian house. He used to move things around, open drawers and cupboards. He'd make loud footsteps, and at night he would walk out of my cupboard and stand at the foot of my bed. One time, when I was working in the kitchen, he even took a knife out of the kitchen drawer. It hovered above me for a second, then dropped between my legs. Not a nice ghost as it turned out. But it left me with an insatiable interest in the supernatural ever since. I read every book on the supernatural I could. I used to love reading the *Reader's Digest* book of myths and folklore as a kid. Then, as I got older, I used to go ghost hunting with my friends. I saw a ghost of a nun walk through a wall at Beneton Abbey once. After that, I decided I wanted to become a writer or journalist and communicate my love of the supernatural with everyone. I got the job with the paper twenty-five years ago, and here I've been ever since."

Ada had listened with interest, but she'd also been thinking all this time. "Okay, Mr Nevery. I'll describe my experience to you. You can print it, but there's something that I want from you too."

"Payment? I can see if the boss will pay something, but he doesn't usually."

"No, not that. I want you to investigate a case of a man that died in the old Victorian police station a hundred years ago. His name is George. He died in 1916. It was put down as suicide at the time, but he claims he was murdered by two policemen who took exception to his German ancestry and the fact that he didn't want to fight."

"He claims?" said Dustin quizzically.

"Yes, he's still there. Stuck in the same police cell where he died."

"What do you want me to do?"

"See what you can find out about him from old archives. Write a story about the injustice of it. I can tell you everything I know about him."

"Anything else?"

"Yes, you could ask people to pray for his soul. Sometimes it helps stuck ghosts to move on. Often, they're stuck here, desperate, lonely. They don't understand why an injustice like murder happened to them. Sometimes it's because they committed suicide. Because George was thought a suicide, he may not have been allowed burial in consecrated ground or a full funeral service. I've not had time yet to find out more."

"Okay, no problem. I'll run it the week after the Spitfire story."

"No, I want you to run it first, please, or no story. I won't tell you of any future experiences either."

"Okay, Miss Baker. You drive a hard bargain but you have my word."

Dustin looked pretty pleased with himself. And why not, with two new stories in the bag and no doubt big dreams of more to come? He grabbed a pencil from his pocket, opened his notepad and licked his finger to turn to a fresh page.

"Okay, fire away."

Ada told him the whole amazing story, though she chose not to mention the connection to Mary in case it compromised the case.

"Well, I'll be blowed! That's quite a story, Miss Baker. They'll give me a whole page spread for it. I have a photo of the Spitfires, would you like to see?" He produced a photo from his inside jacket pocket. It smelt strongly of tobacco, just as Dustin Nevery did. Sure enough, there was the squad of Spitfires and her little plane. The detail was a bit shaky but they were very obviously Spitfires.

"You can keep that one if you like. I have digital versions of it."

"Thank you, Mr Nevery. I'll look forward to seeing your articles."

"Good day, Miss Baker." He handed her a business card. "Here's my number if you think of anything else."

He left the house whistling the *Kojak* tune. He was obviously a fan.

194

"You kept very quiet. I thought you'd take the opportunity to spook him, Dennis?"

"I liked him. I only spook people I don't like."

Chapter 18

Ada's foot was feeling even better the next morning, thanks to her days of rest and an ice pack. She flicked on the morning news. It seemed as if the press might have forgotten about her as some huge political scandal had erupted about a member of the Cabinet having been caught sleeping with a prostitute. It was obviously much more interesting than ghosts for most people. She hoped it would be the end of it.

She thought she wouldn't hear from Matlock yet, so she made her way to Marcus Strang's address. Dennis went with her. He was loath to let her go off on her own. Ada was touched by his concern but realised there was probably also a selfish element to it. Without her, the ghosts would probably never be able to truly touch, smell or feel again.

Marcus lived on the top floor of a converted nineteenth-century mill with huge windows and beautiful architectural features. She pressed the buzzer for his flat and the lower door unlocked. She made her way upstairs and Marcus was standing at the door beaming at her. His trademark sunglasses had been removed and his dark sultry eyes ensnared her and drew her into the apartment. She swallowed hard and could feel her heart beating wildly. Ada hadn't been attracted to anyone for such a long time. He took her hand and kissed it, turning her this way and that as if they were dancing.

"You look ravishing!" he said.

Ada had worn her favourite dress. It was an elegant floaty white dress that moved beautifully as she turned. The top clung and emphasised her figure. She normally kept it for best. She cooed in response to his words and Dennis rolled his eyes.

"A small compliment, a winning smile and women become as soft as butter on a warm day," quipped Dennis.

Ada gave him a glare.

"Where are you going to photograph me?" she asked.

"Over here in my studio area." The flat had incredible light and Ada could see why he'd bought it. The sun must have shone directly into the windows nearly all day.

"I wasn't sure what you wanted when you said the essence of me, so I bought a few things related to me. I have my runes and crystals."

"It's you I want to capture. I want your inner soul to shine out," he said, placing his hand on her heart. Ada could feel her heart beat faster at his touch. He smiled at her.

"Over here on the chaise longue would be good." He arranged her how he wanted, draping the fabric of her dress, until she looked like someone reclining in a masterpiece from some forgotten age. Every element was carefully arranged. He had already set up extra lighting. He took several photographs on a digital camera.

"This is just to make sure I've got the lighting and set-up correct. I'm old-fashioned, I prefer using real film cameras. It has a better quality than digital images, I think."

Marcus arranged her in various poses during the morning. She didn't feel it was the right time to mention Mary again while he was photographing, but they took a break at about one for lunch.

"I thought we'd eat in, if you don't mind. It's only a chicken salad, but I have a nice cold bottle of white wine to wash it down with."

Marcus talked a lot about his art and photography, and Dennis was clearly highly bored. In the end, he said, "I've had enough, Ada. I'm off for a walk and some fresh air. I've learnt more about photography in half a day than I did in a lifetime. Marcus seems okay, do you mind?" She shook her head.

Once Dennis had gone, Ada felt a little more at ease around Marcus.

"They're going to be beautiful images," he said. "Would you like to see my darkroom where I develop the photos?"

"Sure," she said.

He led her through to what might normally have been a bedroom, she guessed, but the window had been completely blacked out. Bottles and jars of chemicals lined the shelves and developing trays were stacked around. Photos were hung up around the room drying. He started to explain the process. "But of course, when I'm developing the photos, I have the red light on so the images don't get damaged." He flicked the red light on and the feeling of the room changed suddenly. Ada could feel a tenseness between them. He reached forward and kissed her gently on the lips. When she didn't pull away, he kissed her deeper and more passionately. Ada was trembling. She hadn't been kissed like that for a long time.

"I'm sorry," he said. "Do you want me to stop? I thought you were interested in me. I always had the feeling when we were at college that you liked me, but I was your teacher so I couldn't do anything then."

"I did... I am interested... It's just been a traumatic week and quite a while since I kissed anyone."

He gave her his most winning smile. "I'll make us a coffee," he said, and left her in the darkroom.

It had felt nice to feel and do something so human and unconnected to her everyday life. She loved her ghost friends, but Ada was still a young woman and she realised how much she was missing connections with living people. How she missed normality. How much she missed a relationship, and if she was being honest with herself, how much she'd missed sex. She hadn't had a relationship of any sort for four years. She felt giddy for a second and put her hand behind her to steady herself. Suddenly, that familiar feeling came over her again, just as she'd felt in Mary's bathroom. Images started to form in her mind. She was back at Mary's house. She saw the back door being opened by a man's hand with a key. The man went up the stairs to the bathroom and there in the bath was Mary, lying dead. The man appeared to be shocked for a few seconds. Then he seemed to check if she was breathing and if she had a pulse. He paused, got out his phone, then put it down. Instead, he reached down into his bag and pulled out a camera. Ada could see Mary through the eye of the camera. The man took several photos, then grabbed his bag, went back downstairs and relocked the door. Then the vision faded away. Ada swung round and looked at what she was touching. It was a photography notebook, listing details of lenses, filters and exposures used, but tucked in the middle of it was a photograph. It was a photograph of Mary in the bath, naked and dead. There was something hauntingly beautiful about it. She walked out into the flat to get a better look at it. Marcus was coming back with the mugs of coffee in his hand. He saw Ada's expression and the photograph in her hand. He put the coffee down on the table and walked over to her, putting his hands on her shoulders.

"I can explain."

"You were there! You did go into the house. You lied

to me. You photographed her when she was dead! You didn't call for help. You photographed her."

He sat down heavily on a chair and put his head in his hands. "I was going to call straight away, but I was struck by how serene and beautiful she looked. She'd been my muse for a while. Somehow it felt right to document it. I could tell she was dead, and there was nothing I could do to help her. I knew that as soon as I called the police the chance would be lost, my films taken from me. The moment would be lost forever. I think it's one of the best photographs I've ever taken, but now I can't even show it to anyone. I would also have been their number one suspect if I'd called from inside her house. I didn't kill her, Ada, though, I promise."

Ada looked at the photograph again. There was indeed a serene beauty in it. She looked like a modern-day Ophelia, her hair floating around her. It was reminiscent of the nineteenth-century painting by Millais.

"You have to go to the police and tell them this. They're searching through William Kent's footage of her house right now. Very soon, they're going to come and speak to you anyway. We should go and speak to Inspector Matlock."

"William Kent?"

"It's a long story. I'll explain on the way. In fact, I know where the inspector lives. He said he wasn't working today anyway. Let's head there now. He'll know the best thing to do."

Marcus nodded. They grabbed their jackets, headed out the door and Marcus drove them. There was no sign of Matlock in his garden when they arrived. Ada knocked nervously at the door. It took a moment for him to answer. He was very surprised to see her, especially with Marcus Strang.

"Ada… What are you doing here?"

"Marcus has a confession. We weren't quite sure what to do and I thought it might be best if we spoke to you first. Sorry to disturb you on your day off."

"Not at all. Come in." He beckoned for them to come through.

Jolly was sitting in his usual spot by the window.

"Ada, good to see you. How are you? How's the foot?" said Jolly.

Matlock, being unable to hear Jolly, repeated almost the same question.

"I'm feeling better thanks. The ankle is a lot better. I'm here because I've been with Marcus today. He's been photographing me, but there's something he needs to tell you about Mary."

Matlock gave Marcus one of his best querying looks.

"I was there. The day that Mary was murdered. I was supposed to be photographing her for a project. I found the key hidden in the tree and I let myself in. It was an arrangement we used a lot. I went upstairs and she was dead. I was going to call the police straight away but I could tell she was dead. She looked so beautiful, so serene, so I took a photograph of her. I know it will seem strange to you, but we capture the moment someone comes into this world and we rarely ever capture the moment that someone leaves it. Why not, I wonder? We're all so afraid of death. We bury it away as something unclean and unfit for conversation. The Victorians photographed their dead loved ones. I thought she looked more beautiful in death than she ever had in life. We give the dead and dying such little dignity. Mary would have understood. She loved art. I was afraid that you wouldn't understand why I'd done it and think that I was the murderer."

"Well, there is always the possibility," said Matlock. "I can't pretend to understand your motives. May I see the photograph?"

Marcus handed it over and Matlock examined it for a while. Inspector Jolly stared over his shoulder at it. "Do you have more photos? Do you have the negatives?"

"Yes, there are a few more. The negatives are in my flat."

"Right, well, I think we'd better go and collect them and take you to the station for questioning. I don't think it can wait till tomorrow. Come on. Ada, do you want a lift home?" Matlock asked. He looked a little cold and disapproving.

"Do you mind if I stay and talk to Inspector Jolly for a while?" she said.

Matlock looked around the room. "No, I guess not.

Just make sure you lock the door on the way out." He led Marcus Strang out and they drove off in his car.

"So, our list of suspects grows ever smaller," said Inspector Jolly.

"It seems so," said Ada.

"Ada, do you have feelings for Marcus Strang? It's not my business, I know. I was just curious."

"How did you guess? Yes, I knew him at art college. He was one of the teachers. He taught me photography. I do still have feelings for him."

"Just wondering, that's all." He smiled and looked wistful. "Subtle ways that you looked at him. That, and the fact you spent the day with him. Don't just settle for anyone, Ada. I married the first woman that took my fancy, but we weren't a good match and we spent many unhappy years together before we finally realised. I missed out on my chance to have children, as she never wanted any. You only have one life. Make the best of it."

Ada looked at him. There were depths to people's souls that weren't always apparent on the surface. Even in the dead.

"What did you think of the photograph of Mary? Matlock clearly wasn't impressed," said Ada, changing the subject.

"Give David a chance, Ada. He sees dead bodies in a different light to most people. They're his work, a problem to be solved, not a work of art, but yes, I could see the artistry in it. He's right, of course. Our modern conception that death should be something hidden behind the curtains, never to be seen, is probably unhealthy. Maybe the Victorians were more in touch with the realities of life and death than we are now, where death is sterilised and whitewashed before it's presented to us. But the question for us now is, if Kent wasn't the murderer and Marcus Strang says he wasn't, who does that leave?"

"Gilbert Orange and Mary's sister Ellen. Or someone that we haven't even thought of yet. I spoke to Gilbert yesterday and found out a bit more about him. I had a vision of him in ladies' clothes with Mary. He's a cross-dresser. He has been all his life. Mary was helping him to set up his new exhibition. I felt he had a deep love for her. I don't think there's any way he killed her. She was his only release to talk about his passion."

"Okay, Ada, let's look at Ellen's motives then."

"Well, they'd never seen eye to eye. Mary's mother didn't seem to like Ellen much. She left her house to Mary and not Ellen. They both act like it wasn't a problem, but I'm not so sure. And…" She paused mid-sentence.

"What, Ada?"

"Well, she seems a little obsessed with Marcus, judging by what he said. She'd been to his show sixteen times already. She did seem rather like a groupie when I chatted to her. I've just experienced obsession and it's not a pretty thing. Kent was obsessed with me, or the idea of me. He truly thought that we could have some kind of relationship. Having been through that, it made me see Ellen in a different light. Perhaps she was jealous of his time with Mary."

Inspector Jolly put his hand on hers to reassure her, but it just passed through. "If you need to talk about it, Ada, I'm always here. Maybe your other ghostly friends don't understand, but I've seen a lot of sorrow in my life. I see how it can destroy lives and be a very unsettling experience. Several officers suffered PTSD after harrowing experiences. Don't bottle it up."

He removed his hand and carried on. "So, it seems that Ellen is now looking like the only one with motive, but there's no evidence to link her with the crime scene and she has an alibi. Did you say that Mary had said Ellen was to inherit the house? It certainly seems like a big motive. Do we know her whereabouts for the time of the murder?"

"No, I never asked that when I went before – she wasn't high on my suspect list. Mary was so sure it must be Kent. What can we do? Talk to her again? She's hardly going to admit to murder. If there's no evidence, the police can't arrest her on motive alone, surely?"

"It would help if we could find out what her alibi is. The police must have questioned her but we don't know what she said. I'll see if I can find out from Matlock."

"I don't think we'll find out anything else useful from Gilbert Orange," said Ada.

"Why don't you get yourself home, you still look tired from your ordeal. I'll walk with you."

They locked up and left. Ada was glad of the company on the way home, although the inspector said very little. They were both deep in their own thoughts.

Dennis was glad to see her when she got in as she'd not been at Marcus Strang's flat when he'd returned. He'd arrived in time to see Marcus being led off to the station by Inspector Matlock. She reassured them she was fine and explained the situation.

Ada spent the rest of the day writing letters or sending e-mails to the loved ones or otherwise of the spirits who had been to see her. Her life was becoming even stranger than it had been.

Chapter 19

The next day, Ada was desperate to know what had happened with Marcus, but neither Marcus nor Matlock were answering their mobiles. She tried to focus on sending the ghosts requests, but it was hard to concentrate and she ended up pacing backwards and forwards.

"At least turn your nervous energy into something positive and do some cleaning," said Rose.

Ada agreed and relaxed her mind so she could let Rose in. Rose's calm, methodical cleaning and humming settled her nerves a bit. She could feel Rose's deep love for a cleanly scrubbed floor and a tidy home. When she'd finished, the kitchen sparkled and shone like new. Rose withdrew from Ada and stood back, taking satisfaction in a job well done.

"It looks marvellous, Rose, thank you."

It was early afternoon when the phone rang. It was Marcus. "Ada, it's Marcus. I wanted to know if you'd come over for a coffee and a chat so I can explain what I did."

Ada paused in thought for a moment. "Okay," she agreed hesitantly.

Dennis was adamant he should come with her again but Ada wanted a bit of privacy to chat with Marcus on her own and so she put her foot down.

When she arrived, he looked harrowed and tired but pleased to see her. He made them coffee and explained what had happened during their time apart.

"The police kept me in the station overnight. They questioned me a lot. I believe they think I might be the killer. I lied about being there. I took a photo of her. They have me pegged as numero uno suspect. They released me on bail this afternoon as I'd been so co-operative, but they still think it's me, I'm sure of it. I don't know what else to say or do, Ada. I really didn't do it. You do believe me, don't you?"

"I know it's been a while since we were close, but I feel I know you, and yes I believe it wasn't you. My vision showed me that it wasn't."

"Do you definitely think it wasn't Kent who did it?" he asked.

"Apart from his extremely creepy behaviour to Mary and me, as far as I'm aware, there is no actual evidence to link him to the scene on the day of the murder. I'm sorry, I don't know what to suggest. We thought about checking out Ellen's alibi. She has the biggest motive of anyone to want Mary dead but I'm unsure how to bring the question up."

"Ellen's harmless, I think. She's all blueberry pie and

chintz. She seems a gentle soul. I can't imagine her doing anything, but I can go and chat to her if you like. She might be more likely to talk to me."

"Well, if that doesn't affect your situation with the police?" Ada replied.

"It can't make it much worse, can it? I've been worried about what you think of me now because of this. Do you think I'm weird? I was worried you might not want to talk to me again."

"I can't pretend to fully understand what you did, but my mother was very artistic and I understand how artists see the world in a different way to everyone else. Despite its subject matter, it was a very beautiful image. I agree. I think Mary would love it."

"I'm glad but I want to forget about it all for the moment. Would you like to help me develop the photos of you?"

"I'd love to."

Marcus showed her into the darkroom, put on the red light and took her through the process of developing. Unlike the immediacy of digital photography, it took time to get an image using film and there was always the chance of the photo being dreadful at the end. It was more expensive, too, than clicking a few digital images. Marcus had studied at the same art college as Ada and learnt the skill there. He'd been given his first camera by his grandfather when he was ten years old, and this had clearly had a profound effect on him. As he put the photo in the solution, she could see the image starting to develop. He hung the photo up to dry and she stared in wonder at it. He had indeed seemed to capture her very soul. He'd made her look mysterious and even a little ethereal. She never knew she could look that pretty. It was as if, somehow, he had brought out her inner beauty.

"You've taken my breath away. It's gorgeous."

"It's easy when you have a beautiful model." He lifted up her chin and kissed her softly again, then more passionately as before. He was an extremely good kisser and Ada felt herself overcome with passion. He held her tightly round the waist and looked into her eyes, tenderly playing with one of her kiss curls.

"Ada, I have always wanted to make love to you, ever since we first met at college. I always thought you felt the same. Do you feel the same?" he said, with an urgency in his voice.

There was a vulnerability and a need in his eyes that she'd not seen before. She didn't want to be yet another conquest but somehow, she felt that this was something more. She bit her lip and nodded. She was nervous, as it had been so long and she'd only had two lovers before. He could see the fear in her eyes.

"I'll be gentle, I promise." He took her hand and led her slowly towards the bed. The flat had no curtains but he assured her that nobody would be watching. Marcus was an expert lover – gentle, thoughtful and beyond anything Ada had ever known before. Her whole body glowed with a soft warmth. She didn't want to leave

Marcus afterwards and spent most of the day with him. She knew if she didn't return though, the ghosts would be tearing their proverbial hair out with worry. He'd wanted to drive her home but she wanted the walk to have time to think, so she kissed him goodbye.

On her route home, however, she suddenly felt rebellious, had a change of mind and found her feet wending their way to Inspector Matlock's home.

There had been soft rain that afternoon and the scent of roses was heavy in the air. She knocked loudly at the door and David Matlock appeared, dressed casually in shorts and a T-shirt.

"Oh, come in, Ada, I was just about to have some dinner. Do you want some?" She hadn't realised how hungry she was till he asked so she agreed and thanked him. He showed her into the kitchen. The oven was on, vegetables had been chopped and were simmering in a pan. Matlock took a large ready-made lasagne out of the oven. "It's my favourite meal. A pack this size normally does me four meals, but it's nice to share it for once. I don't have much time to prepare food, my job keeps me so busy, so I have to live off a lot of ready meals. In fact, I don't have much of a social life... or a love life." Matlock looked thoughtful for a moment. He went to the fridge and handed Ada a cold beer.

"Where's Jolly?" she asked, supping on its icy coolness.

"Oh, is he not here? I wouldn't know. I think he's been trying out his new abilities. I keep finding things have been moved when I return home. I keep saying good morning to George. I'm not sure if he likes that or not. It's hard to talk to someone you can't see."

Ada looked towards the toilet door. George was peering round it and gave her a thumbs up.

"He likes it, he appreciates it. Thank you for thinking of him. It's very lonely being dead with nobody to talk to."

"Some of the prisoners had talked of seeing a ghost in the cells but I'd always ignored them. I thought it was a way to try and get out of the cell. I never believed they were telling the truth."

"Have you got any further in the case?"

"I shouldn't really talk about it, but you've been so involved with it throughout. I don't normally talk this casually with people I've just met but you, you're different somehow. I suppose you've talked to Marcus Strang today?"

Ada looked coy and avoided eye contact with Matlock. "Yes, he told me. He's your number one suspect."

"There's very little evidence pointing to anyone else. We can place him arriving at the scene at about the time we thought the murder happened. He admitted to being there. He even took a photo of the murder victim. It doesn't look good, I'm afraid. We're probably going to charge him with the crime." He paused for a second and looked at her as he sipped his beer. "I need to ask. Are you in a relationship with Marcus?"

Ada was shocked by the blunt question and blushed. "Well, I wouldn't call it a relationship yet…" She found herself opening up to him. "It's been such a long time since I had a relationship. My life is a little odd at the best of times. Most people think I'm crazy when I mention ghosts. You're one of the first people in a long time that's believed me."

"It's hard not to after what I've experienced in the last week. I think a lot more people will be believers after seeing those Spitfires."

"Not just people. The dead have been coming in droves to see me so I can pass on messages to their loved ones. There must have been a hundred of them waiting in the street for me the other day."

Matlock choked on his beer. "Really? Wow! And will you pass on their messages?"

"Yes, of course. I have a gift. I realise now I should be helping as many of them as I can."

"You really are a special person, Ada. I'm glad I met you. Even if it has been in such peculiar circumstances."

Ada felt this was an unusual and sincere moment from the inspector and that he didn't say such things often. Perhaps it was something to do with his relaxed mood today. She looked around his kitchen. It was very ordered and quite homely. On a shelf, she noticed several trophies.

"What are the trophies for? Judo?"

"Kung fu."

"Really? I'm a green belt, what about you?" she

asked.

"I'm a black belt. I've studied it since I was a child. I used to enter a lot of competitions, but I don't have the time these days... or the heart it seems. My parents used to go with me to all the competitions. Since they passed, I've not really had the drive, but it's still a passion."

"So, you're an orphan too, Inspector?"

"I'd not really thought of it like that, but yes, I guess so. Please call me David at home. Where do you train?" he queried.

"With Jian, down at the Chinese restaurant. His dad taught him before he died. I tell Jian and Mrs Lee what Mr Lee wants to say to them and Mr Lee teaches us."

David laughed. "You really do lead an extraordinary life."

Something was playing on her mind. "David, do you not think that Mary's sister might have been guilty of the murder?"

"She's got motive certainly, and we did check her out, but we couldn't place her anywhere near the scene of the crime. Her phone was at home and her friend Mabel from the WI says she was with her at the time of the murder. There are no fingerprints or DNA evidence linking her to the scene. I realise it must be frustrating for you. I'm very sorry, Ada."

They finished the meal and talked of trivial things. When he wasn't being uptight about a murder case, David was quite fun to be around. When they finished, he offered to walk her home. He was quite old-fashioned and she liked that about him.

When they got to her gate, Ada had enjoyed her evening so much she almost didn't want it to finish. She remembered something that Jian had told her. "Jian says that there's a kung fu competition taking place at the local school in three weeks' time. Perhaps if all this is over and you have time, you might like to enter. We could both enter."

He smiled. "I'll think about it."

"If I'm being honest, David, I spend too much time with ghosts and I could use some living friends for a change. It's been really lovely talking to you this evening." She leaned over and gave him a peck on the cheek, which took him by surprise. It was Matlock's turn to feel embarrassed.

"Okay, Ada, but let's get through this investigation first."

She nodded and turned off down the path into her house. The door opened on its own and gently shut behind her.

***

David reached up to his cheek. He could still feel the gentle touch of her lips.

"Hmmm," he said, then pivoted on his feet and walked home.

***

Marcus Strang had given his report of what really happened when he had visited Mary to the police. His soul did feel a bit lighter for telling the truth. He was relieved that Ada hadn't disowned him for it. He even felt like she could be the one worth settling down for. He'd done as she'd asked and given the photos and negatives to the police as requested, but he still had a spare copy of the photographs. After Ada left, he spread them out on his breakfast bar. He got out a magnifier and started looking more closely at them. He looked intensely for some minutes, scanning every little detail. "What the hell!" he said. He picked up his tablet and used its magnify option to take a close-up image of the photo. "Jesus!" he said, and saved it to his backup folder. Then he picked up his phone and started dialling.

Chapter 20

Ada woke the next day and she felt amazing. Warm sunshine streamed in her room and a robin was singing on the wisteria outside her window. She got straight up and opened it. It was a glorious day to match her glorious mood. She got dressed and seemed to float rather than walk downstairs.

"Good morning!" she said, beaming sunnily at the ghosts. "Isn't it wonderful?"

"What is, dear?" said Mrs Entwhistle.

"Oh, just everything! I think I'll have a full monty for breakfast today, Mrs E. Bacon, eggs, mushrooms, the lot, please."

Dennis nudged Rose and gave her a wink. Rose tried to stifle a giggle.

"So, who's the lucky dog?" he asked. "Marcus or the inspector?"

Ada's cheeks blushed rose pink. "I don't know what you mean." She thought on what Dennis had said. She'd certainly never really thought of David like that, although she had enjoyed his company the previous night.

"Full breakfast it is!" said Mrs Entwhistle, not understanding Dennis's lewd comments. She merged into Ada and very soon was cooking up a large fried breakfast. A merry whistling came from the kitchen. "That's very distracting, dear," said Mrs Entwhistle using Ada's mouth.

"Sorry!" said Ada. She stopped whistling and tried not to think about Marcus. Very soon breakfast was ready.

Ada enjoyed the food and ate as if she hadn't seen food for a week. She had hoped Marcus might have texted her already this morning. She kept checking her phone every few minutes.

"That was ace, Mrs E. Thank you so much."

"My pleasure!" said Mrs Entwhistle, bristling with pride. "What's your plan for today then?"

"I thought I might wander over to see Marcus. See how his photographs are looking. He said he might make a photo book for me of the best images. We were going to go through them today and pick my favourites."

"I see," said Dennis.

"Can I come with you?" said Rose. "I'd love to see them."

"I'm not sure Ada wants company," he suggested, giving Rose a wink.

"I don't mind. It'd be a pleasure to have your company," said Ada, glaring at Dennis. "He doesn't know about you lot yet though, so I won't be able to talk directly to you." She paused. "I'm choosing the right moment to tell him that I live with three ghosts."

Rose looked worried for a second. "Ada, if you find love with Marcus or someone else, would you need us to leave?" she said earnestly.

"No, if someone loves me, they need to love my friends too. Living or dead ones. There's no negotiation."

"Thank you!" said Rose, much relieved. "Let's go, shall we?"

"If it's all right, I'd like to come too," said Dennis. "And me!" said Mrs Entwhistle.

Ada and the ghosts left the house and headed off towards Marcus's flat. Ada chatted excitedly all the way, talking about her day with Marcus and her evening with the inspector.

When she got there and buzzed him, there was no answer.

"Strange, it's too early for the gallery. I'm not sure if he's even opening it this week considering. His car is here."

Just then, another car pulled into the space beside Marcus's and a young Indian lady wearing the most beautiful midnight blue sari that Ada had ever seen stepped out. It was threaded all over with silver stars.

"Excuse me," Ada began. "I've come to visit Marcus but there's no answer. I wondered if his buzzer was broken. Do you mind letting me in so I can go up to his flat and knock, please?"

"Certainly, no problem," she said, watching Ada.

"Have you seen him today?" Ada asked.

"No, I've been staying at my parents over a long weekend. I haven't been here for days."

She let Ada in, and the ghosts made their way upstairs. Ada knocked tentatively at Marcus's door, quietly at first. When this received no response, she knocked louder.

"Maybe he's having a shower. Let's wait a few minutes." Ada paced outside the door.

"Perhaps he's nipped down to the shops for a pint of milk?" said Rose.

"Maybe, but wouldn't he be back by now?"

They waited a few more minutes, then Ada's spine startled to tingle with a sense of dread. Was he all right, or was he with another woman perhaps? Maybe he hadn't been as sincere as he'd seemed.

Finally, she said, "I hate to invade his privacy, but Dennis, could you slip in there and see if he's in. Just so I know."

"No problem!" said Dennis, who slipped through the door.

***

The flat was flooded with light as usual, and Dennis turned to look at the kitchen. There, hanging from a cast-iron roof support, was Marcus Strang, his body hanging limp. Dennis didn't need to check for a pulse. Being dead gave you a pretty good idea when someone else was dead or not. Beneath his body was a kicked over stool. The photos of Ada that Marcus had taken were strung across the room. Someone had taken a red marker pen and defaced most of them.

***

A couple of minutes later, he came back. If it was possible for a ghost to lose pallor from his face, then Dennis had.

"Well, is he there?" Ada said.

Dennis nodded.

"Why isn't he letting us in? Is he with someone?"

He shook his head. "Ada... he's dead. He's hung himself."

"What? That's not possible. Just yesterday we spent the whole day chatting. He wouldn't have hung himself. Let me in." She rushed to the door and started pushing it. "Let me in!"

Dennis pulled her round. "Ada, we have to do this properly. You've seen the TV shows. We need to call the police. You can't go in or you'll pollute the scene with your DNA and fingerprints. Call Inspector Matlock. Call David."

"Are you sure he's dead? He might need help?" she said desperately, tears flowing from her eyes. "How has he killed himself?"

"He hung himself, Ada," he repeated.

"Why would he do that?" she said, sobbing.

"Call the police, Ada. It's the best thing you can do for him now."

Ada pulled the phone from her pocket and dialled Inspector Matlock's number.

"Hello, Matlock speaking."

Ada sobbed down the phone.

"Ada? Is that you?" he said, sounding concerned.

"M-M-Marcus... Marcus is dead. Dennis says he's hung himself."

"Where are you?" asked David.

"I'm outside his flat... in the hallway."

"Okay, stay there. Don't get Dennis to let you in. I'll be over asap. Hold on, we won't be long." He hung up.

Ada slid down the wall and sat there crying. "He can't be dead. He can't be dead," she kept repeating over and over again.

It must have only been five minutes before the police arrived, but it felt like forever to Ada. They were furiously knocking and ringing downstairs. The Indian lady came out of her apartment and let them in and was astonished to see Matlock and several police come rushing up the stairs. Ada recognised several of them from the airfield. Matlock went straight to Ada and put his arm around her.

"Come on, Ada, let's take you downstairs. Break the door down will you, Wilson?"

The Indian lady heard him. "Hold on, officer. My

name is Miss Ahuja. I have a key for his flat. I own the building and lease the flat to Mr Strang, so I have a spare." She disappeared for a minute, then came back with a key. "What's the matter?" she asked.

"I'm very sorry to say that we believe Mr Strang may have hung himself. Can you make Ada and yourself a cup of tea and I'll be down to chat to you both later?"

"Oh my goodness!" she said, sounding shocked. "He was such a lovely man. Come on, Ada. What a shock. Let's go get a nice cup of sweet milky tea." She led Ada off to her apartment, putting her arm around her shoulder to steady her.

***

Some of the officers had already suited up and gone into Marcus's apartment.

"He definitely seems dead, sir. He's cold," one of them said.

Matlock slipped coveralls over his clothes and feet and put on some gloves so he didn't contaminate the scene. Then he walked into Marcus's flat. He looked around the flat until he saw Marcus hanging from the iron beam. He walked up to him and reached up to feel if he had a pulse, but there wasn't one and the body felt cold, as if he'd been dead for hours. He'd been hung with a piece of light flex formed into a hangman's noose. It had bitten tightly into his neck and his eyes were bulging slightly. It seemed an unusual choice to choose to hang oneself with. He looked at the stool underneath. It certainly seemed to have been kicked away. Photographs of Ada were hung up around the room. He examined them closely. They'd nearly all been defaced.

"I see," he said out loud.

He wandered over to the bed. A folded note sat on the pillow, addressed to Ada. He picked it up and read it. It was written in capitals.

DEAR ADA, I'M SORRY BUT I CAN'T LIVE WITH MYSELF ANY MORE. I COMMITTED THE MURDER OF MARY WATTS. THE LAW WILL CATCH UP WITH ME SOON SO I'M TAKING THE COWARD'S WAY OUT. I'M SORRY IF YOU THOUGHT I HAD FEELINGS FOR YOU. MARCUS.

"Hmmm…" said David. "Curious."

It took some time for the forensics team to come and check the scene and for photographs to be taken. While they were doing their work, David went downstairs to speak with Ada. He wandered into the apartment.

He looked at his notes. "Miss… Ahuja, may I have a word with Miss Baker in private, please. Do you mind? Then I'd like one with yourself."

"No problem. I'll make us a coffee, shall I?"

"That'd be lovely, thank you." She sauntered off to the kitchen and soon the sound of coffee beans being ground could be heard.

"Ada," he said, putting his hand on hers. "I'm sorry. I know you liked Marcus." She nodded. "Can you tell me exactly what happened? Start with why there are photos of you hanging all over his flat."

Ada had calmed down a little and was no longer sobbing uncontrollably, but talked with the hiccupping talk of someone that had been crying a lot. "He… asked me… over on Monday to take some photos. He said… I was his new muse. I was flattered and curious. We spent… Monday taking the photos. I saw the photo of Mary by accident. I touched it and had a psychic vision of Marcus discovering Mary's body and taking a photo of her."

"Aha, okay, go on, please," he said, furiously scribbling everything down.

"He admitted to me… what had happened… and I told him to go to you and tell the truth… so he did. You know what happened after that till he was granted bail."

"Then what happened yesterday?"

"He phoned me. He wanted me… to come over so that we could talk about what had happened. So I… went over. He was worried that I wouldn't understand why he'd done what he'd done. I said I did understand. Then he asked me to help develop the photos he'd taken on Monday. We did. Then…" Ada paused. She looked up at the inspector and looked away. "Then we made love." She looked up at him. His expression was blank and he was writing down everything she said.

"I see," he said.

"I'm not normally like that, David, I promise. I hadn't said before but I knew Marcus from college. He

226

was my teacher there, and I'd had such a crush on him then. When I met him again, all my feelings rushed back in. It has been so long since there was anyone. He told me he'd always felt the same as me and we just felt a connection to each other…"

"Understandable, I'm sure. I'd prefer 'Inspector' at work though, if you don't mind," he said, a little coolly. "Anything else?"

"Oh, of course, call you Inspector at work. Yes, you did say. We… we were also chatting about who the murderer might be if it wasn't Kent. We wondered about Ellen Watts. Marcus said that he was going to speak with Ellen."

"Impossible," he said. "Marcus was a fit young man. Ellen is only a small woman. I don't think she would have the strength to strangle him and hang him from the roof. What makes you think she's the suspect?" he asked.

"She's connected with both murder victims. She had the biggest incentive to murder her sister. She… she was obsessed with Marcus. When I went to see her, she told me she'd only been to see his gallery exhibition twice, but Marcus said she'd been sixteen times to see it already. She arrived again while I was there. She buys his work. She appeared in a magazine article where he photographed her in her home. She had an unhealthy obsession, I'd say."

"Some might say you have an unhealthy obsession with him too," he said, quite bluntly. Ada felt the sting of this comment and wondered why he'd made it. "At what time did you leave his flat yesterday?" he continued.

"Just a little while before I arrived at yours. I was going to go straight home but I wanted to talk to you."

He paused as he wrote down his notes. "And... and he was alive when you left the flat?"

It suddenly dawned on Ada what he might be thinking. "Yes, he was alive. We'd had a lovely afternoon together. I didn't kill him, if that's what you're thinking. Why would you think that? What motive could I have for killing him?"

"None I can think of, but my job requires that I ask you. You're the last person we know of who saw him alive. Apart from perhaps his murderer. His body was cold, so he'd been dead some hours. The lab will need to determine how long. I'll get one of the officers to run you home after your coffee. You've had a nasty shock."

Miss Ahuja wandered back over with the coffee. "Thank you, Miss Ahuja. We'll take Miss Baker home shortly, and sorry for the disruption. We'll be as quick as we can upstairs. We'll need to keep the key for now. Is this the only other copy?"

"Yes, Inspector, no problem."

Ada finished her coffee and PC Wilson drove her home. She sat in the back seat. Dennis squeezed her hand. She could feel it as a light pressure. Nobody said anything on the short journey home.

"Would you like me to see you in, miss?" She paused

at her gate. "No, thank you, I'm fine," she said dreamily. The car pulled away and she walked up to her front door. Dennis slipped through and opened it from the inside. The door seemed to open of its own accord and Ada wandered in.

Chapter 21

Ada was distraught. Marcus was the first close connection she'd made with a living human being in a long time. Tears started to stream down her face as she walked through the door. Very soon they were a flood as she let out all her pent-up emotion. She screamed out loud.

"Ada, can we do anything for you?" said Dennis tenderly. Just then, there was a rap at the door.

"Can you see who that is please, Den?" she asked. Dennis stuck his head through the door then came back in.

"I think it's the man to read the gas meter. That's what he looks like."

Ada groaned and buried her face in a cushion. "Leave it, he'll go away."

"Is there anything else we can do for you, poppet?" said Mrs Entwhistle.

Ada looked up at her with puffy eyes. "Would you mind if I had some time on my own, please? I need a little space to think."

"Certainly, if that's what you feel would be best for you," she said concernedly. "Come on, Rose, Dennis."

They left Ada on her own to think. She tucked her knees up to her chest and hugged them, her feet on the sofa. She couldn't understand why Marcus would choose to kill himself. There was nothing in his behaviour that had suggested he was even contemplating suicide. He had to have been murdered, but she didn't understand why? Or who? Why would Ellen want to kill Marcus if she liked him so much? It didn't make sense, unless perhaps she was an obsessive like William Kent. Could it be that Ellen was jealous of Ada?

"Oh, it all seems so ridiculous," she said. Inspector Matlock was right, Ellen seemed much more 'peaches and cream' than 'blood and thunder'. She stood up and looked at her reflected image in the mirror. Her puffy eyes made her look hideous. She stared at her reflection, pondering what had happened, hating herself. Had she been the cause of Marcus's death? Where was Marcus's spirit now? Why wasn't he in the flat? Why hadn't he come to her? Perhaps he'd gone straight into the light, but it was unusual for a murder victim to pass straight on. Ada had heard from several ghosts of their experience of seeing a light-filled doorway, but she didn't know what was on the other side of it, as the only ghosts she knew had never gone through the door. Usually because they had been murdered, died suddenly, committed suicide or had some sort of unfinished business.

Eventually, she looked away and up at the clock. Forty-five minutes had passed while she'd been standing there lost in her own soulful thoughts. She hated whoever had done this. She had been sad for Mary and wanted to help her, but now she was more invested in the case than she ever planned to be. She had to find out who had done this. She was more determined than ever. Who was left? Gilbert? Ellen? Or had Kent been the killer all along and just fooled her? Had Marcus been talking to Ellen like he promised he would? It did seem unlikely that she would be able to overpower a fit adult man. Ada was at a loss. The only thing she could think to do was to call Neville. She picked up her phone and dialled his number. It went straight to voicemail.

"Neville, it's Ada... I'm sorry to bother you but something really awful happened today." She paused as she tried to gather her thoughts. "Marcus died. It looks like suicide but I think it was murder. I don't understand why he would kill himself. I've been thinking on it for ages. There's more. I... I went to have some photos taken at his flat. Just straightforward photos. It seems you were right. He had lied. I found out he was there just after Mary had died. He took a photo of her but said he didn't kill her. He went to the police when I asked. And... we were intimate. Oh, it's all a big muddle. Can we meet? Can I talk with you? I know it's not your problem, but I think that we're friends, even though we've only known each other a short while, and I feel lost. I don't know what to do." The phone cut off as she'd reached the maximum message length. She sighed, hugged her knees and started crying again.

Chapter 22

The next morning, the phone rang quite early at about eight a.m. It was Neville. She answered sleepily. She'd found it hard to get to sleep but in the end she had fallen off to sleep through exhaustion. Her eyes were still sore from all the crying.

"Ada, I'm so sorry I wasn't there when you called yesterday. I was working. I'll be straight over. I'm leaving now. See you in twenty."

Ada dragged herself out of bed, had a quick shower and threw on some clothes. When she got downstairs, Dennis had already put the kettle on. She made a large pot of tea and sat staring into her mug, cradling it tightly between her hands.

"How are you feeling this morning, Ada?" asked Mrs Entwhistle. Just then, there was a furious knocking at the door.

"Neville's coming over. That's probably him. Could you check, Dennis, please?"

It was indeed Neville, and he came straight up to Ada and hugged her. He just held her for a whole minute, then pulled himself up onto the chair beside her. She poured them both a tea.

"So what happened? Start at the beginning."

Ada described everything that had happened since she'd seen him the previous week. He listened quietly and thoughtfully. When she'd finished, they both sat there for a few moments in silence.

Neville put his hand on hers. "I'm sorry for your loss. I could see that you liked him but I didn't realise your affections ran that deep. I guess I was wrong about him committing the murder. Have you heard anything from Inspector Matlock?"

"Not yet. I guess they're sifting through the evidence."

"Do you believe he really thinks you're guilty?"

"No, I don't think so. I think he was just following routine procedure. Perhaps if he hadn't experienced so many unusual events recently, he might have done. I don't know if he's found any new evidence, but he'll probably keep it from me now. Perhaps he won't want to see me at all. It's a shame. I enjoyed his company the other night. I had hoped to make a new friend."

"It's odd that Marcus's ghost wasn't there, I agree. Do you really feel up to going further though, Ada? It's been a very dangerous experience so far. What's to say that the murderer won't pick on you next?"

"Nothing, but how does the saying go? All it takes for evil to prosper is for good men to do nothing. What happens if I do leave it? Will the murderer not go on to kill the next person to get in their way? They've already killed twice. I may not be a heroine but I have gifts more than ordinary folk. Matlock might solve it on his own, but I feel it's my duty to try, for Marcus's sake."

"Okay, well then, I think the next step is to speak with Ellen again, but I'm coming with you," said Neville.

"Me too!" said Dennis. "She might not be able to see me, but if she tries anything I'll be there."

"We don't know it's her yet, Den."

"Well, the list of suspects is pretty short now."

"Do you think you feel up to it, Ada?" said Dennis.

"No, but I'm not achieving anything just moping around here. Dennis, Rose, Mrs Entwhistle, if you could have a look around her house while we're chatting, see if you can spot any clues to her guilt. Let's go."

Ada, Neville and all of the ghosts left for Ellen's house. When they arrived, the front door was ajar. Ada could hear voices from within and she gingerly pushed open the door. The 1950s cat clock still ticked its watchful gaze over the room. The voices were coming from the kitchen.

"Hello?" said Ada. The voices stopped. Ada stepped into the kitchen and Ellen was there, pinny on and staring at her.

"Oh! I thought you had company," she said.

"No, just listening to *Woman's Hour* on catch-up. I always talk to the radio," Ellen said, smiling sweetly.

"Forgive me for coming in, but your front door was

open."

"Oh, I must have left it open after the salesman called. Forgive me if I don't make you a drink, I'm in the middle of making bread," she said, wiggling her floury fingers. "Why are you here?"

"I wondered if you'd heard about Marcus?" Ada had been hoping to catch her off guard.

"Yes. The police officers came round last night. Shocking news. Terrible news. Poor Marcus." She wiped the corner of her eyes with her handkerchief. "He was such a talented man. I was his number one fan. All the great artists die young. I suppose people will be rushing to buy his artwork now. It must be a terrible shock for you, dear? Coming across him like that."

"It was. We'd become very close to each other in the last few days." She looked at Ellen, but there was no flicker of emotion in her face. She just kneaded her dough a little more vigorously.

"I also wondered if they'd told you about William Kent?"

"No? What about him?"

"Well, he's dead. It turns out he wasn't a nice guy, but I'm pretty certain he wasn't the killer all the same."

"And how would you know, dear?" she said, becoming ever more energetic in her kneading.

"He kidnapped me. He held me captive. He had no reason to lie to me but he denied it, seemed quite annoyed almost that his little plan had been interrupted."

"That was very careless of you. You should leave it

237

up to the police to solve it, dear. You don't want to end up dead yourself."

Ada ignored her and carried on. "So, the list of suspects is very short. There's only really two people. Gilbert Orange or… or you."

"I thought the police said that Marcus had admitted to it in his letter? He couldn't live with himself any more because he'd murdered my sister. He took the coward's way out. I guess he wasn't the man we thought he was. I'm sure they must be right. Now, Miss Baker, it's been lovely to speak with you again. I'm sorry you haven't been able to solve my sister's murder, but I really must be getting on. I have so much to do. Good day," she said, pointing Ada and Neville to the door.

"Thank you for your time, Miss Watts," said Ada on her way out. Ellen followed behind them and slammed the door shut and they walked off down the road.

"Not quite so sweetness and light this time then," said Neville.

"No, something wasn't right, was it. I think it's her, Neville. She knows we're on to her. Oh blast, hold on… the ghosts."

Ada had forgotten that they'd gone off searching the house. A few seconds later, Ada could see the ghosts emerge and spot her and Neville.

"Did you find anything?" asked Neville.

"Not a lot. There was a whole reel of electrical wire similar to that used to hang Marcus," said Dennis.

"That's not enough to hang her by, though," said

Neville. Ada turned and gave him a withering look.

"What? Oh, sorry! No pun intended," he said.

"Come on, Ada. Let's go home and I'll fix you both a nice spot of lunch," said Mrs Entwhistle.

"That sounds good, Mrs E. I skipped breakfast and I'm famished."

"Me too," said Neville.

When they got back home, Mrs Entwhistle looked in the fridge.

"Not much here, Ada. You haven't done a big shop in a while. Never mind, I have some things we batch cooked in the freezer." Mrs Entwhistle was enamoured of the freezer. Such things weren't a part of homes when she had died, and she had often got Ada to assist her in prepping meals to put in it. It was one of the wonders of modern life that Mrs Entwhistle was prepared to accept. She took out a steak and ale pie and chopped some greens.

***

Neville was fascinated to see her at work. He had never seen a ghost enter a human body. It still looked like Ada but her mannerisms and the way she moved her body was different. She moved as a much older person would, as if Mrs Entwhistle was still afflicted with the same arthritic problems that she'd had in life. Every so often there would be a flicker of a different face on her. He would get impressions of a woman in her sixties with

239

her hair tied back Edwardian-style and wearing a sweep of long skirt. The smell of the pie heating was heaven sent, and by the time it was ready to eat, he could barely contain himself from diving in. A rich, thick brown gravy oozed from his slice. It tasted even more divine than it had smelt.

"What shall we do next?" Neville said finally.

"I think I should go back to Mary. Tell her what's been happening. She'll be devastated about Marcus."

"Oh blast!" said Neville. "I forgot, the care home where I work want me to come in for a few hours this afternoon to help. Will you be okay if I go?"

"Yes, it's only Mary, and I'll have Dennis, Mrs E and Rose with me for emotional support."

Neville thanked Mrs Entwhistle for a fantastic lunch and departed rapidly.

"I guess we should head over to see Mary for a chat," said Rose.

Chapter 23

Inspector David Matlock sat at his desk. He was stuck about what he should do next. The situation was becoming more involved all the time. He picked up Marcus Strang's photos of Ada and flicked through them. Despite the damage to them, and his lack of artistic ability, he could tell that they were good photos. He had been truly talented. She certainly seemed happy in the photos. He paused at the one undamaged image and stared at it for a full minute. He touched his cheek with his hand, then he seemed to snap out of some spell he was in. He picked up the other photos they had taken from the flat. The photo of Mary in the bathtub was another good image, although the subject matter still seemed odd to him. He couldn't quite understand why Ada would think highly of such a man. He'd not really thought about it before, but in the photograph the bath was full of water, yet when they'd found her, it was empty. He couldn't ask Marcus now if he'd let the water out. Then, as he sat there, his drawer opened slowly beside him to reveal his strongest magnifier. The magnifier lifted up slowly out of his drawer and onto his desk.

"Is that you, Inspector Jolly?"

The magnifier moved over the photo. He studied it intently, millimetre by millimetre. He looked at the shaving mirror on the windowsill.

"Bloody Nora!" he shouted, leaping up from his chair. "Sergeant Whisky! Come here, now!"

***

Ada went through the now familiar gate to Mary's house. She walked round the back of the house calling her name. "Mary, love, it's Ada Baker. I've come for a chat. I have some bad news, I'm afraid."

Mary walked out through the French doors. "About Marcus? Yes, Ellen has already told me. He's dead. He's been murdered. She said that you were involved."

"Sorry?" said Ada. "You spoke to Ellen?"

"Well yes, sort of. She's been round a few times to chat to me since you told her I was still here. She can't hear me, I think, but she chats to me. It's very pleasant really. She's here now actually."

The French doors opened and out stepped Ellen Watts. There was something odd about the way she looked. Not quite in control.

"Oh, hello, Ellen, good to see you again. I just came to tell Mary about Marcus Strang's sad death, but I hear you've already beaten me to it. I had no idea you came here talking to Mary."

"Yes, quite a lot. No young man with you this time?" she queried.

"Oh no, Neville had to work this afternoon. It's just me."

"I hear you've been chatting to Mary about her will. Why is that?"

"Just trying to find out the facts, Ellen. A bit like a detective would."

"Only you're not a detective, are you?" she sneered. Ada looked at her. Her face looked enraged, but as she stared, a flicker seemed to pass over it, as if another face was staring back at her. A man's face. Ada gasped and took a step backwards.

"Half the house should have come to me in the first place, but my stepmother always hated me. Just because my mum brought me up well."

"Ellen, that's not true," said Mary. "My mum loved you too. It was just that the house had belonged to her outright before she met your dad. It was a family home. I don't think she meant any ill by it."

Ellen looked to where Mary was standing.

Light was slowly dawning on Ada about what was wrong. "How did you know Mary had been chatting to me about the will, Ellen, if you can't hear her?"

"What do you think?" said Ellen.

"I think you killed Mary. You strangled her with the scarf."

Mary looked horrified. "No, she couldn't, not Ellen.

243

She wouldn't hurt a fly."

"Go on," said Ellen.

"I think you also killed Marcus Strang." Ellen laughed but Ada carried on. "I think you killed him because... well, I'm not sure. Maybe he spoke to you... He said he was going to. Perhaps he found something out he shouldn't have. Maybe... maybe you were jealous of him photographing me. Jealous of our relationship."

"Ha! Relationship? You'd only known him days. I'd known him for months. It really hurt me to have to get rid of him that way, but he was going to blab to the police because suddenly he'd grown a conscience from his hussy. Yes! I know all about your sordid sex with him. You're as bad as Mary."

"I don't think you should be saying such things, dear," said Mrs Entwhistle. "It's not nice."

"Yes, leave Ada alone!" said Rose.

"What are you two going to do? A dead cook and a dead cleaner?" she snapped. "Stay out of it." She turned back to Ada. "I had hoped that your investigations would peter out and come to nothing. There was no evidence till Marcus took that photograph and shared it with the police."

"What evidence?" queried Ada.

"Now, Miss Baker, you have become a real nuisance. I think it's time we were rid of you." She advanced forward, another silk scarf in her hands.

"Piss off and leave her alone. You might be able to

push around a cook and a cleaner, but how about a very important financial consultant from the city!" Dennis rushed forward and forcibly whipped the scarf from her hand. Ellen screamed and her face seemed to recede, and before them they could see the features of a man in his fifties. He looked wiry but very strong. His features were hard and menacing. He snarled at Dennis, then seemed to hit him with a forceful strike that sent Dennis flying back through the air. Then he rushed forward and grabbed Ada, turned her and pushed her face down into an open barrel water butt and held her head down in the water. He seemed to have immense strength, and struggle as she might, she couldn't wriggle free. He had her pinned with his body, one hand holding hers behind her back and the other holding her head down.

Ada could hear the screaming of the other ghosts around her. Rose was desperate to help but had no powers to interfere. Ada struggled wildly to try and free herself from his grip but his hold was so tight. She tried hard not to breathe, but soon she felt she was running out of air and she felt she needed to breathe under the water. She felt pain as she breathed in, but gradually she felt her body relax into a peaceful state as she accepted that she was going to drown. She suddenly felt distant from the struggle and completely at peace and in harmony with the universe. She could feel no pain, and then she felt herself floating up and out of her body. Below her, she could see the figures of the ghosts, Dennis still reeling on the ground from his attack. She felt herself drifting ever upward, lighter than air. She looked up and felt a warmth on her face, and could see glowing beings above her. She felt completely loved, beyond the cares of the world. Then she heard voices screaming from below and it distracted her from her upward journey. What was that noise? It all seemed so far away and insignificant now. She tried to move up towards the light but felt the strong hands of the glowing beings pushing her firmly back down.

***

Rose and Mrs Entwhistle watched with horror as Ada was being drowned by the ghostly spectre, and Dennis was still recovering in the grass from the huge spiritual blow he had been dealt. Mary, who had been shouting at the man attacking Ada, suddenly screamed, "I hate you!" and surged forward. She brought her hands together then thrust straight at him, knocking him off of Ada and forcing him to the floor. The great spiritual force that she had used separated his spirit from Ellen and sent him flying across the floor just as he had done to Dennis.

"You were a bully in life and now you're a bully in death. It was you that killed me, wasn't it, John! Didn't have enough of bullying girls in life, now you want to bully them in death too, just like you bullied me, just like you bullied Mum. Just like you bullied your own daughter Ellen," she said, standing in front of her sister.

"Now you've killed Ada too. Don't you dare come near them. Or so help me, I'll drag you down to hell myself!"

John Watts picked himself up out of the dirt. "You never were of any worth, Mary. Neither was your mother. My Ellen was the only one of any worth. She should have inherited the house. I told your mother it was my express wish, but she ignored it and left everything to you." He looked down at Ellen. "She was a useful vessel for achieving my ends. I took her mild anger and magnified it many times. Half the time she didn't really know what she was doing, but now at least the house will be hers. There's nobody else to interfere." He turned away and walked off into the house, leaving the prone Ada and the group of ghostly figures standing there.

Dennis, meanwhile, had recovered and headed straight over to Ada. He put his hands one over the other and started pressing down on the centre of her chest and made rapid chest compressions. He kept repeating it, again and again. He'd seen it done on a TV show, although he'd never had any training. He couldn't feel for a pulse, but he kept trying chest compressions. Nothing. She wasn't breathing. He tried again. Nothing. He tried again. One, two, three, four… Just then, he heard an almighty racket and Inspector David Matlock appeared around the corner with six policemen.

"There she is! Arrest her," he said, pointing at Ellen. Two officers came forward and lifted up the groggy Ellen, who seemed a bit confused about what was going on. Matlock turned to look at the prone figure of Ada lying on the ground, her top and hair soaked in water. He could see her chest being compressed. He knelt down beside her. "May I try, Dennis?" he said, directing his comment at where he thought Dennis might be. The compressions stopped so he took that as a yes. He felt for a pulse but couldn't feel anything, so he tilted her head back and lifted her chin, pinched her nose and then gave two short breaths, watching her chest all the time. He then started giving her chest compressions. To everyone's delight, Ada started moving. Matlock turned her on her side and she started coughing.

"I need an ambulance right now!" he said.

"Already done," said Sergeant Whisky.

***

Ada coughed and spluttered. Her lungs hurt like hell. Who was she? A memory of a warm, welcoming light held strong in her mind, in contrast to the racking pain she was feeling now. Everything sounded so loud; there was so much noise. She looked up and saw Matlock hunched over her. Behind him she could see fuzzy faces moving around.

"Are you okay, Ada? The ambulance is on the way. You're safe now. We've got Ellen."

"Not safe!" she croaked. "Ellen's father." She coughed and spluttered some more.

Matlock looked at her, puzzled. "She has no father,

he died years ago." He looked thoughtful for a second as he puzzled over her words. "What are you saying, Ada?"

"Possession," was all she could manage to say before another coughing fit started. At that point, the paramedics arrived to take over.

Inspector Matlock said quietly, "I have to go and speak to Ellen at the station, but I would appreciate if you could go with Ada to the hospital." Then he turned away to see to his men.

Mrs Entwhistle, Rose, Dennis and Mary climbed into the ambulance alongside Ada. The paramedics shut the doors and one of them sat beside Ada, who was receiving oxygen. The ambulance sped off down the road, sirens blaring. The ghosts were oddly quiet. Dennis looked across at Mary and squirmed at seeing her naked body parts, which were jiggling with every bump in a most enticing way.

"I think I'll just pop up front to the driver. I can't help here, and I've always wanted to know what it was like to race along in an ambulance." He wandered off through to the cab.

"Does the siren have to be so incredibly loud?" said Mrs Entwhistle, covering her ears.

"It's exciting, I think," said Rose.

Mrs Entwhistle glared at her. "Nothing about today has been exciting. It's all been horrible. I'm sorry we suggested this business in the first place, Ada. We nearly lost you."

Ada mumbled something through her mask that sounded like, "It's okay," before she started coughing again.

They were soon at the hospital and the hospital staff rushed her through for further treatment.

"We'll need to keep her in for observation for a day or two on oxygen. We need to treat the hypoxia. Her oxygen levels are depleted. Let her rest now." The doctor and nurses finished up and left her.

Mary sat on the side of her bed and placed her hand on Ada's. "Thank you, Ada, for trying to help me. I'll stand guard over you. Rest now."

Ada shut her eyes and the ghosts settled down around her to wait. It wasn't long before the soothing click of Mrs Entwhistle's knitting needles started and a very tired Ada Baker fell into a silent slumber.

Chapter 24

When Ada awoke next, it was to see the face of David Matlock looking over her. He smiled at her. "I'm extremely glad to see you in the land of the living, Ada."

Ada tried to talk but she was slightly muffled with the mask on.

"I really think I might need to tie you down to stop you getting involved with this murder. I've come to see you as a friend," he said, proffering her a bunch of grapes. "And also to speak to you about what you said earlier. Ellen Watts is in custody now, but you said something about her father? Her father is dead, and normally I'd think it was some side effect of being drowned, but it's you, so I'm here to find out exactly what happened. Take your time telling me."

"I was just going for a chat with Mary to tell her what had been happening. I wasn't expecting to see Ellen there. She wasn't normal and I could see something was wrong. She was being quite aggressive, and I saw... I saw a man's face superimposed on her own. I think it was Ellen's father. He didn't seem to like me and he rushed forward to attack me using Ellen's body."

"It was my stepdad. John is his name," said Mary. "He was a wicked man in life and now in death too."

"Mary confirms it was her stepfather."

"Go on, anything else?"

She looked wide-eyed at Matlock. "Then he used Ellen to drown me. I went somewhere... somewhere beautiful. I went up, up into a beautiful light, and I could see everyone below me, but I didn't care. I felt warm and loved, but they wouldn't let me in. They said I still had things to do on Earth. I heard your voice and I knew I would be okay. The next thing I knew I was back and my lungs were in agony. You were standing above me."

Matlock put his hand up to his mouth in a thoughtful way. "I see. Do your, er, friends have anything to add?"

"Mary pushed John right out of Ellen! She was wonderful. She told him to pick on someone his own size and stop picking on girls," said Rose. Ada repeated this.

"He's still in the house, Ada. I'm so sorry, I had no idea he was there. He must have been hiding somewhere. Or perhaps he wasn't there all the time," said Mary. Ada repeated this to the inspector.

"We'd been to see Ellen at her house earlier in the day. Neville was with me. She was acting oddly then. She'd left the front door open, and as we walked in, I could hear her talking to someone. When we walked in the kitchen there was nobody there, just Ellen."

"Whatever the truth of this, Ada, you mustn't go

252

back," said Matlock concernedly.

"But what if he decides to leave his house and find me and finish the job?"

Matlock looked stumped.

"I really don't know. Ghost vanquishing is beyond my realm of experience."

"What will happen to Ellen? I don't think she would have committed the crimes unless her dad made her do it."

"I think the court will be lenient. A case for diminished responsibility, mental ill health will probably be put forward. She may not even get a sentence. Hopefully just some medical help, if what you say is true. I have to get back now, I just wanted to see you were okay. Would you like me to put a guard at your door?"

"No, they might do more harm than good if John should take them over. Mary and Dennis are my safest bet."

"Okay, look after yourself," he said, patting her on the hand. "Mary, I don't normally get to talk to the people whose deaths I investigate, but I've always wanted to tell so many of them how sorry I am for their untimely demise. I'm sorry in this case that I can't help you any further. If it's any consolation, your sister may not be able to inherit the house now under the laws of inheritance, so your stepfather didn't achieve his aim after all. It's called the forfeiture rule. You can't inherit someone's property if you've murdered them."

He turned and walked out the door.

"Well, that's very nice of him. He's a lovely young man," said Mrs Entwhistle, who wiped a ghostly tear from her eye.

Mary seemed less moved and rather distracted. "It's no consolation at all. I think my sister is innocent in this. He held power over her in life and now obviously in death too. She'd never have done it without him. We might not have showed it, but we loved each other. What can we do about my stepfather?" she asked. "I can't go home with him there."

Ada turned to look at her. "I don't know, Mary. I'm really tired at the moment. Have a wander around the grounds and think on it. I'd like to sleep some more now and wouldn't mind a little peace." Ada turned over and shut her eyes. She was tired but really she wanted some time to think. She was, of course, concerned for Mary, and the fact that John Watts, her father, was still at large, but she couldn't stop thinking about her own spiritual experience, drifting up to the light. She could still feel its bright warmth even now. She'd always known there was an afterlife, but this was different. It worried her that she hadn't wanted to come back. She'd wondered if Marcus was there in the light. Her lungs still hurt and the world felt so harsh after her experience. She wondered why her ghostly friends hadn't gone to the light themselves. It felt so wonderful. Perhaps she should ask them. She had no idea what to do about John Watts. She'd chatted with ghosts, let them use her body to perform tasks, had visions of things that had happened, but exorcisms, well, that was beyond her normal remit. Poor Ada had been through more experiences in the last few weeks than most people had in a lifetime. She was physically exhausted and soon found herself drifting off to sleep again.

***

When Ada woke next, she could hear voices.

"No, don't wake her, Rose. I'll go to the café for a coffee." It was Neville's voice. Ada opened her eyes and immediately sat up. He gave her a huge grin and came over to hug her.

"It's so good to see you!" she said.

"Likewise."

"How did you know I was here?"

"Well, you're rather famous among the ghost network now. Miss Prim and Inspector Jolly both told me. They're all very shocked at what Mr Watts did. It's not right, the dead attacking the living. What state would the world be in if that happened all the time. I bought you some chocolate bars. I've heard hospital food is pretty bad."

Neville certainly knew the way to a girl's heart. "Thank you so much. They're my favourite. I'm not sure when I'll be allowed to eat them."

"Are you feeling better now?" he asked.

"A lot better, thank you. I feel quite rested and my

lungs hurt a lot less."

"If you don't mind me asking, what was it like? Jolly said you'd experienced an OBE and went up towards a light."

"It was beyond anything I've ever experienced. It felt wonderful. There was no pain, I was warm and I felt loved."

"He also told me who did it. That it was a ghost."

"Yes, Mr Watts, Mary's dad."

"What do we do next?" he asked.

"I don't know. I feel really out of my depth." Ada started to cry. "I'm just making a big mess, aren't I?" He pulled her towards him and gave her a gentle hug. "What happens if he comes for me again?"

"He's going to find it a lot harder without Ellen to help him. He doesn't know where you live either, does he?"

"Actually..." chipped in Mary. "Ada left her business card with her address at my house. It's still on the side. Ellen must have seen it when she was cleaning."

Ada groaned. Her business cards had been her undoing twice now. "It won't be safe to go home then maybe?"

"You can stay at mine," Neville offered keenly.

"Thank you, that's very kind, but your aunt would drive me bonkers. She's a bit of a gossip too, I'm guessing. I wondered if I might be able to stay with the inspector. Inspector Jolly is there too, and John Watts would never suspect that I'd be staying with the police. It might even put him off if he did know."

"If that's what you'd prefer," said Neville, sounding a little crestfallen.

Just then, the doctor came in to see Ada.

"Good evening, Ada. I'm Dr Dixit. You're looking much better. I think you're on the mend. I'm happy for you to have some food tonight. We'll keep you in overnight just to be sure, then you can leave tomorrow. The nurse can help you take your mask off for dinner."

"Thank you, Doctor," said Ada. Dr Dixit turned and left. Very soon after, the dinner arrived and Neville left so that she could eat in peace.

Chapter 25

David Matlock sat at home at his kitchen table eating his meal for one and drinking a beer. He wasn't eating quickly but was using his fork to play with his food, twirling it round and round in the curry. He sighed and looked towards Inspector Jolly's favourite seat. Inspector Jolly wasn't sitting there. In fact, he was sitting directly opposite David.

"Sir, Inspector Jolly, I think this case has gone beyond what I can do to help. I'm worried what the outcome might be. Do you have any ideas?" he said, looking at Jolly's chair.

Inspector Jolly tapped on the table in front of him to let him know he was there. David turned to look at the empty chair.

"I wish… I wish I could see you and chat with you."

Jolly got up and walked over to the chalkboard that they'd used before. He picked up the chalk and started writing. 'U can chat.' Jolly had been practising his poltergeist abilities.

"How do you deal with an unruly spirit?" he asked.

"Are there any spiritual laws?"

Jolly wiped out the last words and wrote anew. All Matlock could see was a stick of chalk seemingly writing on its own. 'None that I know. Only God's law.'

Matlock paused for moment as he thought on this. "If there is a God, presumably he isn't happy about what this spirit has done? Why doesn't he do anything? Is there heaven and hell? Ada spoke of a light."

'I don't know,' wrote Jolly.

"Did you see a light?" asked David.

'Yes,' was scrawled across the chalkboard.

"Why didn't you go into it?"

Jolly thought on this for a moment. 'Unfinished business,' he wrote. Then, as an afterthought, he wrote, 'My murder.'

David nodded. "Yes, I'm sorry about that. I will look into it more, I promise. Right now, I think we need to help solve Ada's problem. Is there a ghostly police force?"

The inspector thought for a second. 'No…' Each dot appeared on the board slowly, as if the inspector was thinking on something.

"Pity. Did you ever read *An Inspector Calls* by JB Priestley at school? It's one of the things that made me want to become an inspector. It's about a ghost detective who comes to a house to investigate a murder."

'No,' was written.

"Oh, it's good. You should. Here, I have a copy on my tablet. I'll leave it open for you before I go to bed so

259

you can have a read."

David had another beer and chatted away to the inspector about life in general. He seemed a little less lonely having someone to chat to. They watched a comedy together and then Matlock went to bed. He was true to his word and left out his tablet. Jolly sat and scrolled through the book. By dawn, he had finished it. The first rays of golden sunshine shone through the window, and like liquid gold, it spread itself across the surfaces of the room. It reminded him of the golden light he'd seen. Why hadn't he gone into it? It was his murder certainly that was stopping him moving on, but he also felt that there was a higher purpose for his remaining. Something that he needed to do. He tapped the tablet and looked at the image of a ghostly inspector drawn on the front page. A ghostly police force. Perhaps there should be. It was an interesting idea. "Hmmm," said Jolly, scratching his chin. Then he grabbed his ghostly hat and strode with purpose out the door.

***

When David came in for breakfast the next morning, he found the tablet still on and the story at the end of the last chapter.

"I hope you liked it," he said, but there was no response.

He had a day off. He read the papers for a while until mid-morning, when he received a phone call from Ada.

"David... Inspector," she said. "I'm being released from hospital today, but I'm worried about returning home. I left a business card with my address on it at Mary's, and after last time... well, I'm a bit scared. Can I come and stay for a few days? Just till I think what to do next? The doctor says I shouldn't be alone for a day or two..."

There was an awkward quiet pause as David thought about this. Ada Baker was becoming ever more entwined in his life. It was beginning to feel like it was beyond his control.

"I can cook, really well. Well... Mrs Entwhistle can. I can make myself useful and I'll buy the food. Please, I'd feel safer if I could," she said hopefully. Matlock had been ready to say no until Ada had said this. He closed his eyes and thought for a few seconds.

"Okay," he said finally. "I'll come round to pick you up. What time are you released?"

"Within the hour I think."

"I'll be there." He hung up. He hurriedly whizzed around tidying his spare bedroom and getting it ready, then left for the hospital.

***

It took longer than an hour for Ada to be released from hospital but finally she was. She was really pleased to see the inspector. He put his arm out for her to hold on to and led her to the car. There wasn't much talking in

261

the car on the way home. Ada had a feeling that the inspector was nervous.

After they arrived, he opened the garden gate for her to go through first. As they walked up to the front door, he said, "I've tidied up the spare room a bit and given it a quick clean. I hope it suits your needs."

"I'm sure it'll be lovely," she said.

"I'll put the kettle on. How many am I making for?" he asked.

Ada smiled sweetly. "Just the six of us, unless you want to make George one."

"Does the inspector want a cuppa?" he asked.

"No, he's not here. At least, I can't see him."

"Oh!" said David. "Okay."

Before long, six steaming cups of tea were standing on the table.

"You don't know where Inspector Jolly is then?"

"No. He spoke to me last night. I think he read the book I suggested. I've no idea where he is. Ada, what do you intend to do? As lovely as it is to have your company, you can't be driven out of your home," David asked.

"I don't know yet. I never dreamed it would lead to anything like this. No ghost has ever tried harming me this way before. I've been wondering, though. How was it that you arrived just in the nick of time? How did you know Ellen would be there? How did you know she was the murderer?"

"The things you said about her kept playing around

my mind. I was studying Strang's photographs. Inspector Jolly was with me, though I didn't know it, and he opened the drawer to my magnifier. I looked more closely at the photos of Mary in the bath. In the reflection of the shaving glass on the windowsill, you could see an image of Ellen standing behind Marcus. I got the lads to look at it in detail on the computer. They clarified the image. It seemed likely therefore that Ellen was the murderer. Strang never reported seeing her there. Presumably she was hiding in one of the rooms. Perhaps it had just happened. We went to her house first but there was no answer. We were going to force entry but one of her neighbours was there and said that she'd gone over to her sister's house to clean it, so we had to act fast. The house was still searchable under the last warrant. I didn't expect to find you there, and I was shocked to see you there on the floor. If Dennis hadn't started CPR on you, I'm not sure you'd have made it."

"Nonsense, it was his CPR that saved you. I lacked the vital breath," said Dennis.

"You both helped me," said Ada. "Thank you both dearly. Now I think I need to perhaps speak with my online spiritualist friends and see if they have an idea of what to do. First I need to fix us some lunch as promised."

"Nonsense, you're just getting better. You focus on trying to solve your problem and I'll heat us up some lunch. It won't be up to your standards, Mrs Entwhistle, I'm sure, but solving your problem is the biggest issue."

He gave Ada his laptop. She thanked him and started chatting to her online friends.

Chapter 26

Inspector Jolly had been inspired by the story he'd read. He'd had a desire since dying to carry on solving cases, but it was hard without a corporeal body or the help of a police force to back you up. Now ghosts were going around murdering living humans. This would never do. He was determined to change this. He was going to create a ghostly police force to police the ghosts. Living people who committed crimes were punished. Why shouldn't ghosts be? He had a good idea where to start looking. He headed towards Dark Street Cemetery. He hadn't been there for a long while because he didn't like to look at his own grave. To see your own name engraved on stone with your death date could put a real downer on your day. When he didn't see it, he could pretend he was still alive. Many other ghosts, though, seemed very attached to their mortal remains and remained with them after death. Inspector Jolly had seen several of them here. The town was quite an old one and had been mentioned in the Domesday Book. A police force had been established quite early as a presence in the town. He knew precisely where to look.

Sergeant Bleaker could always be found patrolling the Victorian part of the cemetery. He walked up and down the regimented rows of graves and had, in fact, been seen by several more psychically gifted members of the public. It wasn't long before the inspector reached him. He was swinging his truncheon, his silver buttons shining brightly against his dark uniform. He had the British pith helmet style of hat and a snake buckle belt. A bullseye lantern was clipped to it. He looked to be in his mid-forties, and a neatly manicured moustache twitched on his top lip. He saw the inspector and waved his truncheon at him in acknowledgement. As he got nearer, Jolly could see that he had deep brown eyes and a light scar on his left cheek.

"Sir!" Bleaker saluted very formally. "It's good to see you here again. Have you returned to patrol the graveyard with me?"

"Quite the opposite, Sergeant. I was wondering if you might like to expand your patrolling? You like patrolling the cemetery grounds, don't you, and keeping an eye on the other ghosts?"

"Yes, sir."

"Well, recently there has been some unsavoury behaviour by a particular ghost in the town."

"I heard, sir. Murdering live human beens. A young woman. It ain't right, sir. It's against the law, sir."

"Sadly, Sergeant, it is not. There's no set of rules for ghosts to live by. No punishments for their

266

wrongdoings. No ghostly police force to enforce it either."

"That's wrong, sir. They should be following a moral code. God's code. Killing is wrong. My old mum taught me that back in the 1840s when I was a nipper. My mum was a good woman. Always taught me right from wrong. It's what made me want to become a policeman."

"I know, Sergeant. How would you like to help change that? How would you like to help capture this wrongdoer, to right this wrong? He didn't just murder one woman. He also murdered a man and was nearly successful in murdering another woman."

Sergeant Bleaker tapped his truncheon gently on his hand. "Well, sir, I reckon I'd like that a lot. I think my old mum would approve."

"Excellent, Sergeant. The first thing I'd like you to do is round up any other former police officers who you think might like to help. Or anyone else you think might be suitable. Explain the idea to them."

"Should they all be from the town, sir?" the sergeant asked.

"No, you can cast your net wider if you like. But I think we need to remain fairly local to start with, until we've established the idea."

"Yes, sir! I'll sort that right away. What are you doing now, sir?"

"I have someone special I want to go and talk to near here. I might be gone a little while, but I'll meet you back here when I'm ready. Thank you, Sergeant."

"Right you are, sir!" The sergeant strode off across the graveyard with a purpose.

Inspector Jolly was pleased that the first part of his plan had come together. Now he needed to travel a bit further to find the next part. It was going to be hard for him to manage all this on his own.

As he strolled through the graveyard, he noticed that there were many ghosts standing around. Some just stared, others were sitting on benches. Some of the children were playing football.

He arrived back on Dark Street. It was thought that it had achieved its name from the rows of gloomy yew trees that lined its edge. It dated back to the eighteenth century. Next, he made his way through town to the number forty-nine bus stop. It was going to be quite a long journey. He sat down at the bus stop and whipped out his e-cigarette and started puffing away.

"Do you mind! No smoking. It upsets my lungs," said an elderly woman dressed in 1940s clothes sitting at the other end of the bus stop.

"My dear, it is water vapour, not smoke, and besides, we are both dead, so it can't affect either of us."

She tutted and the inspector carried on as before. Eventually, the number forty-nine arrived, a small single-decker bus. They both climbed on board, as well as several living people. One of them nearly sat on the inspector until he glared at him, and for some reason he didn't understand, he suddenly thought it would be a very good idea to sit on the other side of the bus.

The inspector watched the country miles rolling by, and it took some time and a couple of changes of bus, but he eventually arrived in the village of Little Waldingfield. He made his way up to the church of St Lawrence and wandered into the graveyard. It was an ancient church with parts that dated to Norman times and with fifteenth-century improvements. He wandered around the graveyard until he found the grave that he was looking for. It had a plain grave marker in the shape of a triangular prism, with no elaborate frills or fancy carved angels. The name on it was Robert Branford. He knelt down at the graveside and prayed for a few minutes. Then he heard a noise beside him, and a man appeared from behind the tree beside the grave. He was smartly dressed in everyday clothes of the 1860s. He appeared to be about fifty, had dark skin, dark hair and dark eyes, and was about five foot ten.

"What is it you want, calling me from my rest?" said the man. He had an East London accent with a slight Suffolk burr to it.

"I need your help, sir. At least for a while. I'm Inspector Jolly. Terrible things have been happening around here recently. A ghost has been murdering living humans. Two successful attempts and one attempted murder. I need your help, sir. I read about you in a book on the history of the police. It said that you possessed a thorough knowledge of police matters in general and seem to have been much respected. You were a superintendent in the Southwark police, I understand, before you retired up here."

"Yes, that's right. What help do you require, Inspector?"

"Well, sir, I would like to form a force to police the dead. To investigate ghosts that break the law and to punish them. I would really like your help in setting up this idea. What laws we should uphold, how we punish the wicked, that sort of thing. It can't be allowed to go unpunished, the dead killing the living. It'd be mayhem. It's a lot of work for me to do on my own and I'd like the authority of someone more senior to talk it over with and help me set it up."

The man walked out from under the trees and looked down at his grave. "Here lies Robert Branford, born 1817, died 1869," he read aloud. Someone had placed a bunch of tulips there recently. "That's nice. Who did that, I wonder. Do you know, I haven't been here for decades? It's always very odd looking at one's own grave. Killing a living human, you say? We can't have that happening. Okay, Inspector, I'll help you. What shall we do first?"

"First, sir, I think we need to draw up some rules. Things may have changed a bit between your time and mine. Let's set out a ghostly set of rules based on the rules we followed in life."

"Here, Inspector?"

"Well, I was thinking the pub. There's a nice-looking pub over there called The Swan. I think it's closed, but we can still enjoy a ghostly pint."

"Great idea, Inspector. I know it well. Lead the way."

The two men headed out of the graveyard and towards the pub for a pint and a chat.

Chapter 27

Ada had spent most of the weekend trying to work out how to stop John Watts' ghost from attacking again. She'd been on online forums, and most just suggested burning sweet grass or white sage and leaving crystals around the room. Somehow, she didn't think that would be enough to stop him. He was a particularly malevolent spirit. She even thought of bringing in some sort of priest or spiritual healer, but that would mean putting someone else at risk. She was loath to go back there and face him on her own with just a smudging stick burning in her hand.

Monday morning came and there was still no sign of Inspector Jolly. David was heading off to work, however. He was munching his morning marmalade on toast and enjoying a cup of tea when Ada emerged from her room.

"Did you sleep well?" he asked the bleary-eyed Ada. "I thought I'd leave you sleeping. I'm off to work shortly. We've obtained an extension so we can interview Ellen some more."

"Is it possible that she might know how to stop her dad? Is she aware of what he did to her?"

"She seems a bit confused at the moment as to why she's there. I think her memory is a bit hazy. She doesn't even remember pushing you under the water. I'll try to ask her more questions today though. She had a mental health assessment yesterday as she sounded so confused and odd, but I can question her today. If I find anything out that I think can help you to lay his spirit to rest, I'll let you know." He grabbed his things together and headed out the door.

Ada felt pretty useless. She resolved to do some food shopping but decided that first she would visit the local crystal healing shop to buy some supplies. All four ghosts decided it was wise for them to go with Ada. They locked up and headed off down to the high street. They were a curious mixture of souls, and if anyone else had been able to see them they certainly would have stared. Dennis and Mrs Entwhistle walked upfront beside Ada, as both felt a little uncomfortable around Mary, but Rose was at the back quite happily chatting away to her. Rose had taken a liking to her and the two chatted as if they were old friends.

They turned onto the high street. Number 36 was called 'Spiritual Haven' and was run by Astrid Starlight. Ada wasn't sure if it was her birth name but it was certainly memorable. The ghosts followed her in. The shop was empty but Astrid was sitting on a cushion in a small room at the back of the shop. Her legs were crossed in a lotus position and her arms were held out palm up in front of her. The smell of sandalwood incense filled the space. A wind chime tinkled in a gentle breeze that blew in from the window. The shelves around the room were stocked with crystals, herbs, incense, divination tools and all sorts of spiritual items. The soothing sounds of a garden played from a Bluetooth speaker to the side. A tremendous energy seemed to flow from the space.

Mrs Entwhistle looked very uncomfortable in such a pagan space, but Rose was fascinated. "I think I'll wait outside if you don't mind," said Mrs Entwhistle, who bustled back out of the shop. Rose, however, was in awe and Dennis indifferent.

Astrid opened her eyes.

"Good morning, Ada. How can I help you all on such a beautiful day?"

"You can see them?" asked Ada.

"No, but I can feel their energies. There seems to be a bit of strife and negative energy around you, but generally I feel you are all good."

Ada only popped in the shop occasionally so she didn't know Astrid very well, but she liked her. She had platinum blonde hair pulled back into a fishtail braid. Her skin was a sun-kissed brown and her clothes were made of loose, floaty white natural fibres. A spiritual calmness emanated from her.

"I'm here with four friends. Three of them live with me and the fourth is a lady called Mary. The negative energy has come from her stepfather. He's an evil man and a danger to the living as well as the dead. He's one of the most powerful spirits I've ever met. He…" Ada paused, gulped and felt a tear run down her cheek.

"He tried to kill me. In fact, he was successful. It's only thanks to my friends that I'm still here."

Astrid raised an eyebrow but still seemed to maintain her ice-cool calm. "I see, a very evil spirit. Normally spirits don't go that far. At least not in the cases we hear about. I think, first, perhaps you look like you could do with some spiritual cleansing." She invited Ada to sit beside her so that she could lead her through the process of cleansing her chakras.

"I think I'll just slip next door to the betting shop," said Dennis. "This isn't really my kind of thing."

Ada, Rose and Mary sat down cross-legged in a semicircle around Astrid. Astrid closed her eyes. "Now, take a deep breath, in and out, in and out. Repeat this till you feel calmer. Now, let's start with our crown chakra at the top of your head. Imagine a bright white light shining down on your crown chakra…"

It took half an hour to go through the entire meditation and chakra cleaning, but Ada felt better, lighter at the end of it, slightly less burdened. Then Astrid offered her a cup of lime flower tea. Ada looked around the shop to find the things she needed: some smudging sticks and crystals. After she'd been through the checkout, Astrid gave her a crystal necklace made of obsidian and quartz. "Here, a gift for you. It'll help keep you safe."

Ada gave her a wan smile.

"Have you used a smudging stick before?" asked Astrid.

"No, I've read what to do but I've never had to remove a spirit with one before."

"Would you like me to come with you to help?" she asked.

Ada paused and thought for a second. "Maybe, but I'm worried that it might hurt you too."

"Don't worry about me. I've smudged lots of houses before and dealt with plenty of troublesome ghosts. Here," she said, pushing a business card her way. "Call me if you need me."

"Thank you, I might do that." Ada took the card and left the shop. She found Dennis next door and Mrs Entwhistle chatting to a lady in similar dress to her. Ada and the ghosts headed into the local Priceright supermarket. Ada grabbed a small trolley and headed off down the aisles, picking up food for the evening meal. The ghosts all had their own preferences for food, and especially teas.

"Ooh, don't forget the Darjeeling tea, Ada," said Rose. Dennis picked a box of tea off the shelf and dumped it in the trolley. They walked forward to the frozen aisle.

"Ooh, we could make some apple crumble," said Mrs Entwhistle.

"I'd love some vanilla ice cream with that. Dennis,

can you get some, please?" asked Ada. Dennis opened the door of the freezer, took a small tub out and dropped it in the basket.

Ada heard an "Eeekk!" from behind her. She hadn't realised that a young supermarket employee was following her. She looked at her name badge. "It's all right, Cassie. He's harmless."

Cassie didn't seem reassured and ran over to her supervisor to tell her what she'd seen. Ada was eyed suspiciously all the way round the rest of the supermarket. Eventually, they checked out and headed back to the old police house.

She spent the rest of the afternoon practising smudging around the police house and cleansing any negative vibes. She was as ready as she'd ever been but since the attack, her nerves had been shaken. She wondered if she should take Astrid up on her offer. She pottered round and cooked tea for the inspector. He wasn't due home till seven p.m. but he seemed thrilled to have his dinner ready for him. It was the first time in a long time that anyone had cooked a meal for him. She'd cooked coq au vin and they drank the rest of the bottle of wine with the meal.

***

David was just starting to unwind and feel quite relaxed. Ada had obviously been cleaning too and the place was sparkling. He wondered if this was down to Rose. Ada was unusually quiet during dinner.

"Is the inspector here?" he asked.

"No, he's not been around all day. I don't know where he is."

He could see that something was troubling her. "What is it, Ada?"

"I have to go there. I have to go back. I know it's risky. I know he might hurt me again, but I can't live my life in fear of him. I have to face him. I have to try to lay his spirit to rest so he can't hurt anyone else. What if he kills the next person to move into the house? It could be a family moving in. I've been practising all day."

"When are you going to go?"

"Tonight."

"I'm coming with you then."

"No, I don't think you should enter. Do you have any spiritual experience? What if he uses you to overpower me?"

"Well at the very least I'm waiting outside in the car so you can find me if you need me."

"That's a very wise idea," said Dennis approvingly. "I'm coming too."

"And us!" said Rose.

"We'll face him together," said Mrs Entwhistle, holding Rose's hand.

"I'm bringing some experienced help too. I've asked Astrid from the crystal healing shop along. She's had past experience with house cleansing rituals and smudging. I sent her a text earlier and she's agreed to meet me there at nine. My friend Neville is coming too. He can't see ghosts but he can hear them, so he might be useful."

"Might John not possess them as well?" he asked.

"He might try, but he was able to control Ellen so easily as she was his daughter. He knew her well and amplified the small grievances she had within her. They're both aware of him and hopefully have no emotional grievances with me. It's a risk we'll have to take. I've got everything ready. Let's wash up and then get going."

Chapter 28

Inspector Jolly had had a good meeting with Robert Branford. He'd found him an intelligent, organised man, who was passionate about policing despite the time gap between them. In fact, in many ways, he found the time gap a boon, as many of the ghosts they might have to police would be from times past. Some of the rules of what constituted a crime and the punishments meted out might have changed but the fundamentals of policing remained the same: stopping and punishing those who committed evil acts. Theft was probably not going to be a big problem, but violent crime or harassment might be.

Robert had agreed to return with the inspector to Sudfield and sort the matter out further. They'd spent a long time discussing what the police force should be and what crimes it should punish. Then they'd moved on to discussing cases from their past that they'd solved. The time had flown by and eventually they arrived back in Sudfield. They chatted amiably as they walked through the town and made their way up to Dark Street

Cemetery. Their ghostly footsteps seemed to resonate through the quiet graveyard. It seemed unusually quiet, quieter than normal, and there weren't so many ghosts hanging around. The inspector and Robert Branford made their way to the Victorian part of the graveyard, walking past a particularly fine sculpture of a weeping angel, to find Sergeant Bleaker, who was standing on a bench amid an assembled horde of ghosts all murmuring and chatting excitedly. Some of them were just the ordinary ghosts of the graveyard, but looking among them, they could see many men and women in uniform. Sergeant Bleaker saw them and raised his hand, causing everyone to turn and look. Bleaker stepped forward and pushed his way through the throng, which must have been at least a hundred strong.

"Inspector, you're back. I've been busy, as you can see."

"Are all these people here to join our ghostly police force?" the inspector asked.

"Sadly not, but a lot are. I've rounded up a few good choices though, I think. I've been doing preliminary interviews. I'd really like you to meet Sergeant Brewer. He did sterling work in the area during World War Two but sadly died during an air raid. He's as excited as me about the idea."

"Very good, Sergeant. I need to speak to everyone, please."

"Stand aside for the inspector!"

The crowd parted and Jolly and Branford made their

way to the bench.

"Good afternoon, everyone. I'm pleased to see that you're all showing an interest in my new idea. I'd like to introduce Superintendent Robert Branford, who worked in Southwark for many years, firstly as a constable, then making his way up to sergeant and finally superintendent, before his final retirement to Suffolk and his death in 1869. He brings a great deal of experience and knowledge of policing with him. We have been setting out rules that we feel all ghosts should be living by… Ahem, no pun intended. It is our belief that ghosts should be coexisting in harmony with living people, not harming them. We had our time as living people, now that is past. We do not expect spirits to vacate the homes they once lived in but to coexist peacefully as they were expected to do in life. Our main rules are as follows: one, no ghost shall harm a living person; two, intentionally hounding a living person and forcing them to leave their own home is forbidden; three, no ghost may possess a living person without their clear consent; and four, no ghost shall kill a living person."

"We may revise these rules at a later point, but right now we have a problem. We have a ghost in this very town who has broken all four of these rules. He has possessed, he has harmed, he has driven people from their homes. He has also killed two people and nearly killed a third. Many of you may not know the people he has harmed, but who's to say that he will stop at killing

282

these people? It might be one of your relations or friends next. It could be your daughter." He pointed at someone. "Or your great grandson," he said, looking at another. "We followed these sorts of rules in life because we all realised it was the right thing to do, and we should follow them in death too. The living need our help with protection from these troubled souls, and we the…" He paused for a few seconds, looked at the sergeant and whispered, "Have you thought up a name for us yet, Sergeant?"

"The North Essex, South Suffolk Ghostly Constabulary," said Sergeant Bleaker.

"Really? Bit of a mouthful, isn't it? Okay, well we might work on the name. Now, are there any questions, and who would like to be a part of this new organisation?"

Lots of hands shot up. "Yes, you?" he said pointing at a small weaselly looking man at the back.

"Why should we listen to what you say? It's bad enough we had to listen to you lot in life. Now you want to control us in death too!"

"Well for the very reasons I listed earlier, and because we all know it is morally right. Nearly every religion and society in the world agrees that these things are wrong, and it is up to us to ensure that wrongdoers such as John Watts are stopped."

Hands went up again. "What punishment will be meted out to the guilty?" asked a particularly large, beefy man.

"That will depend on the crime. Causing a person distress so that they leave their home will result in the ghost's removal from their home. If they harm or kill a human, their souls will be sent to hell."

A small murmur of shock went up from the assembled crowd.

"What experience is necessary to be part of the constabulary?" said a woman.

"If you were a police officer in life, that would be ideal, but anyone who had a respectable role in life can request to join – security guard, soldier, nurse, teacher, doctor, that sort of thing."

"What about pay for being part of this constabulary?"

"I'm afraid there's no pay, just the knowledge that you're helping to make the world a better place. What else are you going to do for the next hundred years? Being part of this new constabulary will give meaning and purpose to your afterlife. I may be able to ask Ada to pass on messages to your loved ones as an added bonus. Who'd like to join?"

A group of about fifty men and women stepped forward.

"I'm so pleased so many of you support the idea. Right, Sergeant Bleaker, write down everyone's name and details and swear them in. Superintendent Branford, we have some planning to do in working out how to tackle Watts."

Jolly and Branford stepped down and the crowd thronged forward to speak to Sergeants Bleaker and

Brewer.

"What now, sir?" asked Jolly.

"Where are we going to use as our base of operations, Inspector? Have you thought about that?"

"We could use the old police house, but it might be a bit small. What about basing ourselves in the new police station? That way we'd have first-hand knowledge of any crimes that are happening and we can use their resources to help find things out."

"Sounds perfect. Arrange it, Inspector."

"Yes, sir. It'll take a while to organise this lot and swear them in too."

"Well, once we've signed everyone up and briefed them fully, I suggest we go and have a conversation with this Mr Watts, don't you, Inspector? Someone needs to tell him that he's been a very naughty boy," said Superintendent Branford with glee.

The inspector nodded and walked over to speak to his sergeant.

Chapter 29

Inspector Matlock was amazed to find himself in the situation he was now in. He thought back a few weeks to when everything was very different, life was ordinary and ghosts didn't exist. Now he was driving Ada and a bunch of ghosts to a house to cleanse it of an evil ghost. The David of a month ago would have thought him mad.

He pulled up outside Mary's house. The two back doors of the car opened on their own and shut again. He didn't think he'd ever get used to that. Ada was beside him and seemed to be steadying her nerve. He put his hand on top of hers. She flinched at his warm touch but left his hand there.

"You call me or come and get me if you need to, and if you're not out within half an hour, I'm coming in to get you no matter what." He gave her hand a squeeze to reassure her. He looked out the window and an attractive blonde woman was sitting on the wall outside the house chatting to a man who he assumed was Neville. Ada got out and shut the door quietly and walked over to greet her. Very soon, the three of them disappeared through the gate and round the back of the house.

David sighed. He felt a bit useless.

***

Ada, Neville, Astrid and the ghosts made their way round to the back of the house. Astrid had already lit the smudging sticks and told Neville what to do. He claimed to have used them once before, back in his days at university.

Mary slipped into the house and unlocked the French windows, and they entered the house as quietly as possible. There were no sounds to be heard, and Ada felt her pulse racing as she remembered what had happened to her here only a few days ago. Every part of her felt like turning around and running away, but she knew she would never be free of the fear if she didn't face it head on. She'd started it so she needed to finish it.

They started in that room. First, they made sure every drawer, cupboard and curtain was open and Astrid placed a quartz crystal in each corner of the room. Ada, Neville and Astrid waved smoke with their hands into every corner and crevice of the room while Astrid began a chant: "Blessed smoke, cleanse this home, make it safe for all to roam, usher out all hate and fear, only good souls may linger here."

Once they had been through that room, they made their way into the dining room and repeated the process. Ada paid close attention to the nude portrait of Mary.

There was still no sound or sight of John Watts. They cleansed the whole of the downstairs in this way, making sure to reach every corner, then made their way slowly up the stairs. The ghosts went up first, then Astrid, followed by Ada and lastly Neville. Ada's heart raced faster still. Each step they made was slow and measured. Ada listened intently for any noise or indication of John Watts' presence. Astrid continued her chant. At last, they reached the top step and Astrid turned to face the bathroom. Then she made her way across the hall. Moonlight shone in through the pale translucent curtains, which fluttered softly in a breeze that blew in through a crack. Mary was standing there in a moonbeam, and her raven tresses seemed to flow and shine with an ethereal beauty. Then she did an unusual thing. She stepped into the bath and sat there, just as she'd been found.

"Smudge me too, Ada. This is where all this started and where it needs to end too. I think if you do it, I'll feel more at peace."

Ada wafted the sage smoke all over her body.

***

John Watts drifted slowly down from the attic where he'd been resting. The effort of trying to kill Ada had taken a lot out of him. He'd not heard them enter the house, but as they approached up the stairs, he'd felt their presence. The air felt different somehow, unwelcoming; it didn't feel like home any more. Somehow it felt sanctified like a church. It reminded him of the time he'd been to St Peter's in the Vatican City. The place had a feeling unlike anywhere else he'd been. It had felt holy and spiritual. He'd hated it and tried to leave as soon as possible, but Mary's mother Emma had insisted on the visit.

He looked at Ada as she wafted the smoke over his stepdaughter. How he hated them both. The boy Neville had his back to him. He sensed that he would be quite easy to control. He sensed that Neville was someone who was used to being told what to do. He stepped forward silently with ninja-like stealth and took control of the young man's body, and he managed it pretty easily. Neville just made a small, surprised sigh as he took control. He turned to face Ada, who didn't seem to have noticed. The only thing Neville had in his hand was the smudging stick, but he could feel something in his pocket: a fold-up knife. The blade was only four inches long but he thought it should be enough. He opened it up and gripped it tightly in his stronger hand and advanced towards Ada. He would put an end to this witch once and for all. Hatred seethed through every part of his body. The blonde woman had her head facing the window, Mary's eyes were shut and Ada was looking down at her. He raised his hand ready to strike the blow.

**

There was a scream from the hallway. Ada recognised it; it was Rose. She looked up in time to see Neville standing over her, a knife in his hand, looking ready to plunge it down. Ada knew instinctively that this wasn't Neville but John Watts. She dropped her smudge stick in the bath as she reached up to try and stop him, getting both hands on his attacking arm, but Neville, amplified with the power from John Watts, was surprisingly strong. He used his other hand to try to pull her hands away. She could see Neville's face but somehow it wasn't his eyes that stared back at her. Two dark circles seemed to swirl within his irises. She screamed to attract attention. Astrid swung round and seemed deeply shocked to see Neville attacking her, but seemed to realise straight away what had happened. She took her smudging stick and pushed the burning end of it onto his face. He pulled back for a second and clutched his face. Then he slapped her hard, sending her spinning, and she fell, knocking her head on the side of the bath. Mary opened her eyes and leapt up out of the bath. Then she rushed forward and grabbed hold of Neville, trying to pull her stepfather from his body, but this time he seemed to be holding fast. He pushed a big burst of energy towards Mary, throwing her backwards. Next, Dennis came rushing in from the bedroom and ran straight for Neville. He grabbed the hand with the knife and tried desperately to keep it from plunging into Ada, but John was strong and the knife seemed to get lower and lower till its tip started pressing into her skin and made a small cut. A jewel of ruby-red blood ran down her beautiful skin. Ada screamed again with panic. She could see the desperation in Neville's eyes to finish her but also the stronger determination in Dennis's to stop him. John was too strong for him though, and the knife slipped down, but not where John had intended and it gashed the side of her head. John screamed in frustration and raised the knife again. Dennis tried his best to hold him, but he had a power beyond his own. He aimed down again, this time towards her stomach. Like watching in slow motion, his arm seemed to descend slowly but inexorably towards Ada's stomach. Dennis couldn't stop him, only slow him, and the knife plunged down again, this time towards her lower abdomen. She felt it push in and she screamed with pain. John Watts lifted his hand again and pushed Dennis aside. Ada saw his hand plunge down again, this time towards her heart, and she felt the world slow around her. A heartbeat felt like an eternity as the knife dropped towards her and the last few seconds of her life.

A hand shot forward and grabbed Neville's arm. It was Matlock. He was stronger than Neville but no match for the two. She could see the panic in his eyes as he realised what was about to happen.

Then, on the edge of her hearing, Ada could hear a strange screaming, whistling noise. It got louder. Then there were shouts and hollering. Half a dozen arms stretched forward and grabbed hold of Neville. They didn't seem to have hold of Neville himself but rather had reached within him. Strong arms grabbed hold of John Watts and dragged him out of Neville, who collapsed on the floor beside Ada, dropping the knife and clutching his head. Matlock, not realising what was going on, held him still with his hand behind his back.

Ada focussed on John Watts, who was screaming and shouting at his captors and trying every way he could to get free and attack Ada.

"Oh, I don't think so, sunshine, do you?" said Sergeant Bleaker, ably assisted by Sergeant Brewer and another man. "Like picking on young ladies, do we? Well, there's a special place somewhere nice and hot that's reserved for people like you."

Another constable came along and helped force him out. Then he was dragged forcibly down the stairs. Ada tried to get up but winced with pain. Neville whimpered as Matlock twisted his arm further. "It's okay, David, it wasn't Neville himself, it was John Watts. He's gone now. They've taken him away."

"Who has?" Matlock enquired, still not letting go.

"I don't know who they were. They looked like policemen."

A voice came from the hall. "They are the North Essex, South Suffolk Ghostly Constabulary," said Inspector Jolly, as he walked into the bathroom. "It's a little scheme I've been cooking up. It looks like we were just in time. I didn't expect you to strike so soon, Ada. I'm sorry you've had to go through this again."

Matlock could see Ada watching something move around the room.

"Who is it?" he asked.

"It's Inspector Jolly. He brought a ghostly police force with him."

As Matlock followed her gaze towards the window, there in the moonlight he could see the ghostly shape of the inspector in front of him. Not quite visible, but still with a sense of solidity about him.

"I can see him!" he said excitedly, and he let go of Neville's arm, who let out a groan. "Inspector!"

Inspector Jolly turned to look at him and smiled.

"Well done, David," he said, smiling. David Matlock sat down on the ground and tears sprang from his eyes. "I must go now, David, work to be done." Then the inspector moved from the moonlight and vanished from his vision. David recovered and remembered that Ada had been hurt.

"Are you okay?" he said, concerned.

"I think so. It looks worse than it is, I think. Bloody hurts though."

David took a clean handkerchief from his pocket and pressed it to the wound. Neville sat up beside them, holding his head and groaning.

"Poor Neville!" said Ada. "Are you okay?"

"Why does my head hurt, and why did you have my arm pinned behind me?" He looked down and saw his bloody knife on the floor and the wounds on Ada's side. "Oh, Ada! My God, I'm sorry!" He looked at the blood on his hands with horror as he realised what had just happened.

Astrid stood up. "I'll carry on cleansing, you sort yourself out." She paused for a moment to look at Inspector Matlock. "You have a beautiful aura, you know? It's all sorts of rainbow colours." She smiled and carried on, relighting her smudging stick and chanting around every area of the house.

Matlock helped Ada up. Mary and Dennis were still slightly stunned but Rose rushed forward.

"Ooh, Ada, we're so glad you're okay. We went and got the inspector. I managed to knock on his window to alert him! Me! I've never done that before."

"Thank you, everyone, all of you, for your help. I wouldn't be here without you. Right now, I'm quite tired and I want to go home."

Matlock shook his head. "Hospital first, then home. We need to get those knife wounds cleaned and checked. You'd better come too, Neville and Astrid, though I don't know how we're going to explain this. They'll be saving you a permanent bed if you carry on like this, Ada."

Ada put her arm on his shoulder and he gently put his arm around her waist and helped her slowly down the stairs. Ada felt the warmth of his strong arm supporting her and turned and smiled at him. At last, she had some real friends, someone alive to turn to for help when she needed it. People who seemed to love and care for her. At last, it seemed the ordeal might be over.

Outside, Inspector Jolly watched as the four policemen shoved John Watts into the back of an old Maria horse-drawn police van. Sergeant Bleaker shoved spectral manacles on his hands and feet and shut the doors. The van moved forward and started trundling off towards the graveyard.

"A good start to our little scheme, don't you think, Inspector?" said Superintendent Branford.

"Indeed, sir."

Another car pulled up. This time it was at least a bit more modern but still looked like something out of the 1920s.

"What amazing new technology!" said Branford climbing in.

The inspector smiled. "Oh, just you wait and see, sir. A lot has changed since you were last here. Right now, I think we need to send some scum off to hell, don't you? To the cemetery, please, PC Smitty," he said to the driver.

"Well, I'm not missing this!" said Rose. "The inspector's looking after Ada. Come on, Mary."

Rose, Mary, Mrs Entwhistle and Dennis got into another police car and followed them down the road.

Chapter 30

The old police van went hurtling through the gates of the graveyard, drawn by two speckled white horses. Their well-brushed white manes shone silver in the moonlight. It slowed down as it passed the larger monolithic tombstones and finally came to a halt in the centre of the graveyard by an old yew tree. Inspector Jolly and Superintendent Branford drew up behind it, then the officers jumped down from the cab and opened the back of the van. Ghostly manacles bound Watts' hands and feet, and the officers who were inside with him roughly manhandled him out. The ghostly horde of the graveyard drifted forward and pressed in around the prisoner.

He was made to sit down on a bench, and from among the throng stepped a man in long red robes and a white wig.

"Lucky you," said Inspector Jolly to John Watts. "You have Judge Jebediah 'Bloody' Blackthorne presiding at your trial. He was one of the eighteenth century's most notorious and bloodthirsty judges during the time of the 'Bloody Code'. It should be a quick trial at least."

John Watts still looked defiant and struggled to free himself from his bonds.

Judge Blackthorne came forward and stood on the steps of a high tombstone and leant over the top, looking down at John Watts.

"You may begin," said the judge, looking to a man on his left.

A bewigged clerk stepped forward. "John Watts, you have been brought to this court today accused of the heinous crimes of murder and attempted murder. Further, of taking possession of the body of your daughter Ellen Watts to commit these murders and then that of a young man Neville Lightfoot."

"Do we have any witnesses to these crimes?" asked the judge.

"I call forward Mary Watts – John Watts' daughter and one of the murder victims."

Mary Watts stepped forward. "Miss Watts, please tell us what you know of these events."

Mary poured out the sad details of her own death and the attempted murder of Ada, which was only unsuccessful due to the quick thinking of Dennis and the inspector. Fat ghostly tears rolled down her pale cheeks as she spoke of her sadness at her life cut short by her wicked stepfather. She weaved a tale of his ill treatment of them as children and how it had now continued after his death, and of poor Ellen, forced to do his bidding.

By the time she'd finished, there wasn't a dry eye left in the graveyard.

"I see. John Watts, what do you have to say for yourself? Do you have any witnesses to defend you?"

John Watts' nostrils flared and his eyes were like a wild horse's. "She was a wicked child, born out of wedlock, a hussy just like her mum. She deserved to die. She stole from my child, Ellen. As for that nasty little witch, Ada. She deserved to die. Thou shalt not suffer a witch to live! My Ellen's in jail because of her interfering. I intend to go back and finish the job!" he said, spitting on the ground.

The onlookers reeled back in horror.

"Ladies and gentlemen of the jury," said Judge Blackthorne. "How do you find the defendant?"

There was a murmur from the crowd, as many voices talking in hushed tones all at once, before the large, beefy man of the previous day stepped forward. "We find him guilty, your honour!"

"John Watts, I sentence you to be sent to hell to spend eternity atoning for your sins, of which there are many. May your body be ripped apart by swine daily and your innards fed on by their piglets. Reverend Hargreaves, please carry out the punishment."

From out of the crowd stepped a vicar who looked like he was all blood and thunder. In a booming voice, he began, "In the name of God, we cast thee John Watts down to hell to burn in the fiery pits of damnation and be tortured for eternity! Lord our God, open a portal to hell so that this unworthy soul may enter."

With these words, the ground began to quake and a hole opened up in front of him. It was like a sinkhole suddenly appearing, but there was a red glow and an intense heat, as if they were standing over a volcanic vent. Screams of the wretched could be heard.

John Watts turned to the inspector and looked fearful for the first time. "I'm not going in there. You can't make me! What right do you have to send me down there? I refuse!"

A large, red taloned pair of hands appeared over the edge of the pit and a horned creature with eight black eyes and a mouth full of needle-sharp teeth appeared behind him. "John Wattsss?" it rasped. John Watts turned to look at it and screamed. "I'll take that as a yessss." It grabbed his legs and pulled him with a bump over the edge of the pit and down into the fiery hellfire. The pit disappeared and sealed over in a few seconds as if nothing had ever been there.

The haunting cry of a male tawny owl could be heard through the otherwise still quiet night and the world returned to how it had been before.

Superintendent Branford turned to the inspector. "Well, that was dramatic! Trials were never like that, even in my day."

"And brief. Yes, a little different from a modern trial, but I'm sure we can iron out the creases as we go along. It's quite hard to unite law enforcers from all ages. Trials were short in the eighteenth century, I'm afraid."

"And normally the murder victim doesn't give evidence at a trial into their own death," said Superintendent Branford.

"Still, he's gone to the right place I think. Can't have killings like that taking place. I'm sure word will spread and it'll make a difference," said Jolly.

"I hope you're right. Thirsty work this lawmaking. Fancy a pint?"

"Don't mind if I do. The White Horse is a good pub. It's been there since 1664," said Inspector Jolly.

"Sounds perfect," said Branford.

"Do you want to come?" said the inspector to Dennis, Mary and the other assembled ghosts.

"I think I could use a drink after that," said Mrs Entwhistle, still crossing herself.

"Me too," said Dennis.

Most of the crowd dispersed after the trial, but a few followed them to the pub.

***

David Matlock's brow remained furrowed during the drive to the hospital. Driving Ada to hospital was starting to become a habit. He stared across at her in the passenger seat. Her eyes were shut and she looked exhausted. The ghosts, if they were around, were quiet all the way there. He felt an overwhelming urge to protect her from harm and keep her safe. He helped her out and sorted all the paperwork for her, and there were questions about what had happened to her and Neville. He left the ghosts out of the story and made up the rest. They seemed to believe him once they knew he was an inspector.

The wound was, as Ada had said, not too bad, and hadn't touched any vital organs. Neville was a little disorientated, but David was a little ashamed to note that his shoulder had been dislocated. He must have held him a bit too hard. Other than that, he seemed no worse for his ordeal. He hoped that the horrid events of the past few days were now over, but he needed to find out from Jolly what had happened.

After they'd been patched up, Matlock drove them both back to his home. They both went to bed, and David gave Ada his own bed. He could keep a better eye on them here and make sure they were okay. He guessed it would probably be a while before he heard from Jolly, so he cracked open a beer. He felt he deserved it after this evening.

"I'm not sure what the ghost etiquette on beer is or even if you're in the room," he said aloud. "This is the only beer I have, but thank you to you all and I wish you all the best. Cheers!" He held up his bottle. "Let's hope we've seen the last of him." It was a cold spring night and Matlock had lit the fire in his wood burning stove. He watched the entrancing flames as they danced in front of him, and he slipped off into a slumber.

***

Arthur Scallion nervously crept down the stairs of the White Horse pub. He'd been woken from his sleep by the sound of many voices talking and laughing and glasses clinking. The pub was an old one, and he'd been told many tales of ghosts frequenting it over the years, but this was the first time in his two years running the pub as landlord that he'd heard anything. As he got nearer, the voices got louder. He nervously pushed open the door to the lounge and the voices stopped. Unusually, the fire was still burning in the wood burner. If anything, it seemed bigger than when he'd gone up to bed. He walked in and was going to sit down in one of the chairs in front of the fire but decided against it at the last minute. Instead, he grabbed a bottle of water from the fridge, looked around the room again, then shut the lounge door and started climbing up the stairs to bed. When he was halfway up, he could hear the voices again, but this time he decided not to investigate. He went back to bed, pulled the covers over his head and pretended not to hear.

Chapter 31

The next morning, David awoke relatively early, about seven a.m. He checked in on Ada and Neville, who both still seemed to be sleeping soundly. He was too tired to work and phoned in to book the day off for personal reasons, something he'd never done before. Ada had stocked his fridge up with all sorts of goodies and he was pleased to see some bacon and eggs in there. It felt like a morning for a fry-up. He was more of a no breakfast kind of person, but today it was needed. He put the bacon in the sizzling hot pan and its delicious aroma soon wafted through the whole house. Fried bread, eggs and tomatoes cooked gently in pans next to it. No audible alarm was needed, and soon his guests were up and making their way into the kitchen. Ada slumped down in the chair at the end of the table. Neville sat somewhere in the middle.

"Good morning!" David said merrily. "How are you both feeling today?"

"Like someone stabbed me in the gut," said Ada.

"Like a ghost possessed my body, then several

303

people tried to fight me and someone dislocated my shoulder. Oh, no, wait a minute, that did happen!"

"Sorry about that," said David.

"I feel... I feel unclean," replied Neville. "Can I use your shower in a bit?"

"Sure, just remember to ask George to stay sitting on the loo."

"Sure, okay. Err, who's George?"

"The ghost of a man who was hanged by corrupt police officers in the bathroom a hundred years ago, except it was his cell then," Ada said.

"Oh, er, I see. Thank you... I think."

"Breakfast first though."

David put three plates of food down on the table and poured them all a mug of tea. "How many extra teas today?" he asked.

Ada smiled, appreciating his effort to include the ghosts. "Actually, they're not here. I'm betting they've gone out to find out what's happened to John Watts."

"I'm here!" shouted George from the bathroom.

"Except for George, who's always here in the loo."

David poured another mug and took it down to the bathroom.

"Thank you!" said George loudly.

Everyone was quiet through the rest of breakfast. They were hungrier than they realised. Very soon, there were three full and very satisfied people around the table.

Neville yawned. "I could have another sleep now,"

he said, rubbing his belly.

"You can if you want. You're welcome to stay till you're sure that you're better."

"Thank you. Very kind. I'd really like to know what happened with John Watts before I go anywhere."

"There's one thing I still don't know," said Ada, with a sad lilt in her voice. "What happened to Marcus Strang's spirit? I find it odd that he would up and leave without saying goodbye at least. I know we didn't know each other very long, but usually, like Mary, people are desperate to know what's happened to them when they're murdered. My parents died without coming to see me and it's always bothered me. I saw my grandparents. They all came and said goodbye before they went. Does it mean they didn't think I was worth saying goodbye to?" she asked.

"I'm sure it's not that, Ada. Perhaps it wasn't possible for some reason, or maybe they all thought it would be too upsetting for you. You nearly went without saying goodbye, you said so yourself," said David, trying to reassure her.

"Yes, I suppose so. I just would have liked time to say goodbye to them all." She brushed away a small tear from her eye.

"Well, what now?" asked Neville.

All of a sudden, a newspaper was pushed through the letterbox and flopped down on the doormat. David walked over to pick it up. "Have a read of the paper?" he volunteered. "It's the *Sudfield Times*."

Ada eagerly took the paper from his hand and turned to the 'Strange East Anglia' section of the paper, licking her finger as she turned each page. At last, she found it and read it aloud:

Ghost of murdered local CO still haunts his police cell

The ghostly stirrings of George Brent can still be heard in the former cell of the old Victorian police station in Sudfield, which closed a couple of years ago. George was the son of local gardener Thomas Brent and his wife Mathilde, who was of German descent. They lived in one of the houses on Coronation Avenue that was destroyed during World War Two. In 1916, George Brent was called up to join His Majesty's forces, but Mr Brent refused to join on the grounds that he was a Quaker and therefore also a conscientious objector. On the night of 20 June 1916, Mr Brent was arrested by local police officers and taken to the prison cell. In newspaper reports of the time, it was recorded that George Brent committed suicide by hanging.

Local psychic Ada Baker says differently though. "George told me that he was cruelly murdered by corrupt police constables in his cell, partly because he was half German and also because he was a conscientious objector."

The terrible mob justice that was meted out on George has meant that he's been unable to leave his cell ever since. For a hundred years he's endured the punishment of being in that cell for the crime of being half German and not wanting to kill a fellow human being.

Conscientious objectors were treated appallingly during the war. They were imprisoned, given hard labour and virtually tortured with curious punishments. To this day, they have never received an official apology from the British government. I spoke, however, to the local chief of police, who said that if such a terrible injustice had occurred while George was in custody, he apologised profusely and was appalled that this could happen. His own grandfather had also once been a conscientious objector. He would be asking his church to pray for Mr Brent's soul at church on Sunday and said that they had decided to have a fete to try to raise funds for a plaque or statue in tribute to local conscientious objectors. Let us hope that this will do some good and Mr Brent will soon be able to depart his earthly prison.

Dustin had even found an old photograph of George to put with the article.

Ada heard a shuffling noise down the corridor and George appeared in the room beside them.

"George! You're out of the cell. I hope you didn't mind me doing that. I was so appalled by what had happened to you.'

"Did he really say that? Are they really going to do all those things?"

"Yes, I believe so. How have you left the cell?"

"I don't know. I listened to the words and I felt my soul feel so much lighter. I feel… unburdened. I think I'd like to see my family now. It's been a long time since I saw my mother. She'll be wondering where I am."

Ada thought for a few seconds, then said, "Would you like help crossing over, George? I can help, I think."

George nodded. "I would, Ada. I'm so tired of being on Earth. I need a rest now. Will it be okay? Will they be there?"

"I think so, George. I'm going to think about a door. You need to step through that door."

Ada closed her eyes, cleared her mind, then thought only of a door. A door for George to go home and visit his family. The outside door to the kitchen suddenly morphed into a different door. An old, rickety cottage-style door with a simple latch, which seemed very out of place in the old police house. It glowed with a brilliant light that seemed to shine through every crack and knothole.

"That's the door to my mum's house. There used to be a lovely garden outside. She'd grow fruit and veg and cottage garden plants. The bees were there all the long days of summer. It was lovely. Do you think she'll be in the garden?" he asked.

"I think she might, George. Why don't you go and see?"

George stepped forward nervously and put his hand on the latch. He turned to look at Ada. "Thank you, Ada Baker, for helping me to move on. It's been a lonely hundred years. I'm so pleased it will finally end. I'm finally going to get to go home." He turned and lifted the latch. The door swung open and Ada was blinded by golden light. The fragrant scents of summer wafted into the kitchen and Ada thought she could see the faint outline of flowers. George stepped through the door and it slowly shut behind him. Then, the light dimmed and the door began to fade, until it was the same door that it normally was.

"He's gone," said Ada. Tears streamed down her face, and she blessed Dustin for running the article as requested.

"I could smell flowers," said David.

"Yes, I think there was a garden." She smiled. "One less ghost for you to live with, Inspector."

"Yes," he said wistfully. "Though I was kind of getting used to the idea of living with him, I'm glad he's at rest now. God rest his soul.

Chapter 32

An hour after George had left, the other ghosts came rolling in. Ada could tell straight away that they were intoxicated as they were laughing and cheering loudly. She didn't even know that ghosts could get drunk. The kitchen door sprang open and they all swept in.

"Ada!" cried Rose, who ran over to her.

"What's all the celebration about?" asked Neville.

"He's gone, Ada! He's really gone. There was a trial and now he's gone," said Rose.

"A trial?" asked Ada.

"Yes, it was the inspector's idea. He's got together a ghostly police force to help punish wayward ghosts. There was a judge and everything," Rose replied.

"Where's he gone?" asked Neville.

"By the look of the fellow that came up from the fiery pit in the ground – red skin, horns, many eyes, big teeth – I'd say he's gone to hell. I don't think he'll be troubling you again," said Jolly.

Ada's jaw dropped and Neville went pale and clammy. "I-I-I…" she stammered.

"What's wrong?" said David Matlock, concerned and unable to hear the conversation.

"Inspector Jolly says that they sent him to hell."

"Good! That's where he deserves to be."

"No, you don't understand, literally hell. A demon came out of the ground and dragged him into hell." Ada had always thought and known that it had existed, but having someone tell you that they'd seen the entrance to it was quite a different thing.

"Ah," said David. "I see. Well, it's still good for you and the other residents of Sudfield. Are you going to go home now?"

"I guess so, but I don't need to go just yet, unless you want me to?" said Ada.

"No, I'd love you to stay. Both of you. All of you."

"I have to get back home I think. I have work tomorrow and I need to get ready for it," said Neville.

"I'd just like to go home," said Mrs Entwhistle. "My head is spinning."

"I'll see you home, Mrs E," said Dennis.

"I'll come too," said Rose.

Very soon, it was just Ada, David, Mary and Inspector Jolly.

"I must go too, Ada. I can't thank you all enough for your help solving my murder. I feel at peace now," said Mary.

"What do you want to do now, Mary? Will you pass on, do you think?" asked Ada.

"I'm not sure. I think I want to see a little more of the

world first. I can't go back to the house, it has too many bad memories. I think I'll see if I can influence Ellen's trial and try to help her all I can. Then I might travel round for a bit, visit some art galleries. Perhaps see Gilbert's exhibition. Galleries are where I feel at home. I think I'll go to see Ellen now, if you don't mind."

"Not at all."

Mary got up and walked straight through the wall.

"Where's George?" said Inspector Jolly all of a sudden.

"He's gone home, Inspector." She pushed the newspaper report across to him to read.

"A door appeared for him and he stepped through. I guess he just wanted recognition that what was done to him was wrong. Hearing those words helped him move on."

"Ah, I see. I was hoping to have a chat with him. He was quite a nice sort of fellow." The inspector suddenly seemed a little crestfallen and lonely.

She put her hand out to him. "I'm sure Inspector Matlock will carry on looking into your own death, Inspector, and I'll help if I can. You have your police force now, too, to keep you occupied, and you can come and see me, Dennis and the others any time."

"I promise I will, sir. I know I can't hear you but you can always write me a message," said David.

"Thank you both," said Jolly.

"Would you like a drink of coffee?" Ada asked.

"No, I think I'll go and spend some time in the

garden. Thank you." He rose and left the house, walking straight through the wall.

"He says thanks but he's gone outside to think. Do you really think we can catch his killer?" she enquired.

"Yes, I think I can. Ada, I appreciate your help, but it's put you in some pretty dangerous situations. I think you need a break and should leave this case up to me."

Ada agreed with David but knew she would find it hard to resist helping. Her curious nature was already thinking through the possibilities. She treasured this new friendship, though, and she resolved to try. They spent a lot of the day happily chatting about what they'd experienced and other things that interested them both.

Ada cooked them some dinner and eventually, at about nine p.m., David walked her home. At the gate to her house, she said, "Thank you so much for everything over the last couple of weeks. You've saved my life twice now. Maybe I'll save yours someday." She smiled sweetly and gave him a hug and another peck on the cheek. She stared up into his eyes and smiled. Then she pushed open the gate and went into her house, waving as she went with a light skip in her step. David waved back and walked off slowly up the street.

***

Across the street, a dark shadowy figure sat in a car that had recently pulled up. It opened the glove box, withdrew a notebook, and started writing.

9.15 p.m. – Ada Baker arrives home accompanied by a man. Who is he?

The figure put a pencil to its lips in thought for a moment.

Ada has been a very naughty girl. Ada must be punished.

The ghost of William Kent put down his pencil and snuggled down in his car to watch and wait.

The Real Robert Branford
by Stephen Bourne

The Robert Branford who features in this novel is based on a real person, whose story was discovered by writer and historian Stephen Bourne, back in 2017. Stephen has been writing books about Black British history for over thirty years (www.stephenbourne.co.uk) and has been kind enough to provide a written account of his discovery and a brief history of the real-life Robert Branford.

On 15th August 2017, I travelled to the picturesque village of Little Waldingfield in Suffolk to attend a memorial service for a Victorian gentleman who had broken down barriers in the Metropolitan Police. His name was Robert Branford, and he now has the distinction of being the earliest known mixed-race police officer in the Met. I first came across Branford in Clive Emsley's book *The Great British Bobby*. When I undertook further research, I discovered that he had faithfully served the people of the London Borough of Southwark for more than twenty-eight years, from 1838 to 1866. As a Southwark resident, I was intrigued and searched for more information. His police pension record states that he was born on 6th May 1817 in Stoke-by-Nayland, a village in the Suffolk countryside. However, according to census records and his death certificate, Robert was more likely to have been born in 1820, and simply added three years to his date of birth to enter the Met.

Robert was illegitimate. His mother was white, but we know nothing about Robert's father and his heritage. Robert named his grandfather, Daniel Branford, as his father on his application to join the police, as in those days, children who were born outside of marriage were stigmatised. Robert joined the Met's M Division in Southwark on 14th September 1838 and rose through the ranks to become a superintendent in 1856. He was based at Stone's End police station near Borough High Street (not far from London Bridge) and it was during the 1850s that he commanded a young police constable by the name of Timothy Cavanagh.

Mr Cavanagh, who rose to the rank of Chief Inspector, speaks of him fondly in his memoirs *Scotland Yard Past and Present* published in 1893. Acknowledging Mr Branford as a man of colour, he says: "Mr Branford was not an educated man; but, what to my idea was of much greater importance, he possessed a thorough knowledge of police matters in general. I should say he was about the only half-caste superintendent the service ever had."

Mr Cavanagh's use of the term 'half-caste' is used in its original 1893 context. This was before the term, which is now considered offensive, was replaced with mixed-race, bi-racial or dual heritage.

While we should not rule out the possibility of other mixed-race police officers in Victorian England, it has to be noted that Mr Branford was an exception to the rule.

Robert Branford retired on 17th October 1866. He was described in his pension record as 5ft 10in tall, with a dark complexion and black hair and eyes. At this time, Mr Branford and his wife Sarah were living in Southwark but, on his retirement, they moved to Suffolk. They made their home in Little Waldingfield but Mr Branford's retirement was short-lived. He died on 14th August 1869. Sarah died in 1885 and she was buried with Robert. The Branfords did not have any children.

Acknowledgments

Sudfield, the town in my book, is fictional, but it is based loosely on the market town of Sudbury in Suffolk and the surrounding areas. I dearly love the area, with its colourful forest of thatched timber-framed cottages, and it has been my great delight to set my novel in this part of the world.

This book could never have existed without the help and inspiration of a great many people. I'd like to thank my beta readers, Aoife Woodhouse-Spillane, Squiff Stephanie Drake, Gary Drake, Zibby Miles, Paul Allcock, Tracy Lee and my brother Martin Scott-Jupp. I'd especially like to thank my muses, Lenette Warren, my husband Wel, and author Helen JR Bruce. I'd also like to thank Haz of Haz John Art for her professionalism and amazing cover art. Above all these, I would like to thank my mum, Evelyn Scott-Jupp, who nourished my love of books from a young age. A big thanks goes to psychic Mike Baker for predicting which publisher I should approach. I'd like to offer a big thanks to Cranthorpe Millner too, for taking a chance on my little novel.

I also owe a great debt of thanks to the noisy poltergeist who rattled around my Edwardian flat all those years ago, and who is my inspiration for the character of Dennis.